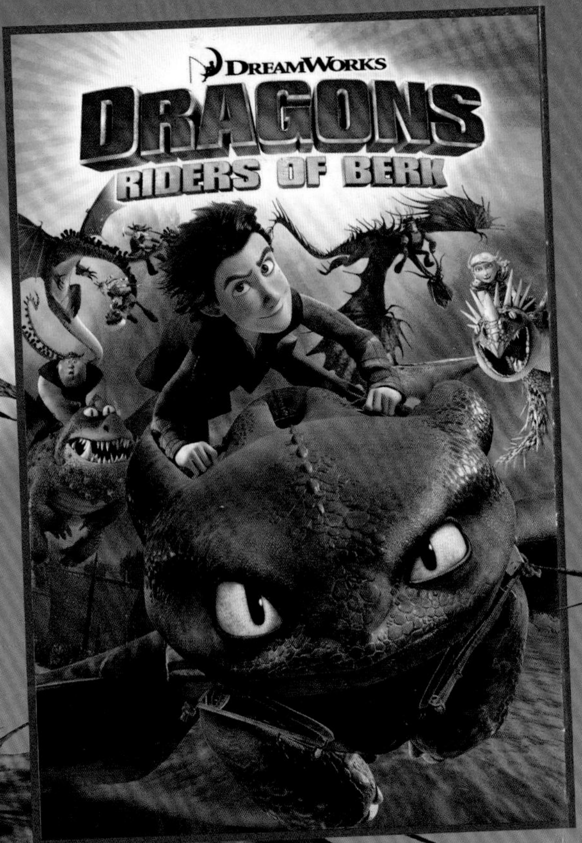
DREAMWORKS
DRAGONS
RIDERS OF BERK

DRAGON DOWN

Snotlout's dragon, Hookfang, goes missing! Can Hiccup and his friends find him before their enemy does…?

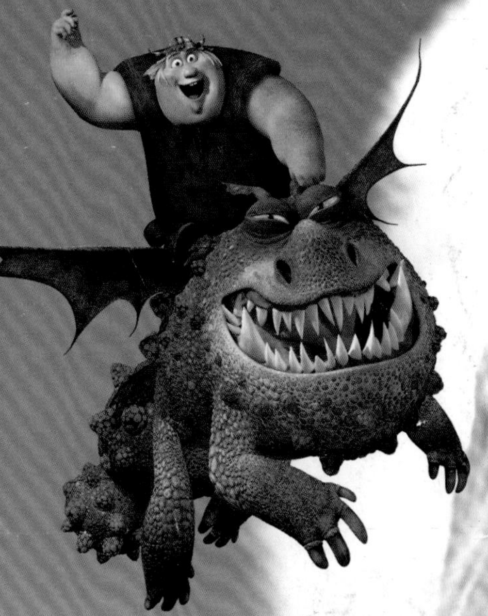

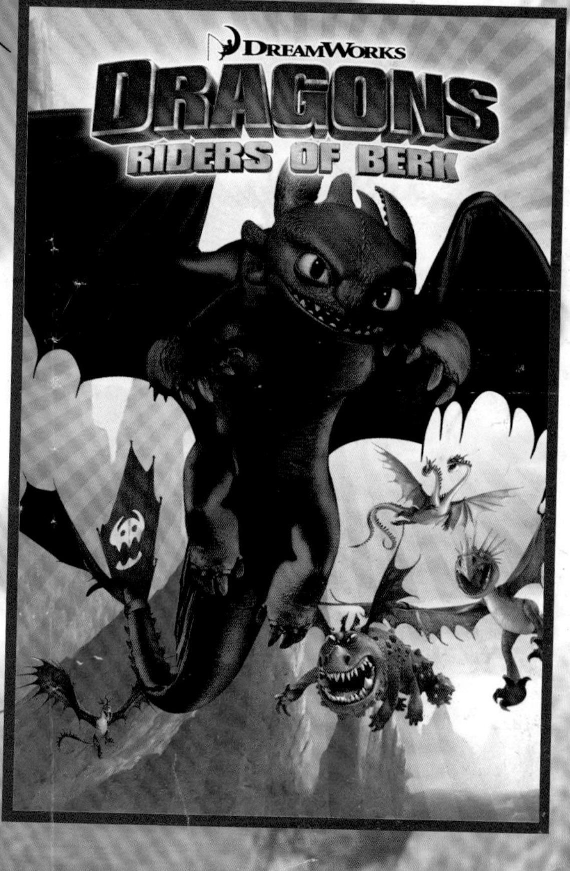
DREAMWORKS
DRAGONS
RIDERS OF BERK

DANGERS OF THE DEEP

Something very scary lurks in the mysterious Veil of Mists – and Hiccup, Stoick and his Vikings are about to face it!

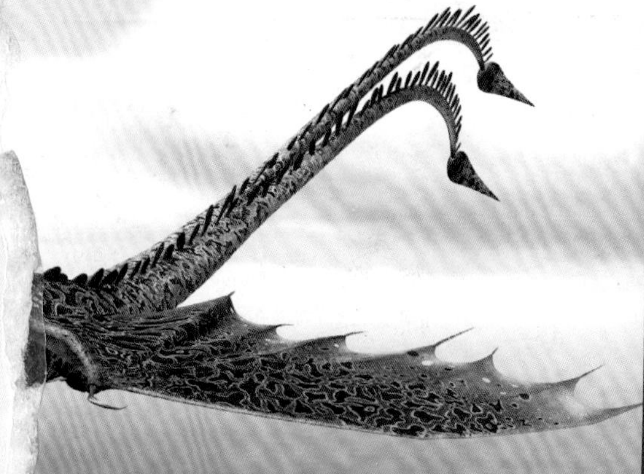

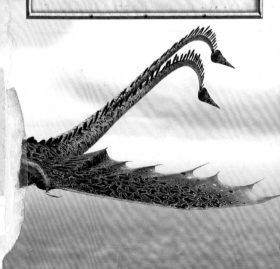

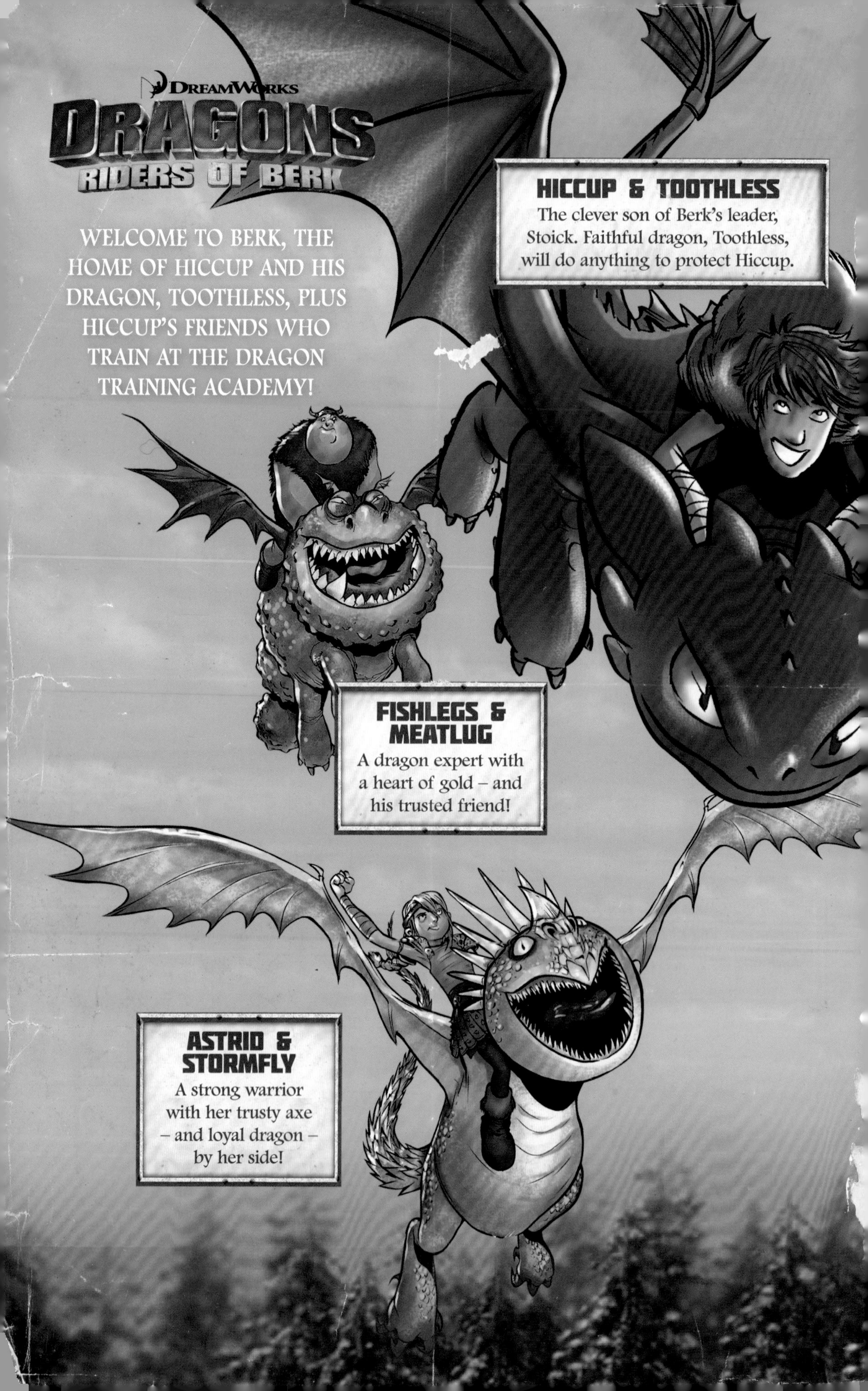
DREAMWORKS
DRAGONS
RIDERS OF BERK
WELCOME TO BERK, THE HOME OF HICCUP AND HIS DRAGON, TOOTHLESS, PLUS HICCUP'S FRIENDS WHO TRAIN AT THE DRAGON TRAINING ACADEMY!
HICCUP & TOOTHLESS
The clever son of Berk's leader, Stoick. Faithful dragon, Toothless, will do anything to protect Hiccup.
FISHLEGS & MEATLUG
A dragon expert with a heart of gold – and his trusted friend!
ASTRID & STORMFLY
A strong warrior with her trusty axe – and loyal dragon – by her side!

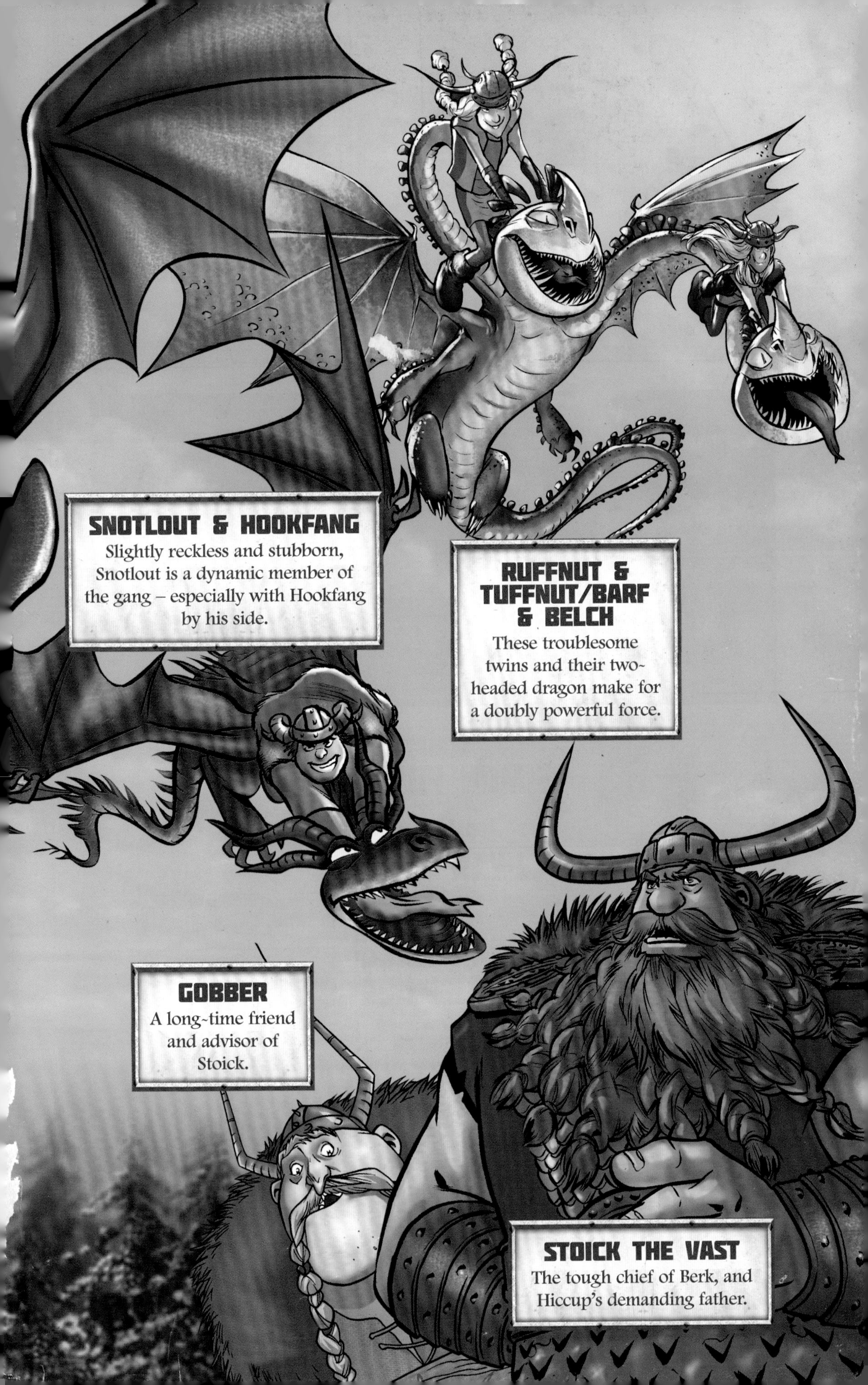
SNOTLOUT & HOOKFANG
Slightly reckless and stubborn, Snotlout is a dynamic member of the gang – especially with Hookfang by his side.
RUFFNUT & TUFFNUT/BARF & BELCH
These troublesome twins and their two-headed dragon make for a doubly powerful force.
GOBBER
A long-time friend and advisor of Stoick.
STOICK THE VAST
The tough chief of Berk, and Hiccup's demanding father.

DRAGON DOWN

SCRIPT
SIMON FURMAN

PENCILS
IWAN NAZIF

INKS
IWAN NAZIF
WITH BAMBOS GEORGIOU

COLORING
NESTOR PEREYRA,
DIGIKORE & JOHN CHARLES

LETTERING
DAVID MANLEY-LEACH

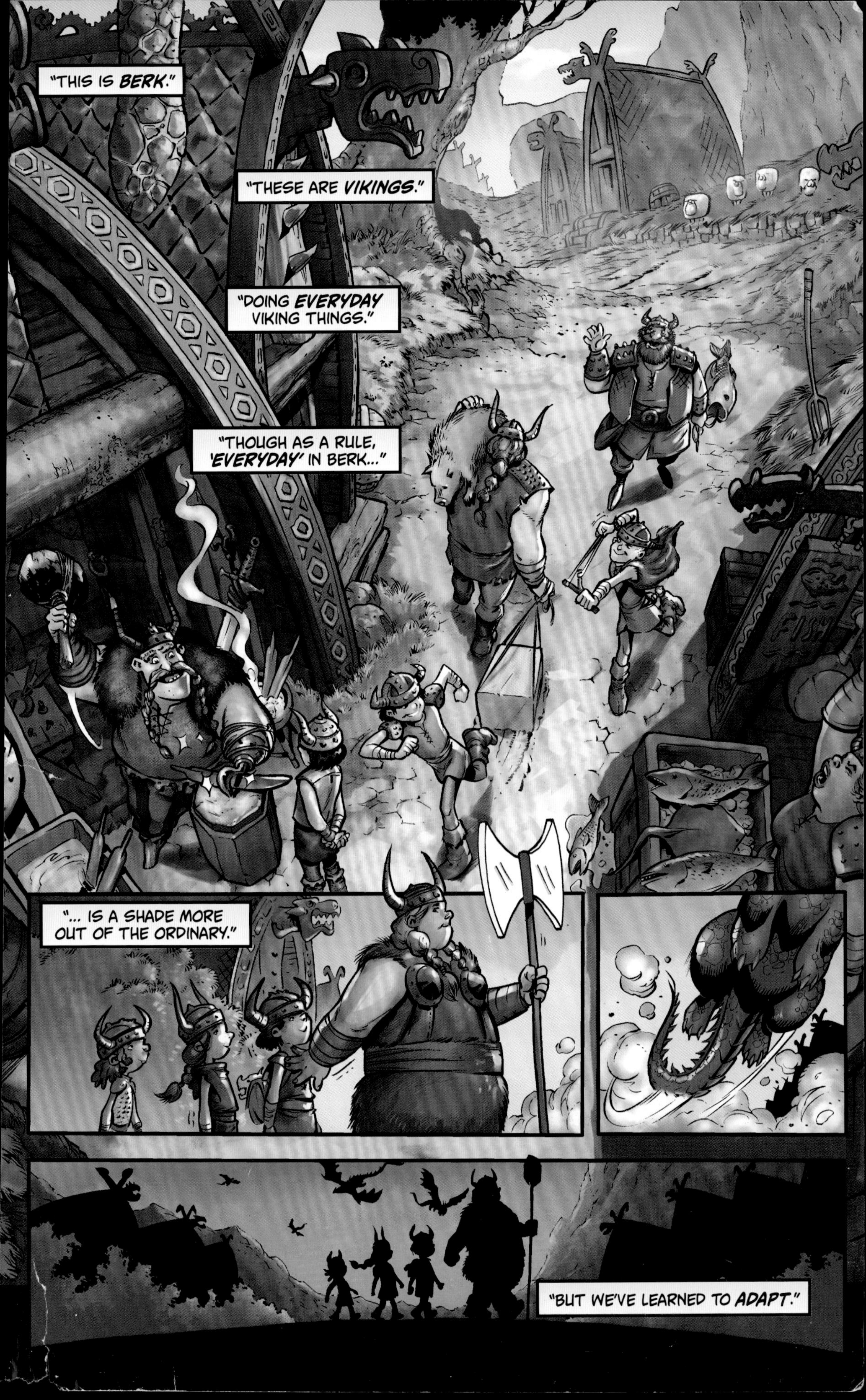
"THIS IS BERK."
"THESE ARE VIKINGS."
"DOING EVERYDAY VIKING THINGS."
"THOUGH AS A RULE, 'EVERYDAY' IN BERK..."
"... IS A SHADE MORE OUT OF THE ORDINARY."
"BUT WE'VE LEARNED TO ADAPT."

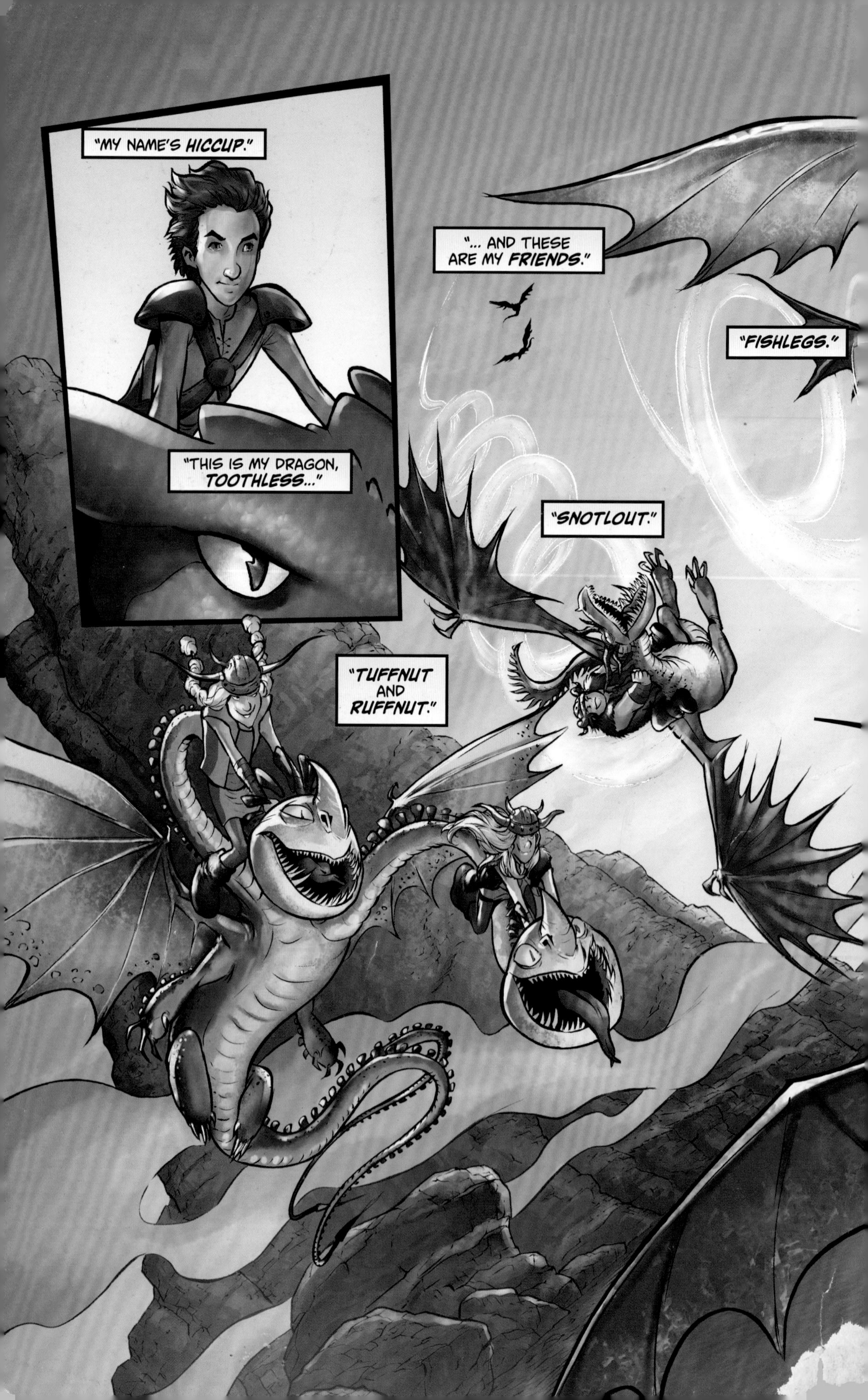
"MY NAME'S HICCUP."
"THIS IS MY DRAGON, TOOTHLESS..."
"... AND THESE ARE MY FRIENDS."
"FISHLEGS."
"SNOTLOUT."
"TUFFNUT AND RUFFNUT."

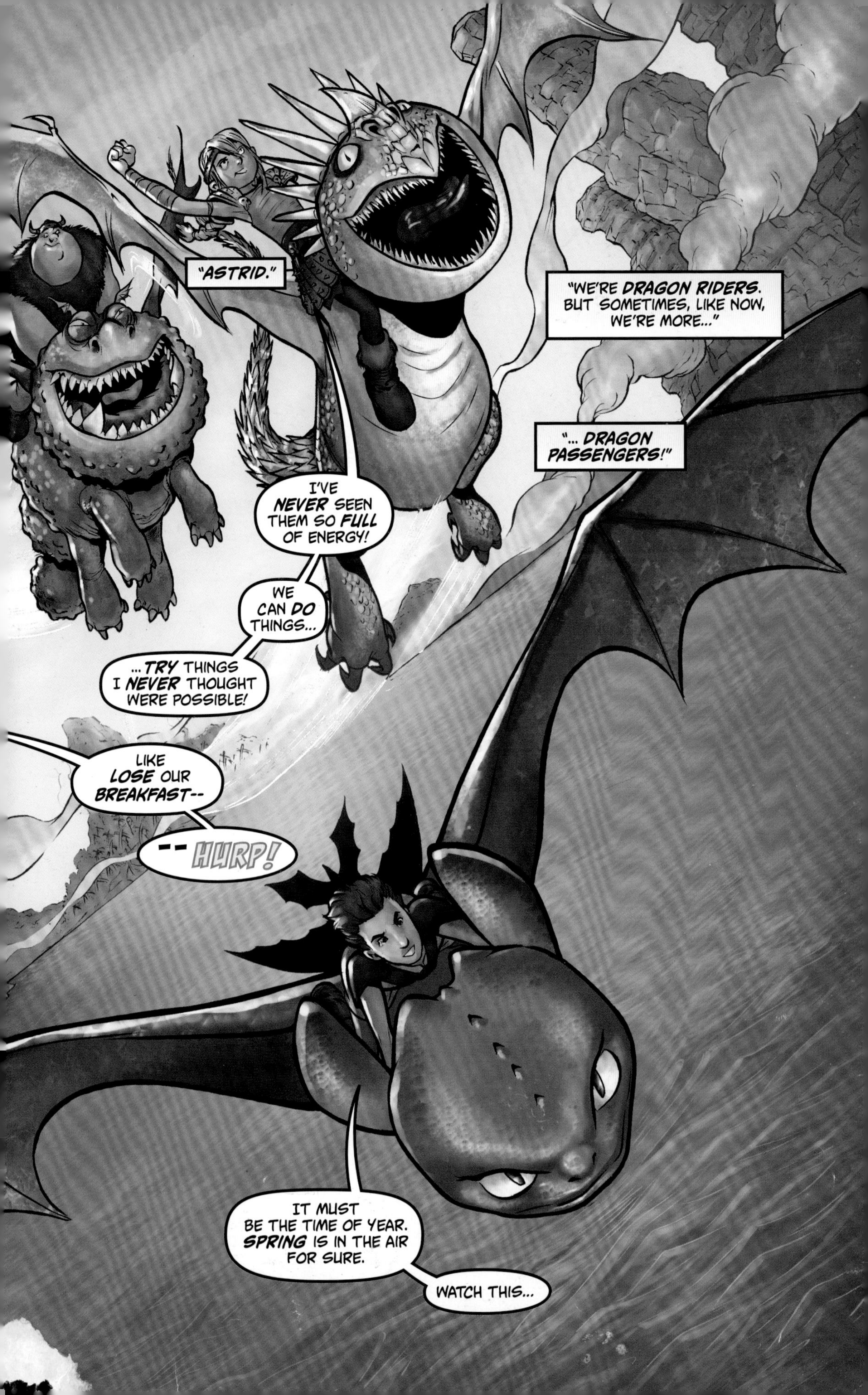
"ASTRID."
"WE'RE DRAGON RIDERS. BUT SOMETIMES, LIKE NOW, WE'RE MORE..."
"... DRAGON PASSENGERS!"
I'VE NEVER SEEN THEM SO FULL OF ENERGY!
WE CAN DO THINGS...
...TRY THINGS I NEVER THOUGHT WERE POSSIBLE!
LIKE LOSE OUR BREAKFAST--
--HURP!
IT MUST BE THE TIME OF YEAR. SPRING IS IN THE AIR FOR SURE.
WATCH THIS...

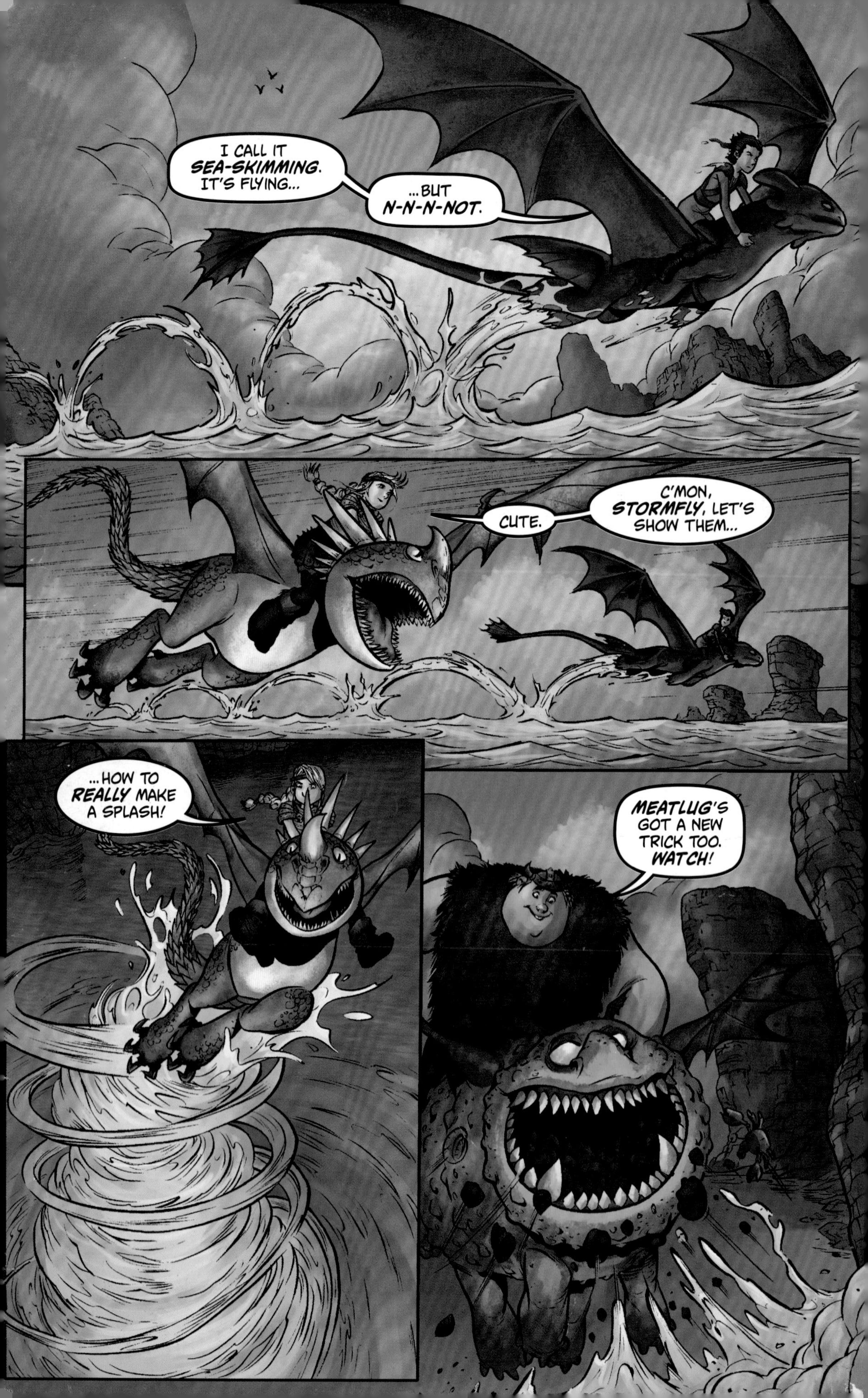
I CALL IT SEA-SKIMMING. IT'S FLYING...
...BUT N-N-N-NOT.
CUTE.
C'MON, STORMFLY, LET'S SHOW THEM...
...HOW TO REALLY MAKE A SPLASH!
MEATLUG'S GOT A NEW TRICK TOO. WATCH!

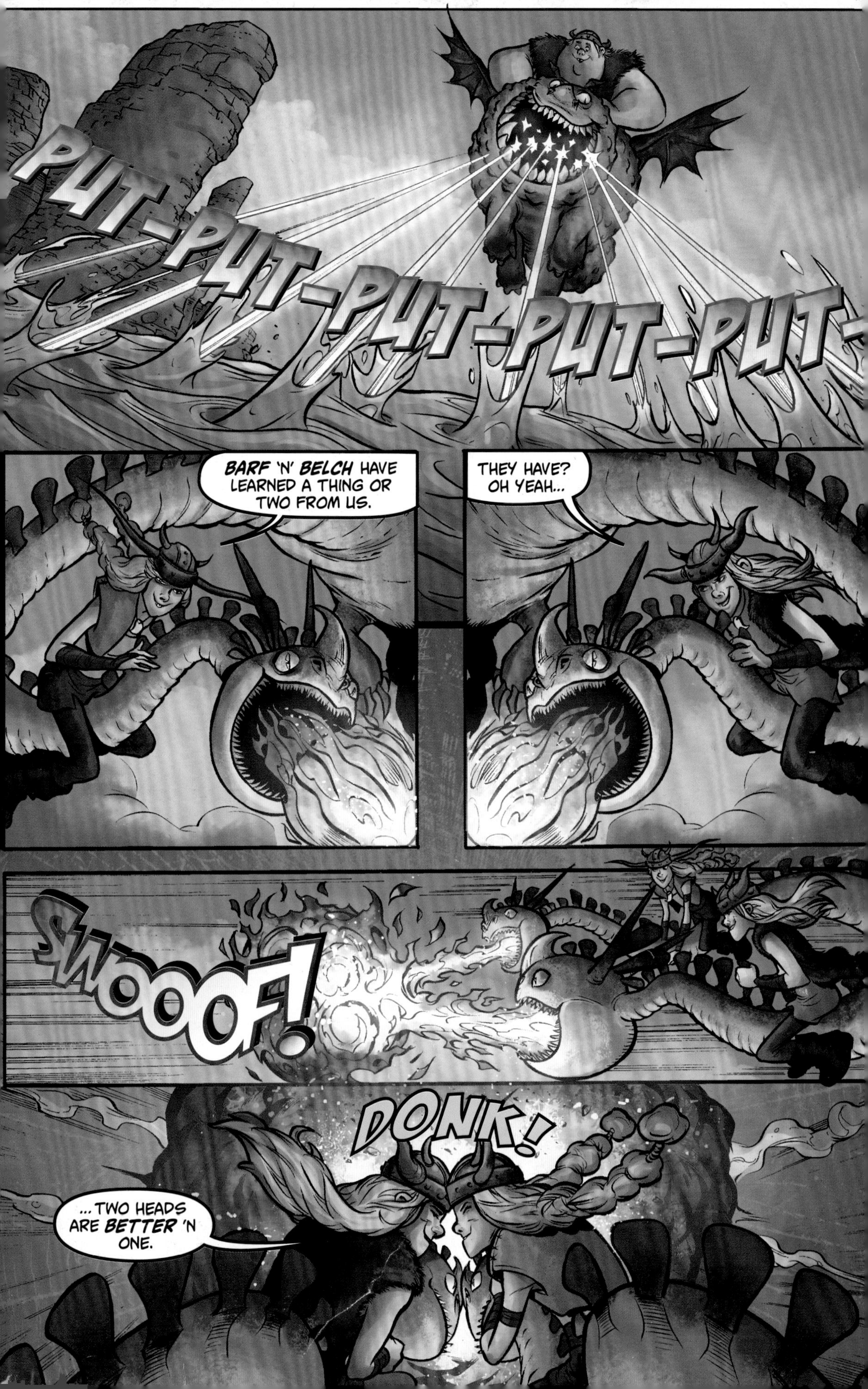
PUT-PUT-PUT-PUT-PUT-
BARF 'N' BELCH HAVE LEARNED A THING OR TWO FROM US.
THEY HAVE? OH YEAH...
SWOOOF!
DONK!
...TWO HEADS ARE BETTER 'N ONE.

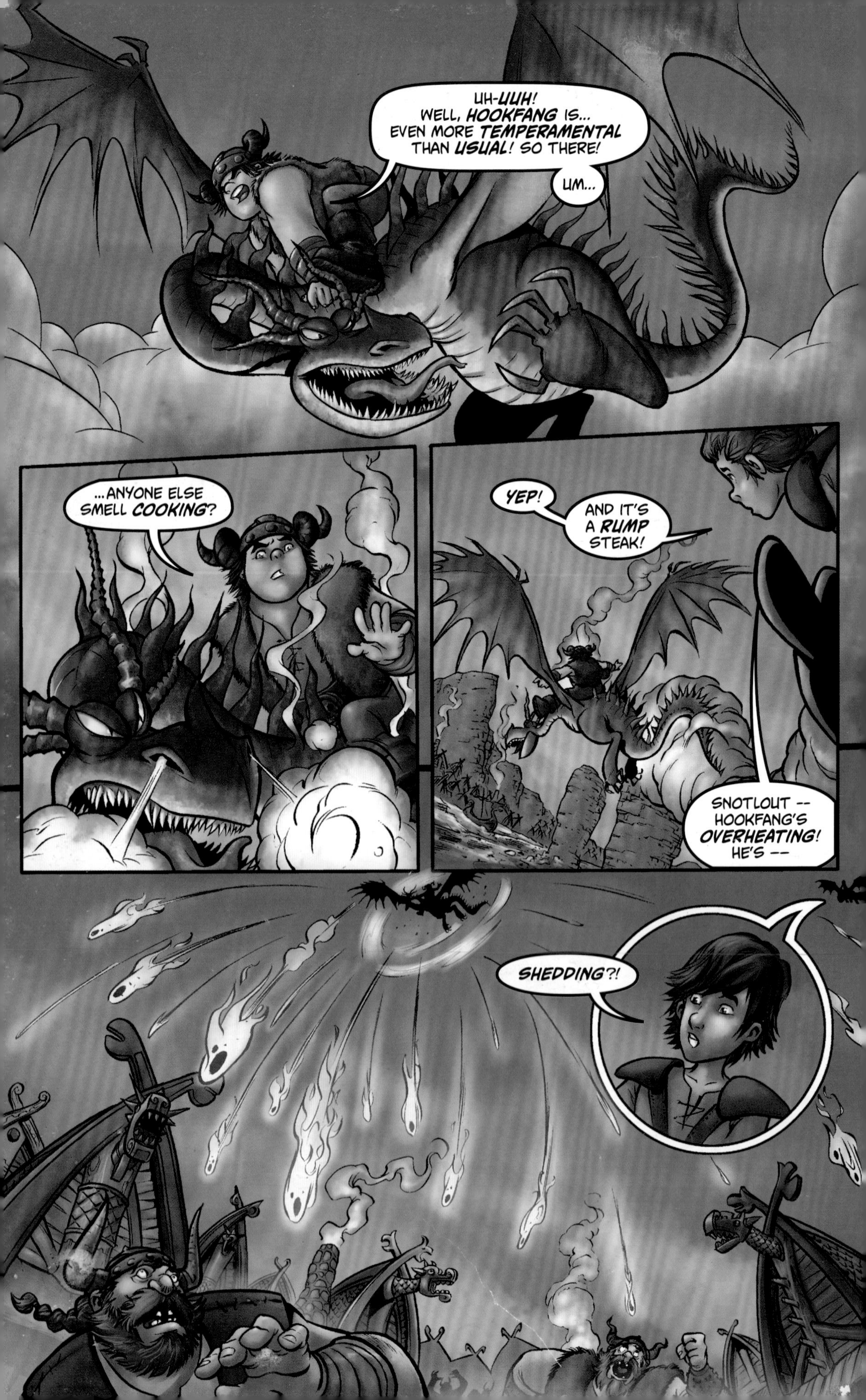
UH-UUH! WELL, HOOKFANG IS... EVEN MORE TEMPERAMENTAL THAN USUAL! SO THERE!
UM...
...ANYONE ELSE SMELL COOKING?
YEP!
AND IT'S A RUMP STEAK!
SNOTLOUT -- HOOKFANG'S OVERHEATING! HE'S --
SHEDDING?!

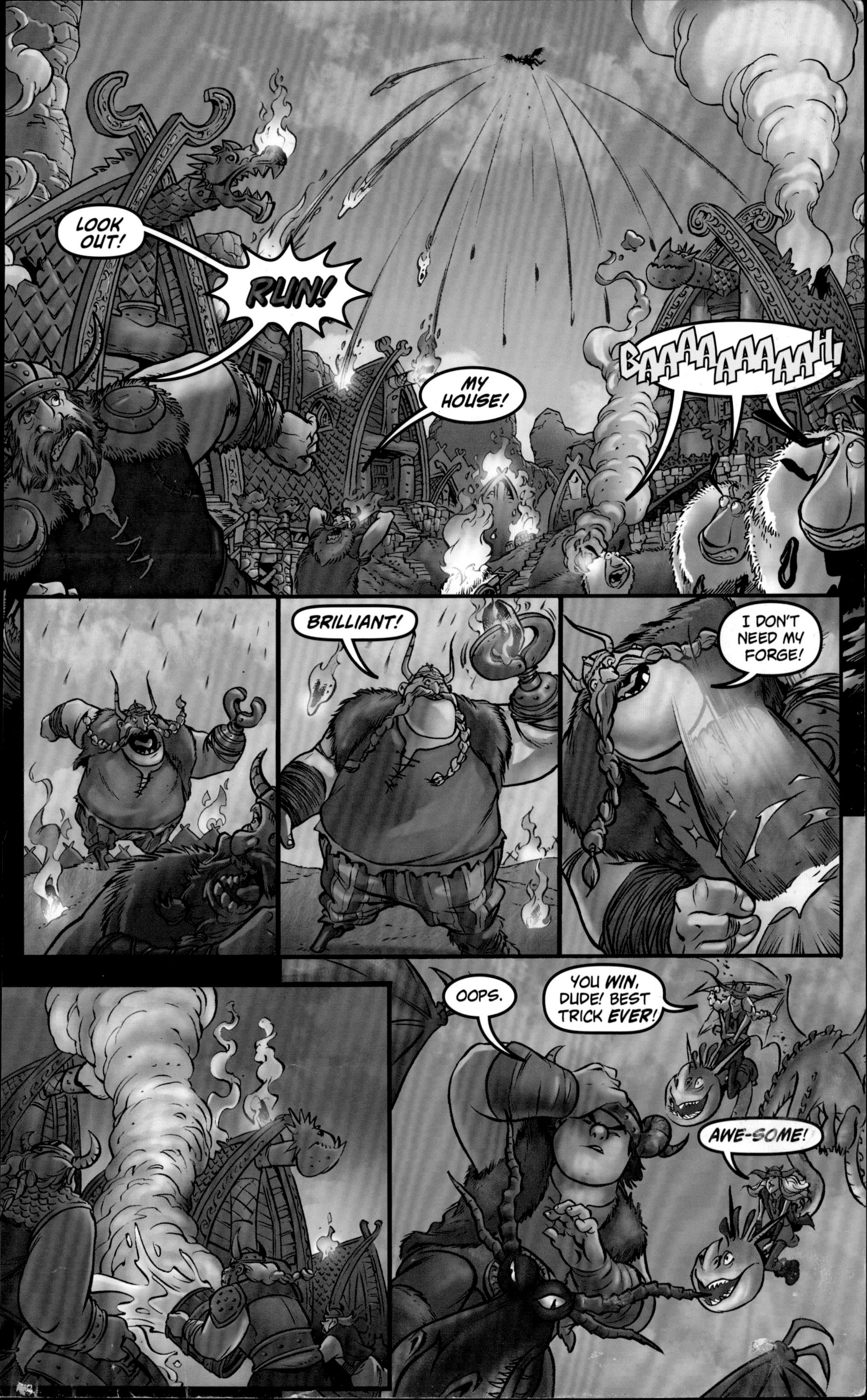
LOOK OUT!
RUN!
MY HOUSE!
BAAAAAAAAAH!
BRILLIANT!
I DON'T NEED MY FORGE!
OOPS.
YOU WIN, DUDE! BEST TRICK EVER!
AWE-SOME!

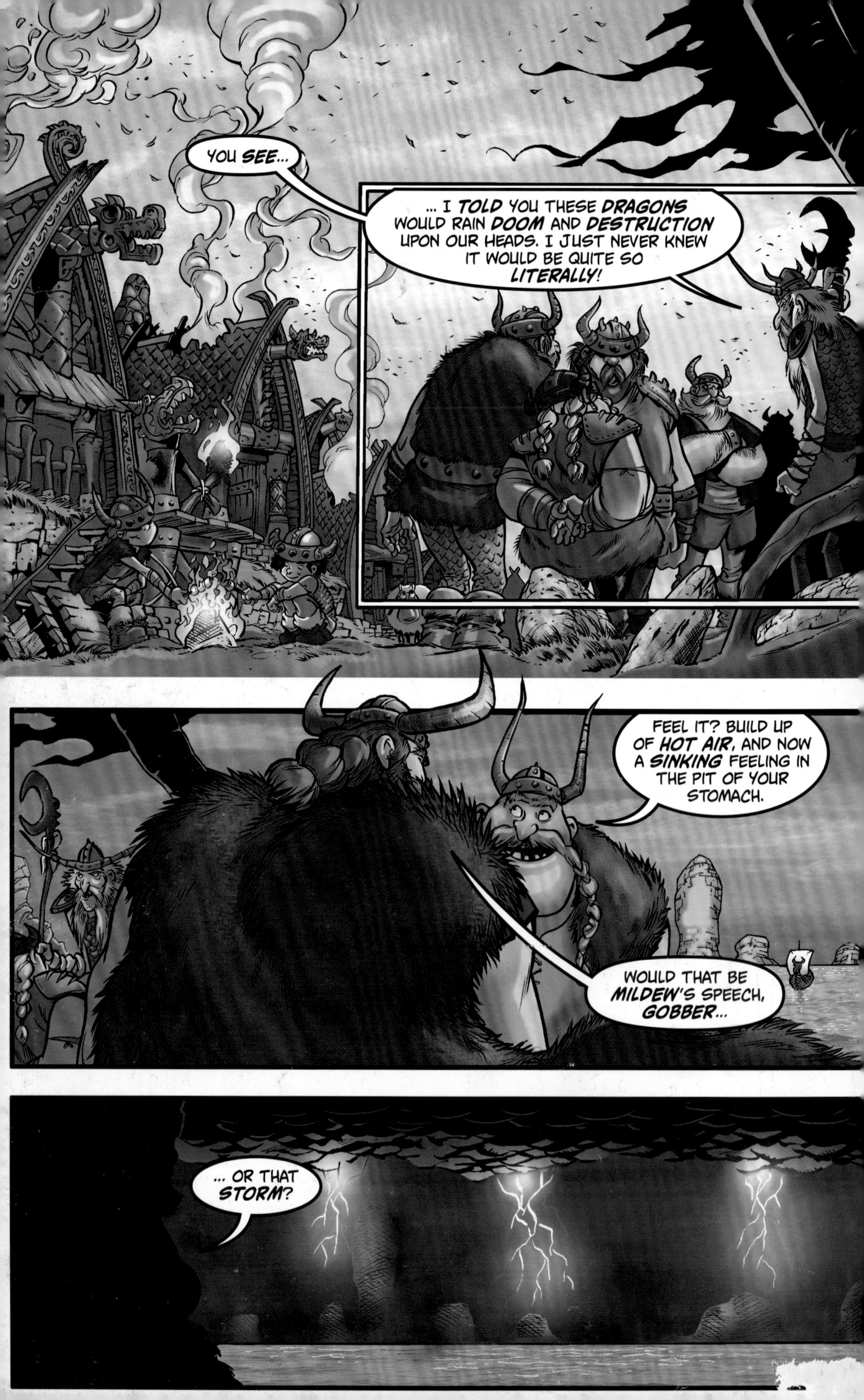
YOU SEE...
... I TOLD YOU THESE DRAGONS WOULD RAIN DOOM AND DESTRUCTION UPON OUR HEADS. I JUST NEVER KNEW IT WOULD BE QUITE SO LITERALLY!
FEEL IT? BUILD UP OF HOT AIR, AND NOW A SINKING FEELING IN THE PIT OF YOUR STOMACH.
WOULD THAT BE MILDEW'S SPEECH, GOBBER...
... OR THAT STORM?

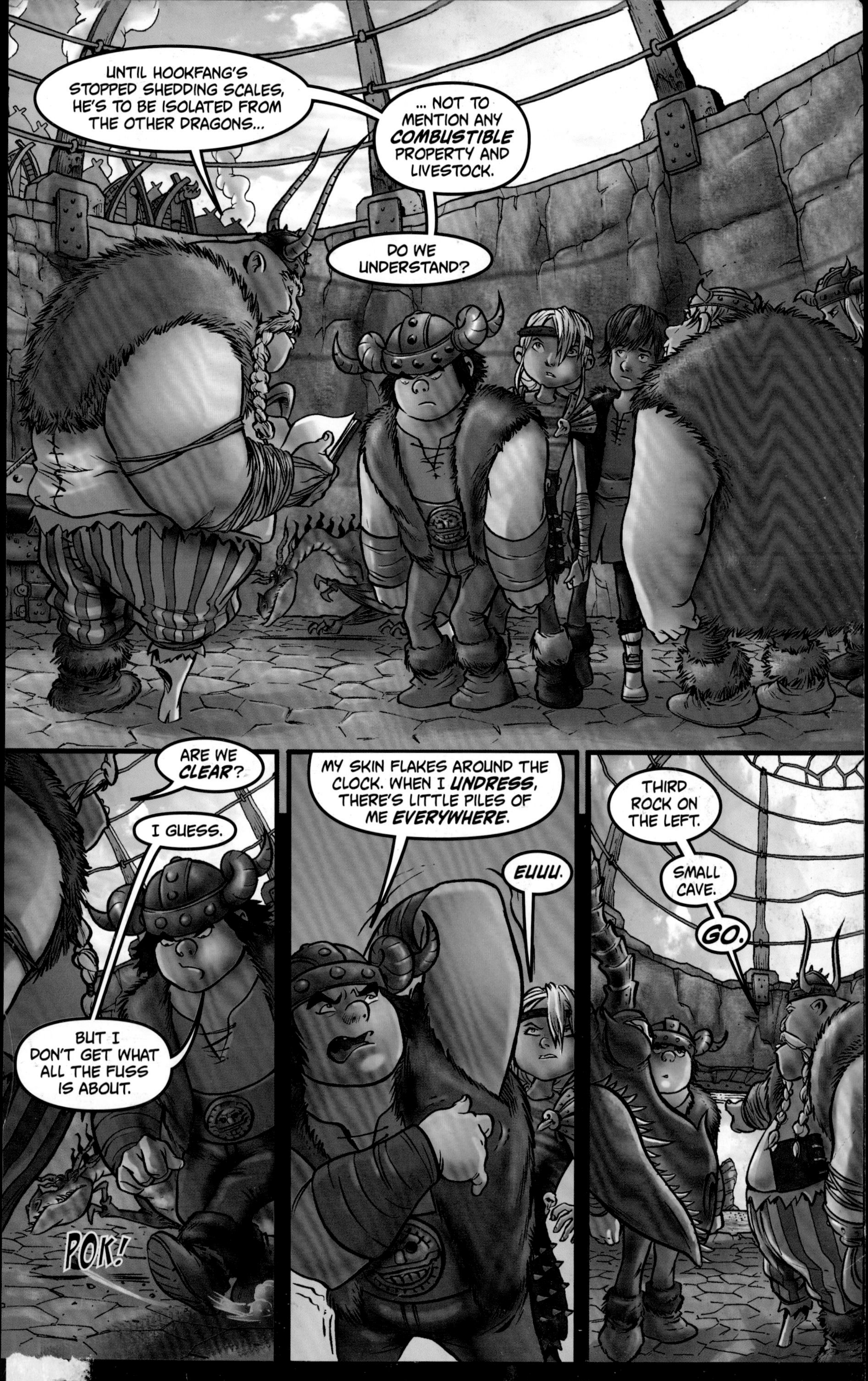
UNTIL HOOKFANG'S STOPPED SHEDDING SCALES, HE'S TO BE ISOLATED FROM THE OTHER DRAGONS...
... NOT TO MENTION ANY COMBUSTIBLE PROPERTY AND LIVESTOCK.
DO WE UNDERSTAND?
ARE WE CLEAR?
I GUESS.
BUT I DON'T GET WHAT ALL THE FUSS IS ABOUT.
POK!
MY SKIN FLAKES AROUND THE CLOCK. WHEN I UNDRESS, THERE'S LITTLE PILES OF ME EVERYWHERE.
EUUU.
THIRD ROCK ON THE LEFT.
SMALL CAVE.
GO.

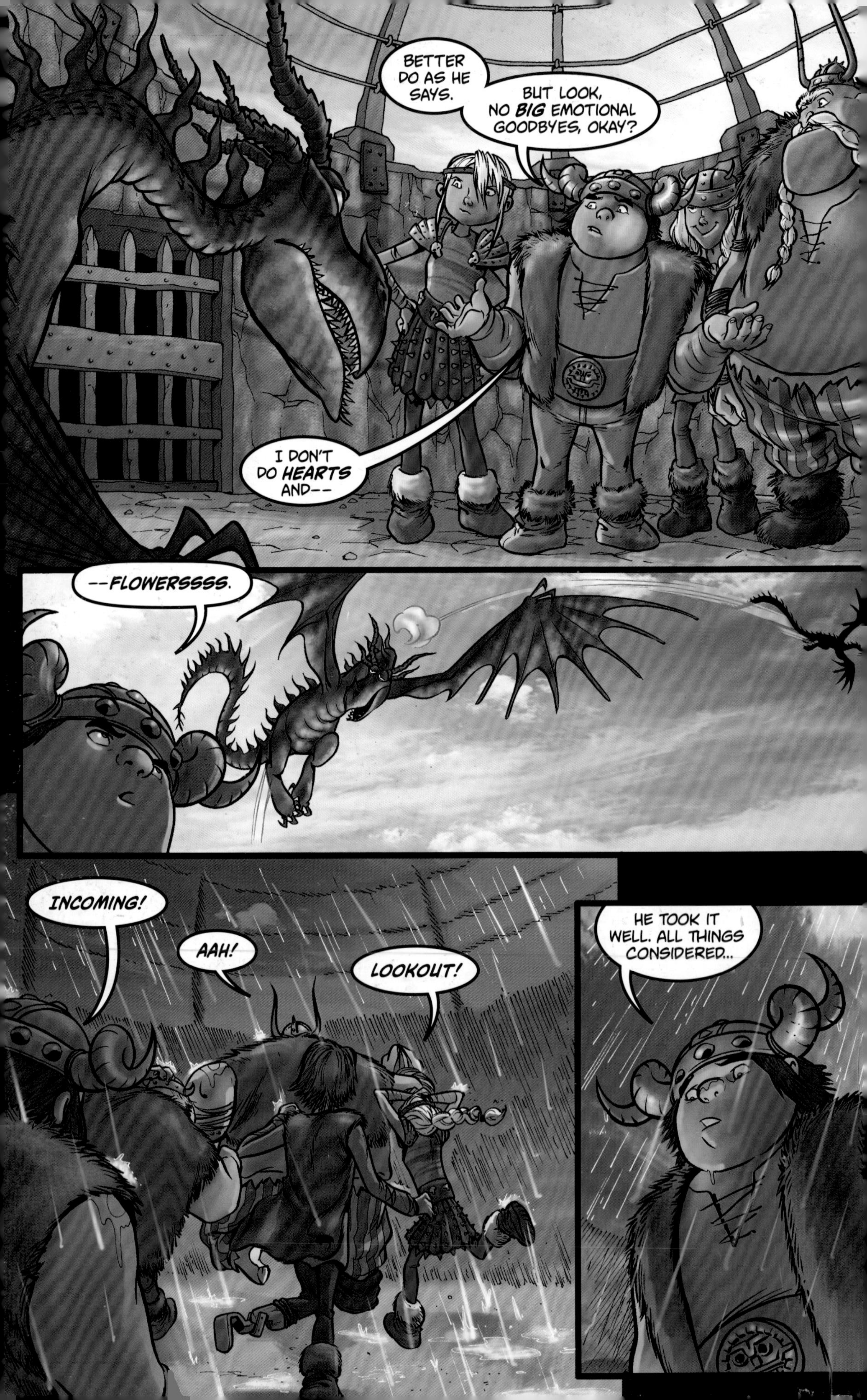
BETTER DO AS HE SAYS.
BUT LOOK, NO BIG EMOTIONAL GOODBYES, OKAY?
I DON'T DO HEARTS AND--
--FLOWERSSSS.
INCOMING!
AAH!
LOOKOUT!
HE TOOK IT WELL. ALL THINGS CONSIDERED...

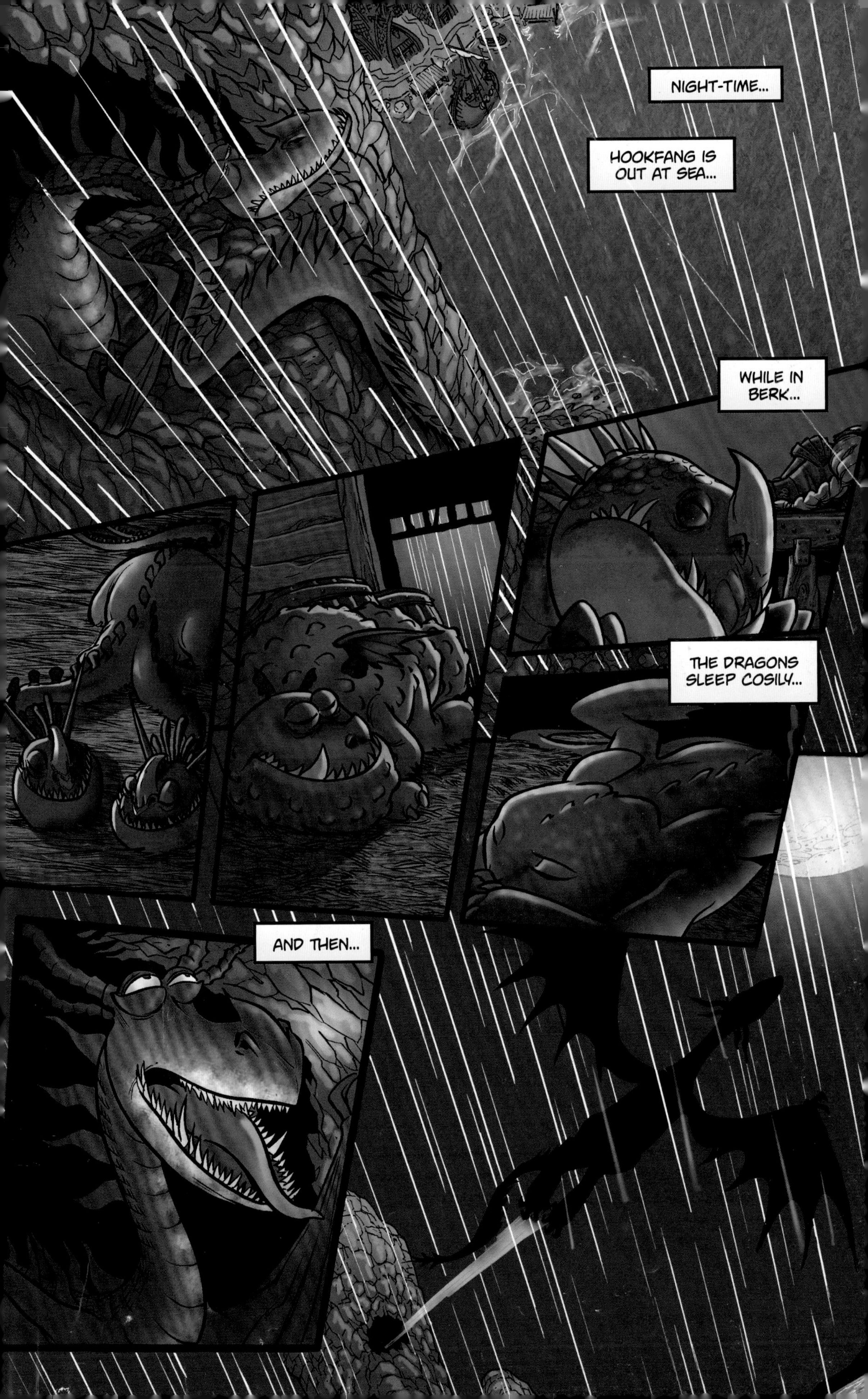
NIGHT-TIME...
HOOKFANG IS OUT AT SEA...
WHILE IN BERK...
THE DRAGONS SLEEP COSILY...
AND THEN...

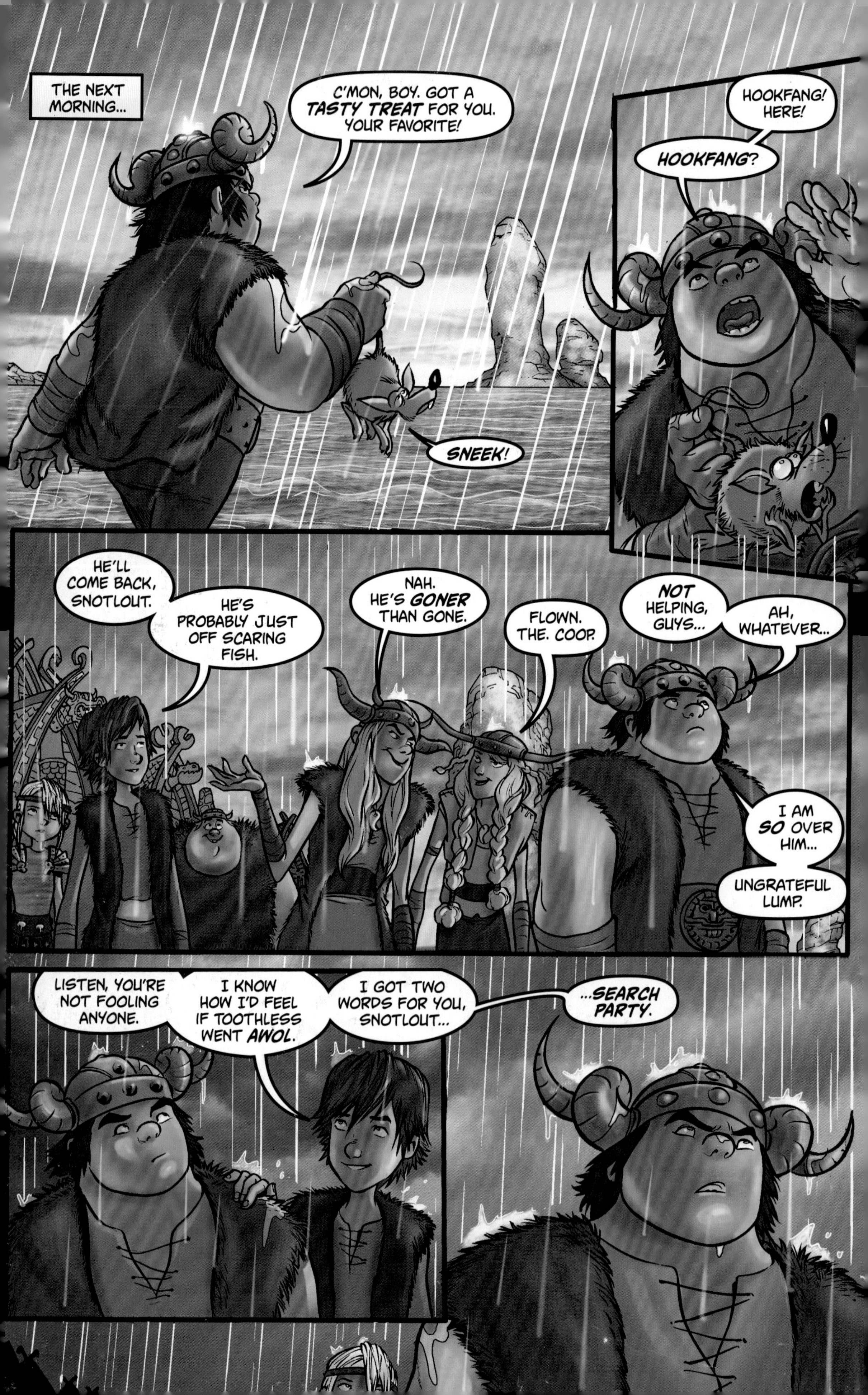
THE NEXT MORNING...
C'MON, BOY. GOT A **TASTY TREAT** FOR YOU. YOUR FAVORITE!
SNEEK!
HOOKFANG! HERE!
HOOKFANG?
HE'LL COME BACK, SNOTLOUT.
HE'S PROBABLY JUST OFF SCARING FISH.
NAH. HE'S **GONER** THAN GONE.
FLOWN. THE. COOP.
NOT HELPING, GUYS...
AH, WHATEVER...
I AM **SO** OVER HIM...
UNGRATEFUL LUMP.
LISTEN, YOU'RE NOT FOOLING ANYONE.
I KNOW HOW I'D FEEL IF TOOTHLESS WENT **AWOL**.
I GOT TWO WORDS FOR YOU, SNOTLOUT...
...**SEARCH PARTY**.

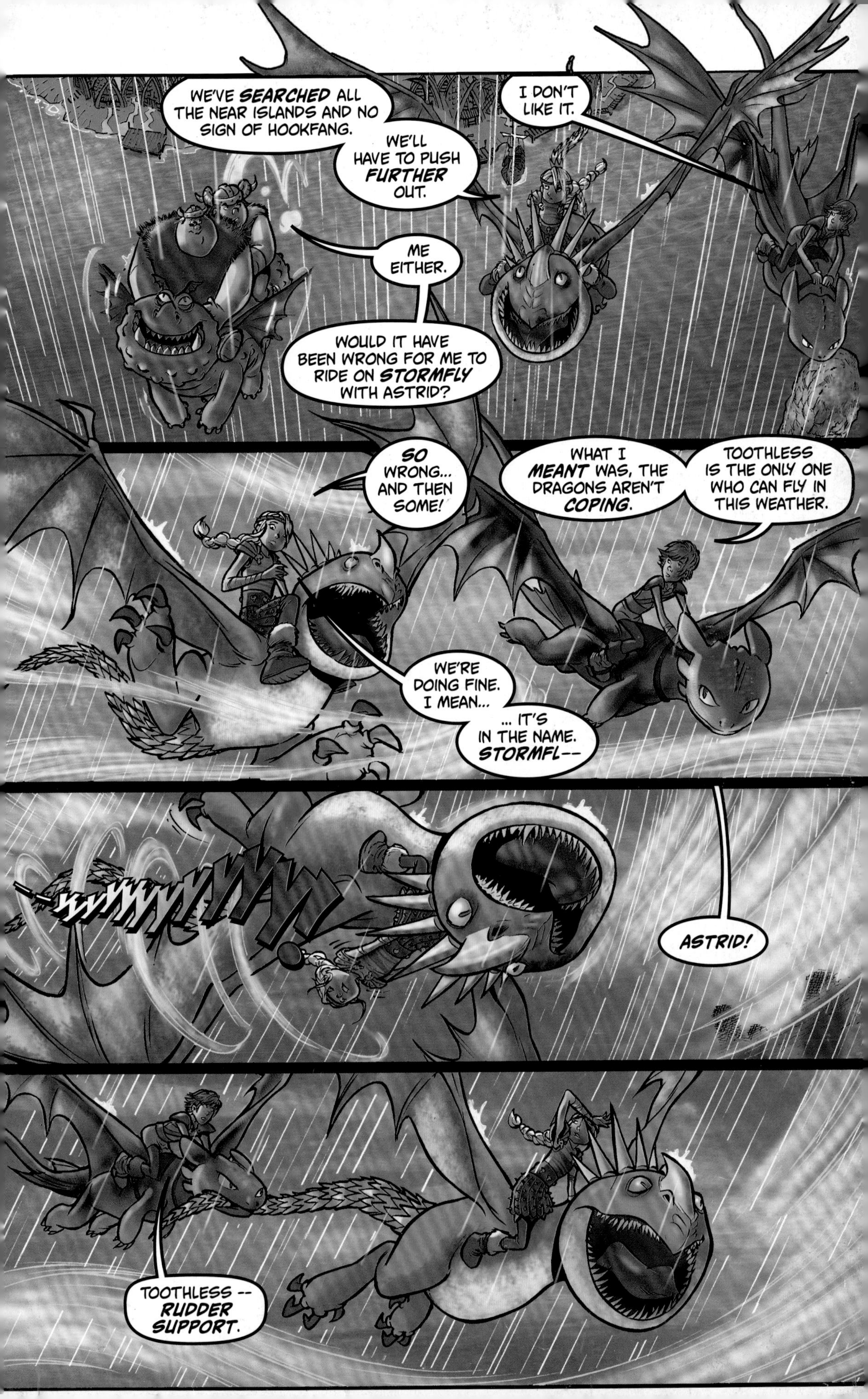
WE'VE SEARCHED ALL THE NEAR ISLANDS AND NO SIGN OF HOOKFANG.
WE'LL HAVE TO PUSH FURTHER OUT.
I DON'T LIKE IT.
ME EITHER.
WOULD IT HAVE BEEN WRONG FOR ME TO RIDE ON STORMFLY WITH ASTRID?
SO WRONG... AND THEN SOME!
WHAT I MEANT WAS, THE DRAGONS AREN'T COPING.
TOOTHLESS IS THE ONLY ONE WHO CAN FLY IN THIS WEATHER.
WE'RE DOING FINE. I MEAN...
... IT'S IN THE NAME. STORMFL--
YYYYYYYYYYY
ASTRID!
TOOTHLESS -- RUDDER SUPPORT.

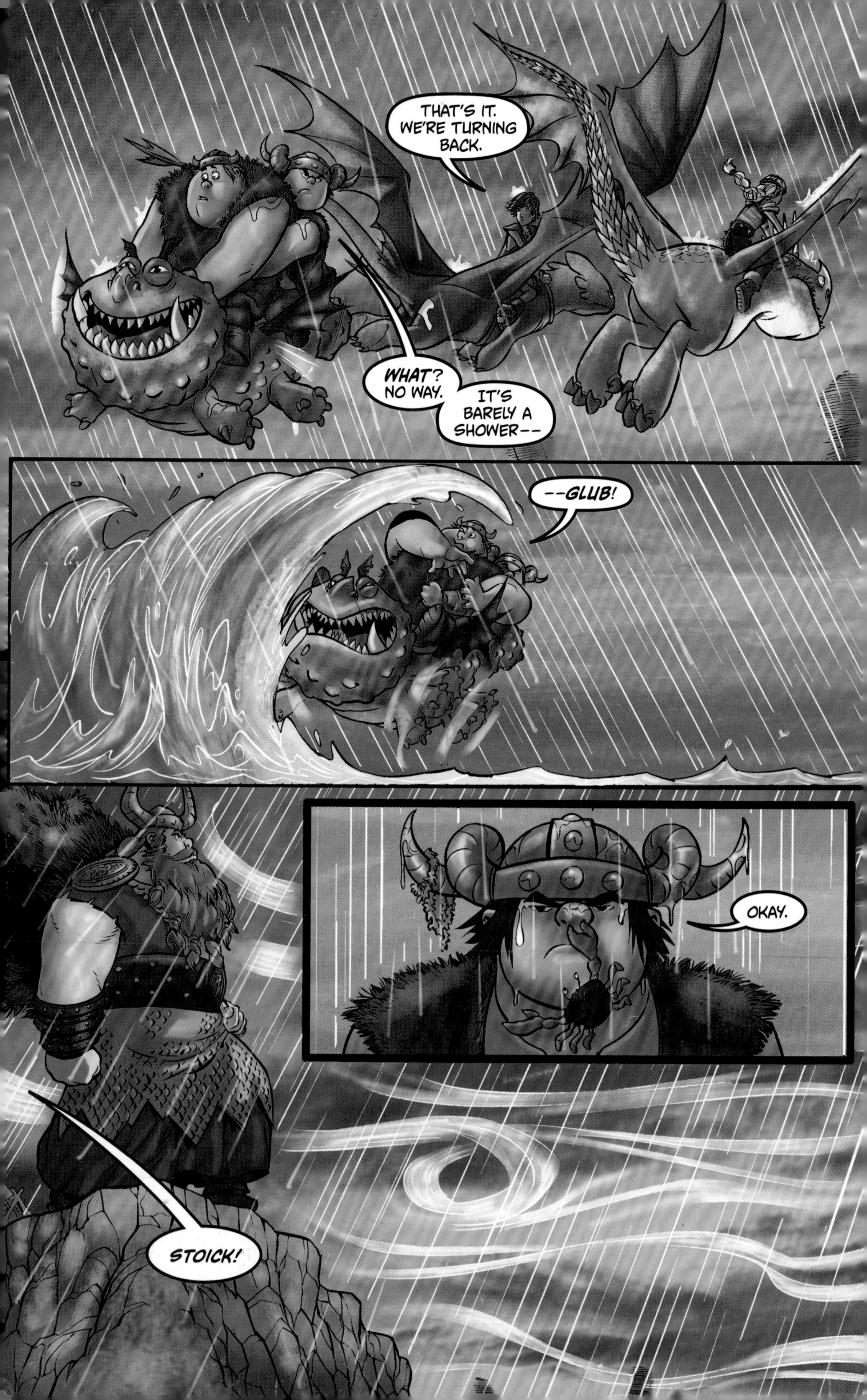
THAT'S IT. WE'RE TURNING BACK.
WHAT? NO WAY.
IT'S BARELY A SHOWER--
--GLUB!
OKAY.
STOICK!

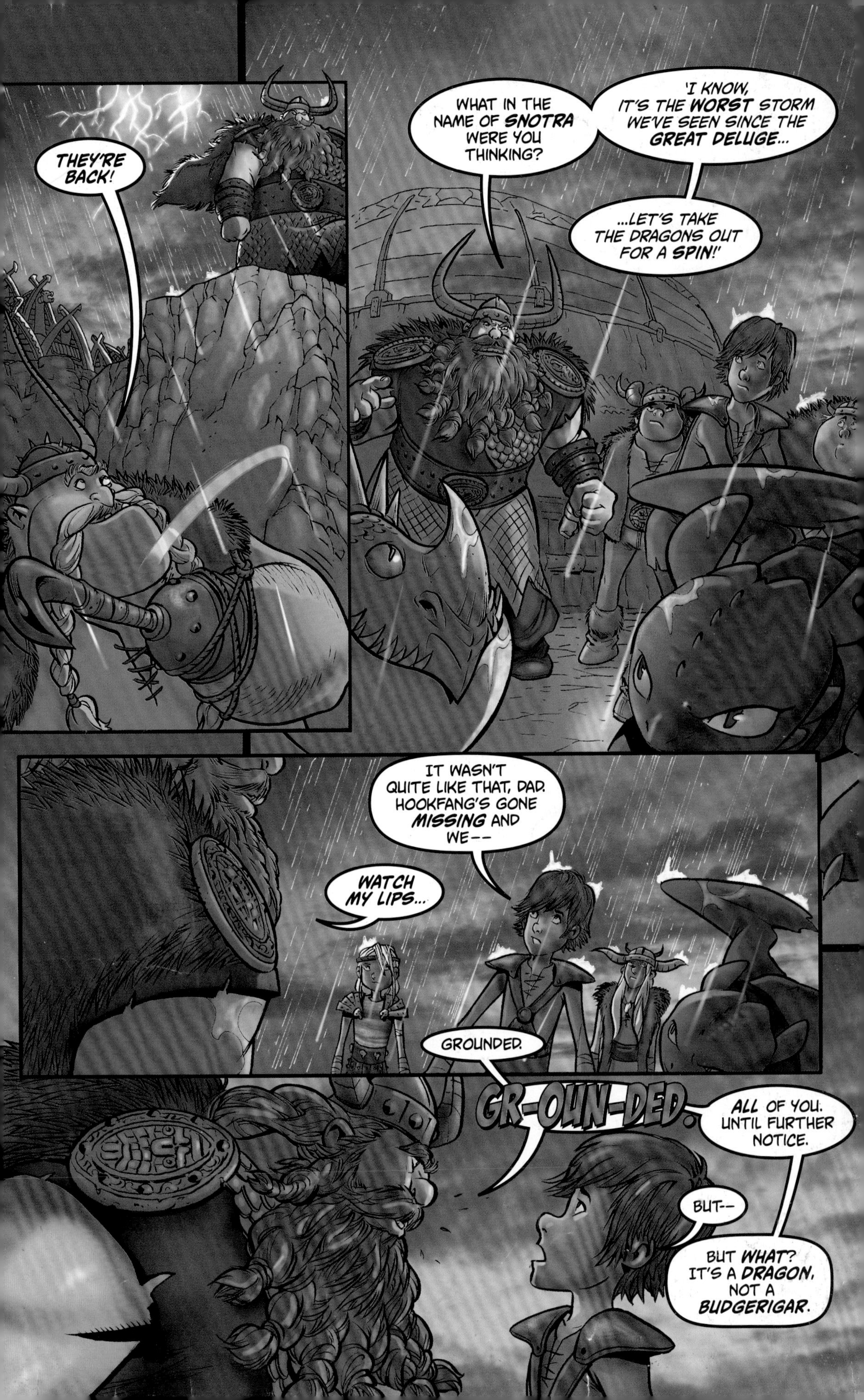
THEY'RE BACK!
WHAT IN THE NAME OF SNOTRA WERE YOU THINKING?
'I KNOW, IT'S THE WORST STORM WE'VE SEEN SINCE THE GREAT DELUGE...
...LET'S TAKE THE DRAGONS OUT FOR A SPIN!'
IT WASN'T QUITE LIKE THAT, DAD. HOOKFANG'S GONE MISSING AND WE--
WATCH MY LIPS...
GROUNDED.
GR-OUN-DED.
ALL OF YOU. UNTIL FURTHER NOTICE.
BUT--
BUT WHAT? IT'S A DRAGON, NOT A BUDGERIGAR.

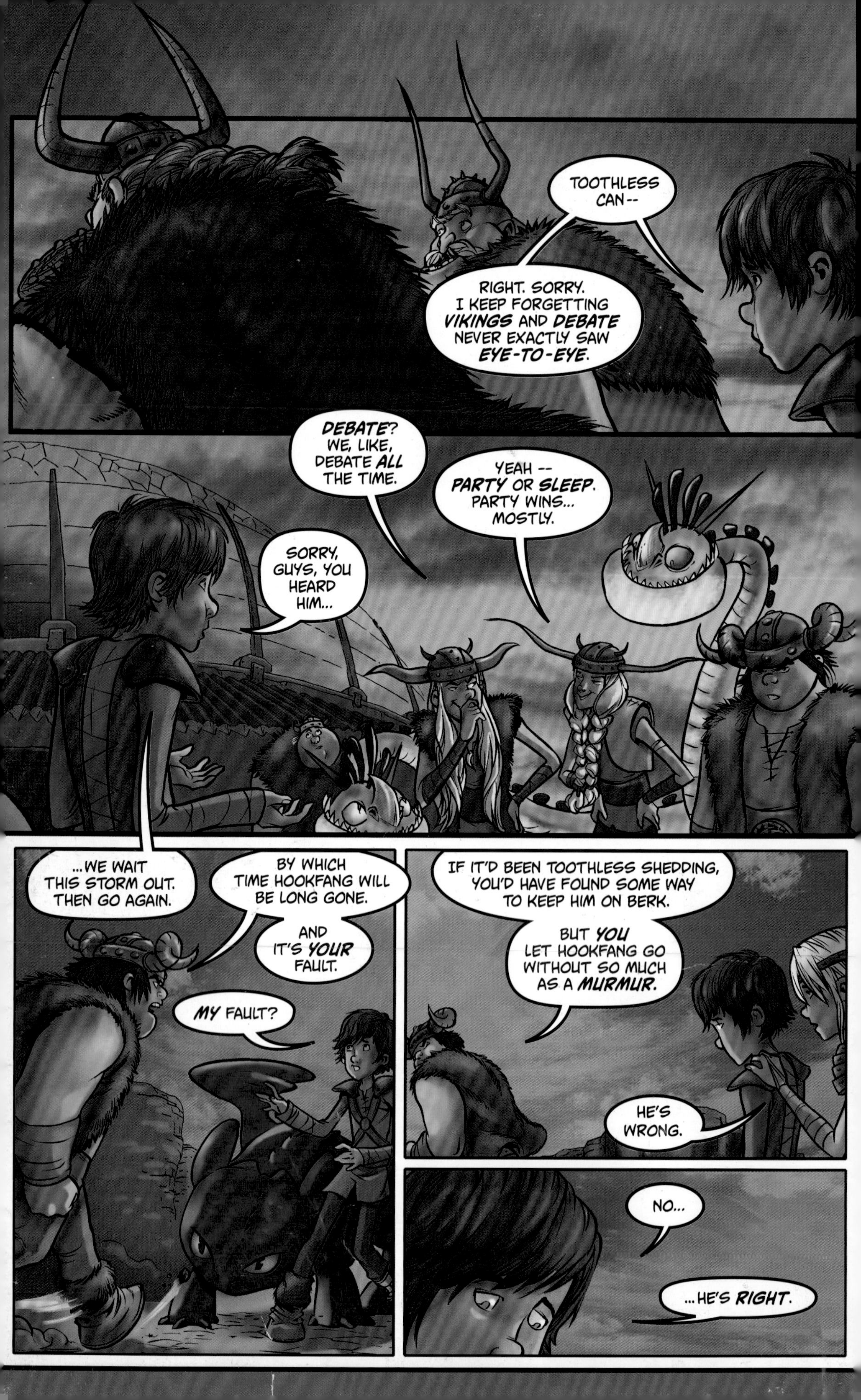
TOOTHLESS CAN--
RIGHT. SORRY. I KEEP FORGETTING VIKINGS AND DEBATE NEVER EXACTLY SAW EYE-TO-EYE.
DEBATE? WE, LIKE, DEBATE ALL THE TIME.
YEAH -- PARTY OR SLEEP. PARTY WINS... MOSTLY.
SORRY, GUYS, YOU HEARD HIM...
...WE WAIT THIS STORM OUT. THEN GO AGAIN.
BY WHICH TIME HOOKFANG WILL BE LONG GONE.
AND IT'S YOUR FAULT.
MY FAULT?
IF IT'D BEEN TOOTHLESS SHEDDING, YOU'D HAVE FOUND SOME WAY TO KEEP HIM ON BERK.
BUT YOU LET HOOKFANG GO WITHOUT SO MUCH AS A MURMUR.
HE'S WRONG.
NO...
...HE'S RIGHT.

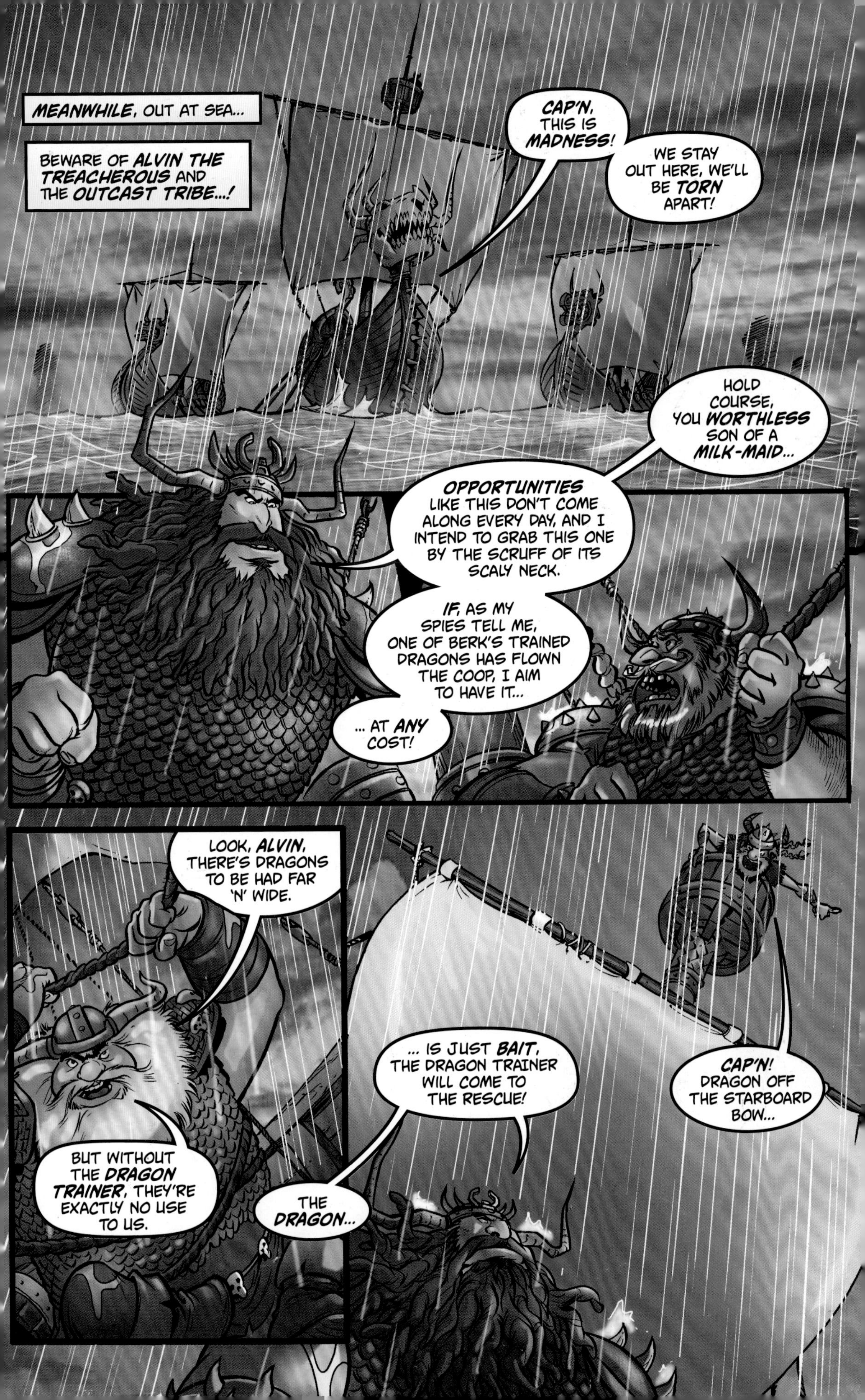
MEANWHILE, OUT AT SEA...
BEWARE OF ALVIN THE TREACHEROUS AND THE OUTCAST TRIBE...!
CAP'N, THIS IS MADNESS!
WE STAY OUT HERE, WE'LL BE TORN APART!
HOLD COURSE, YOU WORTHLESS SON OF A MILK-MAID...
OPPORTUNITIES LIKE THIS DON'T COME ALONG EVERY DAY, AND I INTEND TO GRAB THIS ONE BY THE SCRUFF OF ITS SCALY NECK.
IF, AS MY SPIES TELL ME, ONE OF BERK'S TRAINED DRAGONS HAS FLOWN THE COOP, I AIM TO HAVE IT...
... AT ANY COST!
LOOK, ALVIN, THERE'S DRAGONS TO BE HAD FAR 'N' WIDE.
BUT WITHOUT THE DRAGON TRAINER, THEY'RE EXACTLY NO USE TO US.
THE DRAGON...
... IS JUST BAIT, THE DRAGON TRAINER WILL COME TO THE RESCUE!
CAP'N! DRAGON OFF THE STARBOARD BOW...

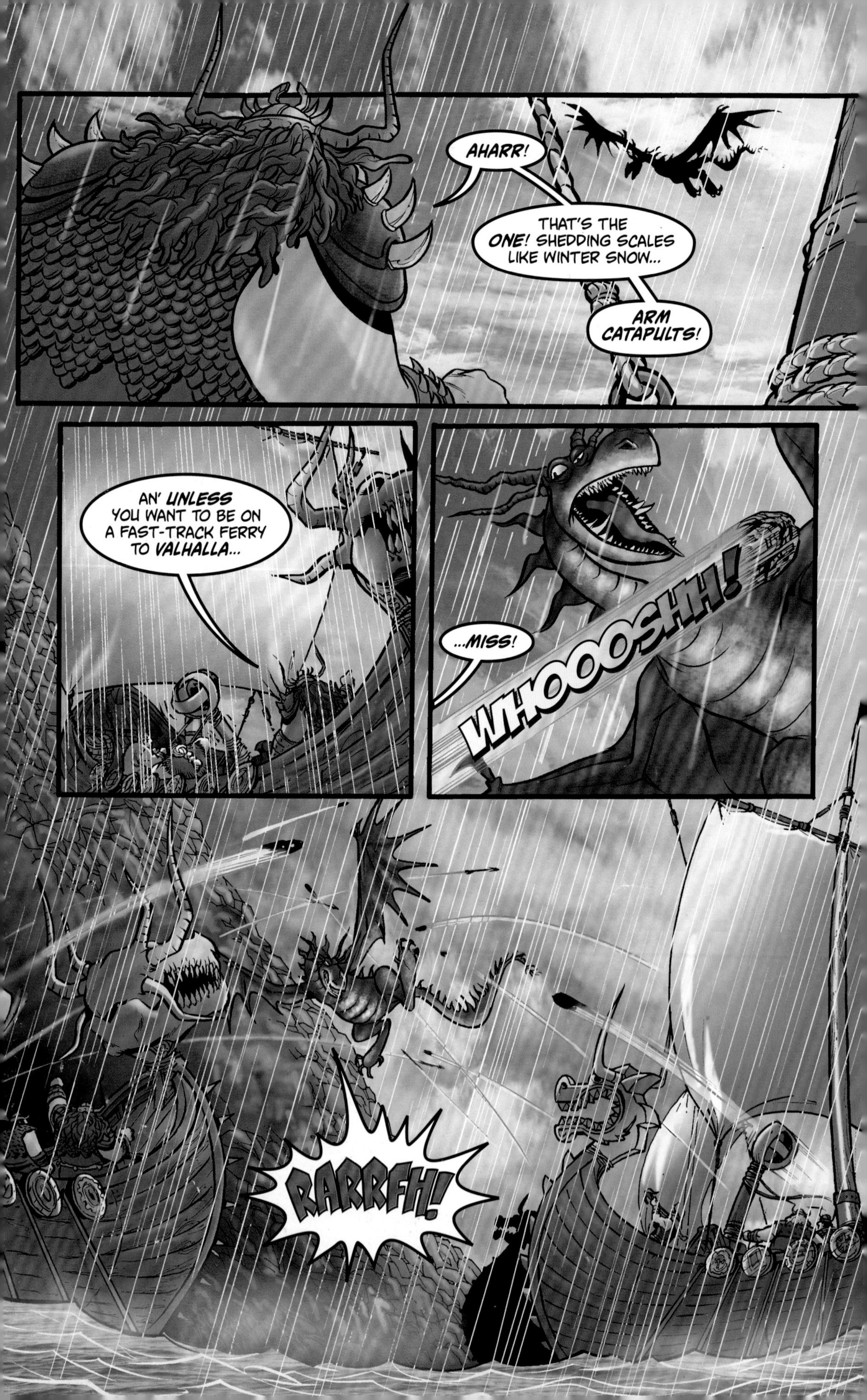
AHARR!
THAT'S THE ONE! SHEDDING SCALES LIKE WINTER SNOW...
ARM CATAPULTS!
AN' UNLESS YOU WANT TO BE ON A FAST-TRACK FERRY TO VALHALLA...
...MISS!
WHOOOOSHH!
RARRFH!

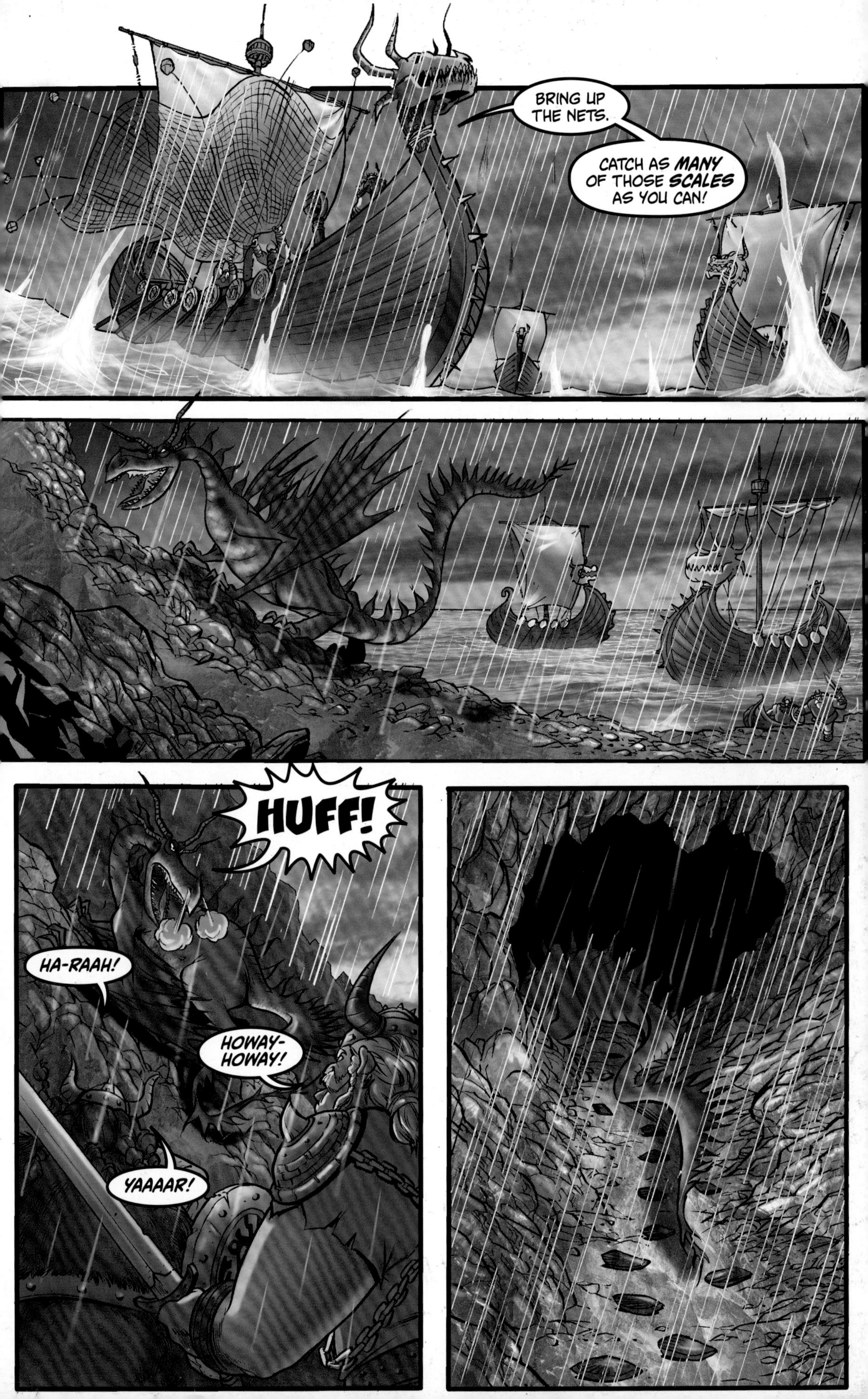
BRING UP THE NETS.
CATCH AS MANY OF THOSE SCALES AS YOU CAN!
HUFF!
HA-RAAH!
HOWAY-HOWAY!
YAAAAR!

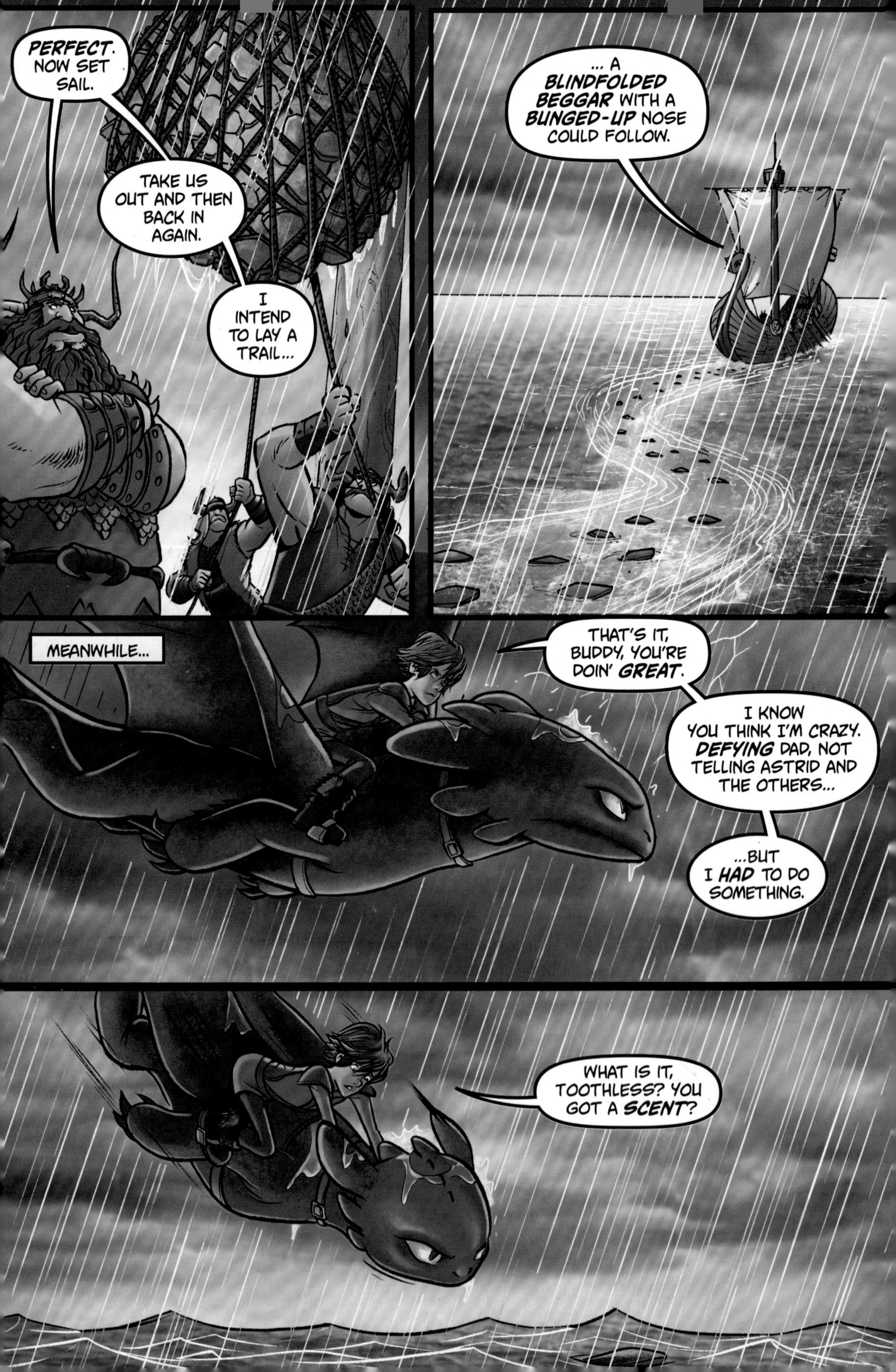
PERFECT. NOW SET SAIL.
TAKE US OUT AND THEN BACK IN AGAIN.
I INTEND TO LAY A TRAIL...
... A BLINDFOLDED BEGGAR WITH A BUNGED-UP NOSE COULD FOLLOW.
MEANWHILE...
THAT'S IT, BUDDY, YOU'RE DOIN' GREAT.
I KNOW YOU THINK I'M CRAZY. DEFYING DAD, NOT TELLING ASTRID AND THE OTHERS...
...BUT I HAD TO DO SOMETHING.
WHAT IS IT, TOOTHLESS? YOU GOT A SCENT?

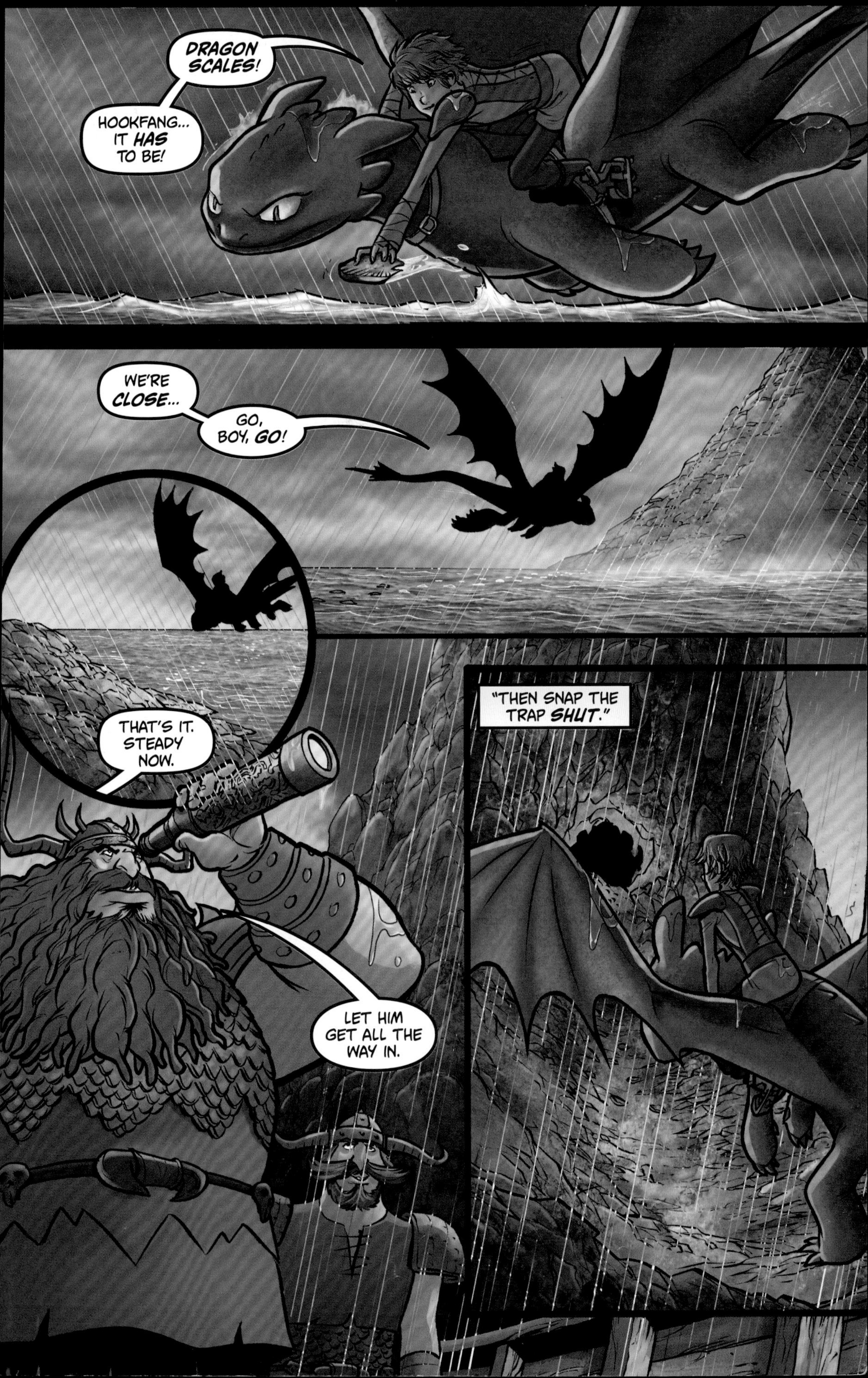
DRAGON SCALES!
HOOKFANG... IT HAS TO BE!
WE'RE CLOSE...
GO, BOY, GO!
THAT'S IT. STEADY NOW.
LET HIM GET ALL THE WAY IN.
"THEN SNAP THE TRAP SHUT."

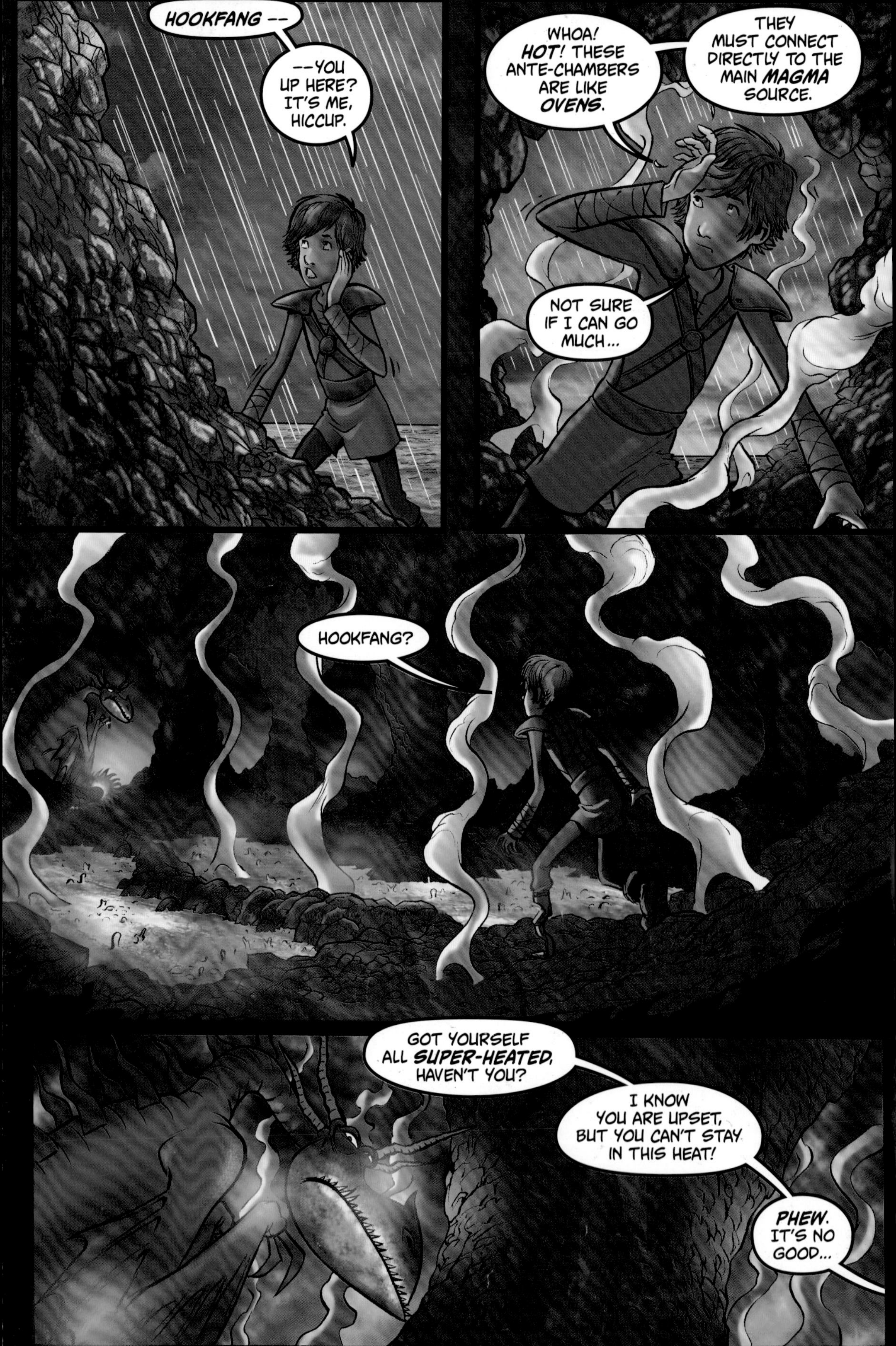
HOOKFANG --
--YOU UP HERE? IT'S ME, HICCUP.
WHOA! HOT! THESE ANTE-CHAMBERS ARE LIKE OVENS.
THEY MUST CONNECT DIRECTLY TO THE MAIN MAGMA SOURCE.
NOT SURE IF I CAN GO MUCH...
HOOKFANG?
GOT YOURSELF ALL SUPER-HEATED, HAVEN'T YOU?
I KNOW YOU ARE UPSET, BUT YOU CAN'T STAY IN THIS HEAT!
PHEW. IT'S NO GOOD...

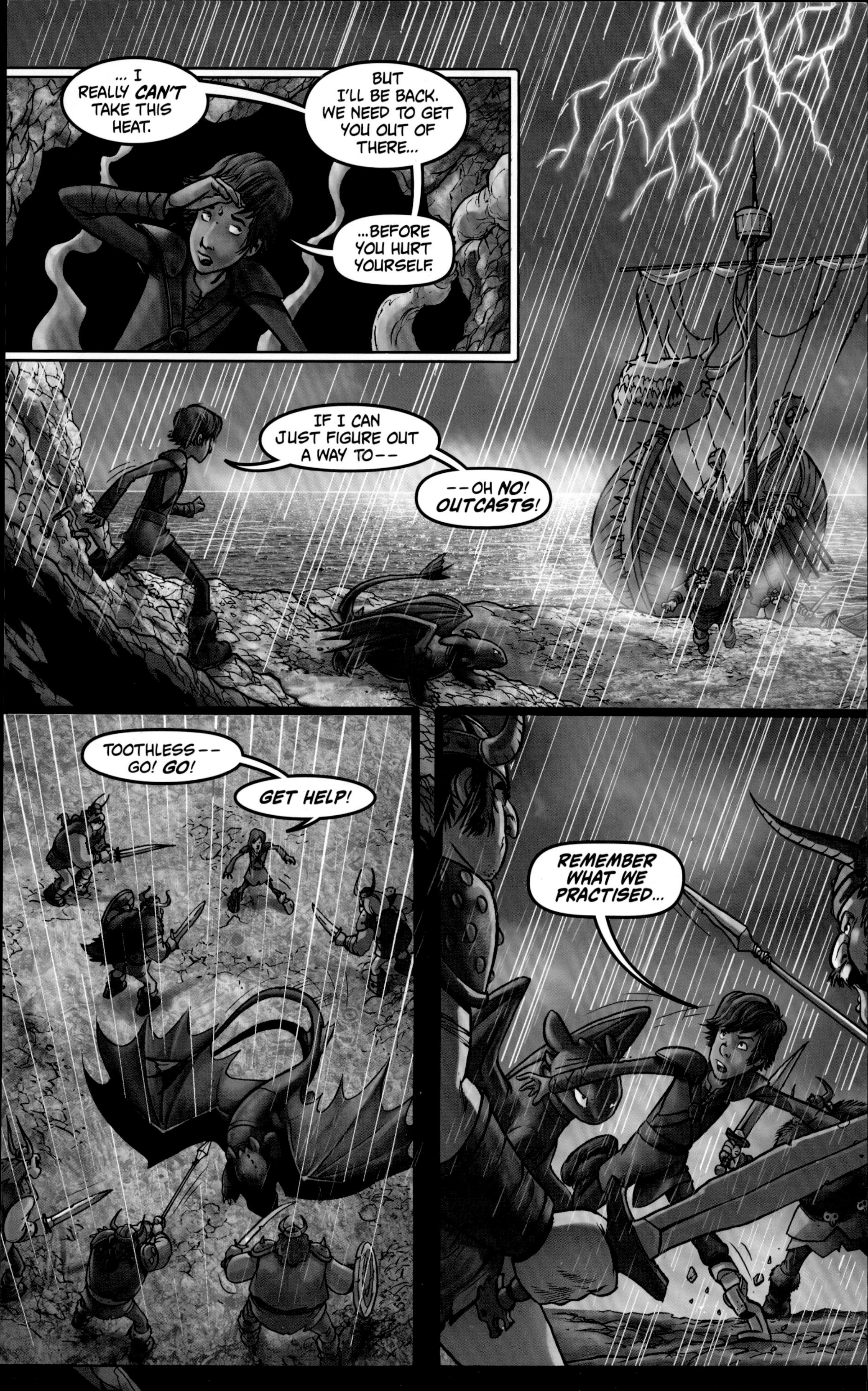
... I REALLY CAN'T TAKE THIS HEAT.
BUT I'LL BE BACK. WE NEED TO GET YOU OUT OF THERE...
...BEFORE YOU HURT YOURSELF.
IF I CAN JUST FIGURE OUT A WAY TO--
--OH NO! OUTCASTS!
TOOTHLESS-- GO! GO!
GET HELP!
REMEMBER WHAT WE PRACTISED...

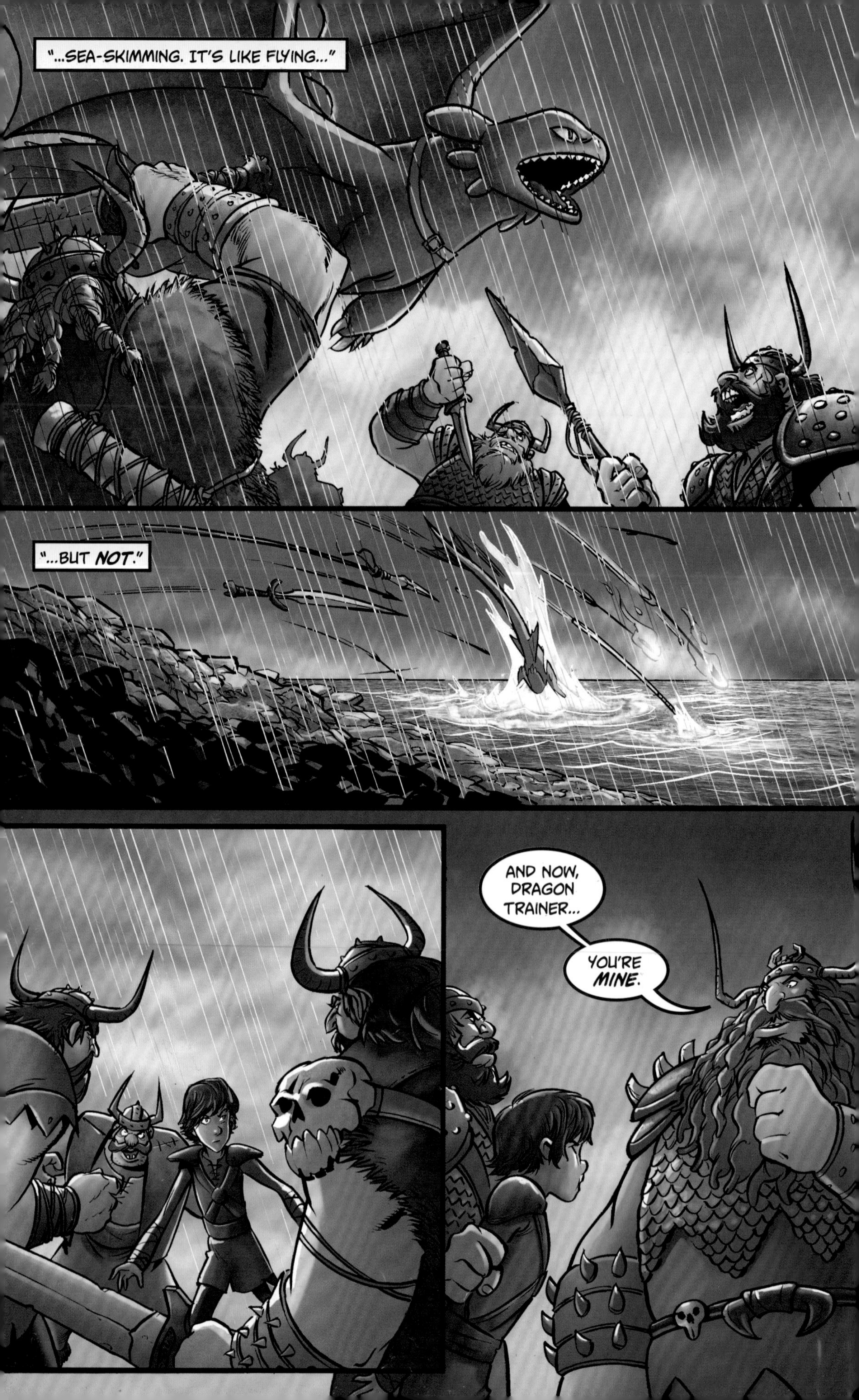
"...SEA-SKIMMING. IT'S LIKE FLYING..."
"...BUT NOT."
AND NOW, DRAGON TRAINER...
YOU'RE MINE.

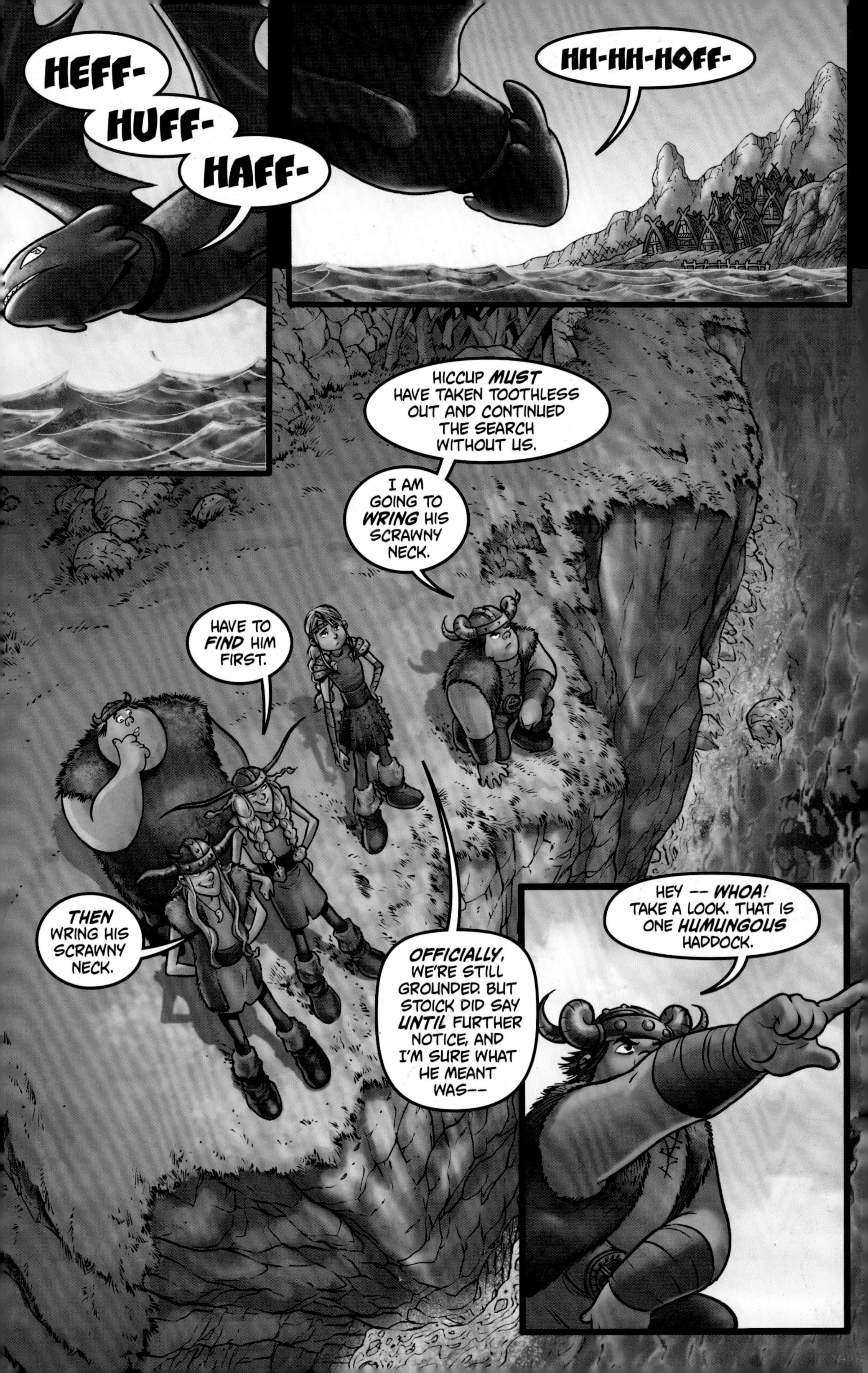
HEFF-
HUFF-
HAFF-
HH-HH-HOFF-
HICCUP *MUST* HAVE TAKEN TOOTHLESS OUT AND CONTINUED THE SEARCH WITHOUT US.
I AM GOING TO *WRING* HIS SCRAWNY NECK.
HAVE TO *FIND* HIM FIRST.
THEN WRING HIS SCRAWNY NECK.
OFFICIALLY, WE'RE STILL GROUNDED. BUT STOICK DID SAY *UNTIL* FURTHER NOTICE, AND I'M SURE WHAT HE MEANT WAS--
HEY -- *WHOA!* TAKE A LOOK. THAT IS ONE *HUMUNGOUS* HADDOCK.

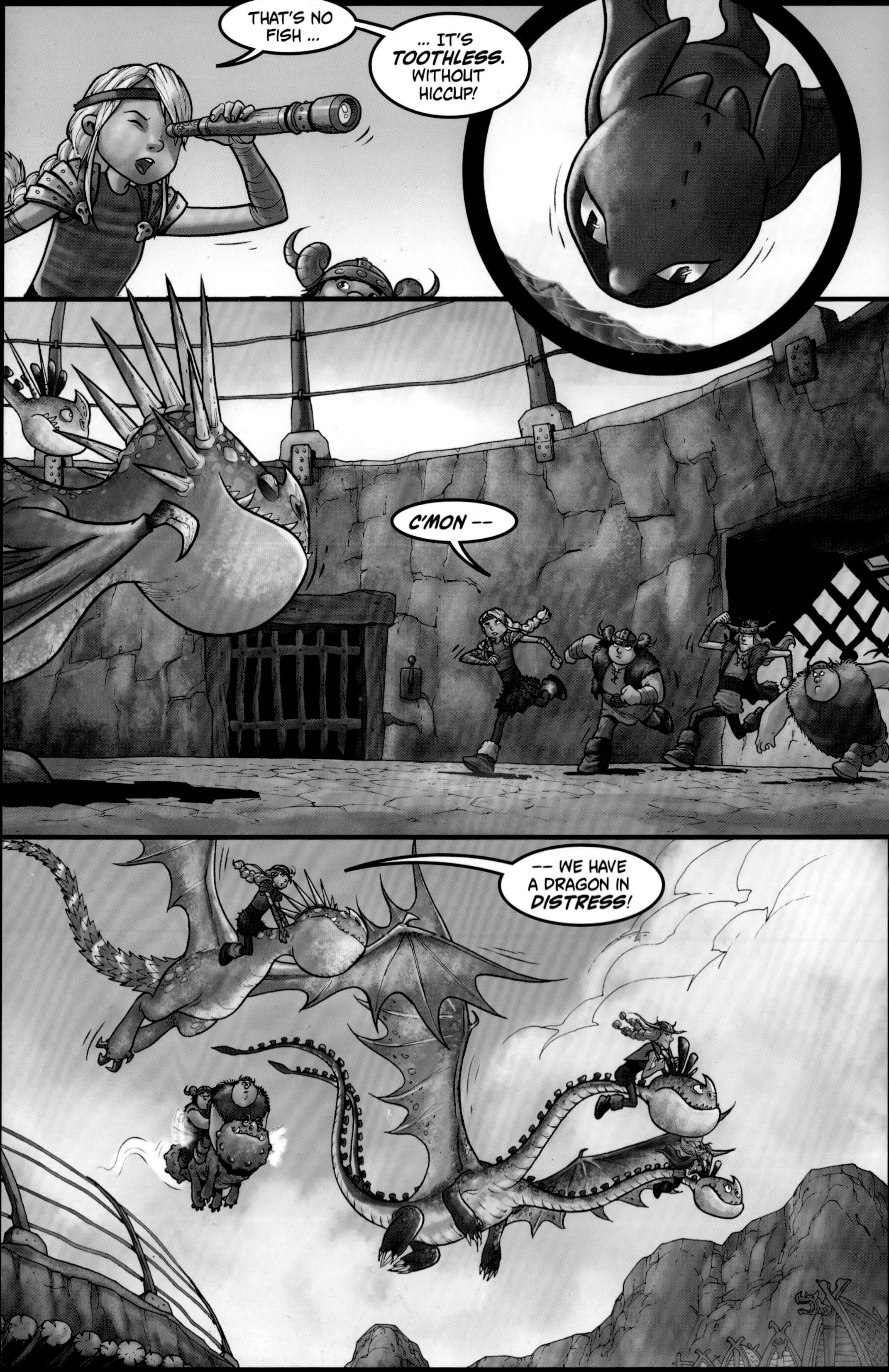

THAT'S NO FISH ...
... IT'S TOOTHLESS. WITHOUT HICCUP!
C'MON --
-- WE HAVE A DRAGON IN DISTRESS!

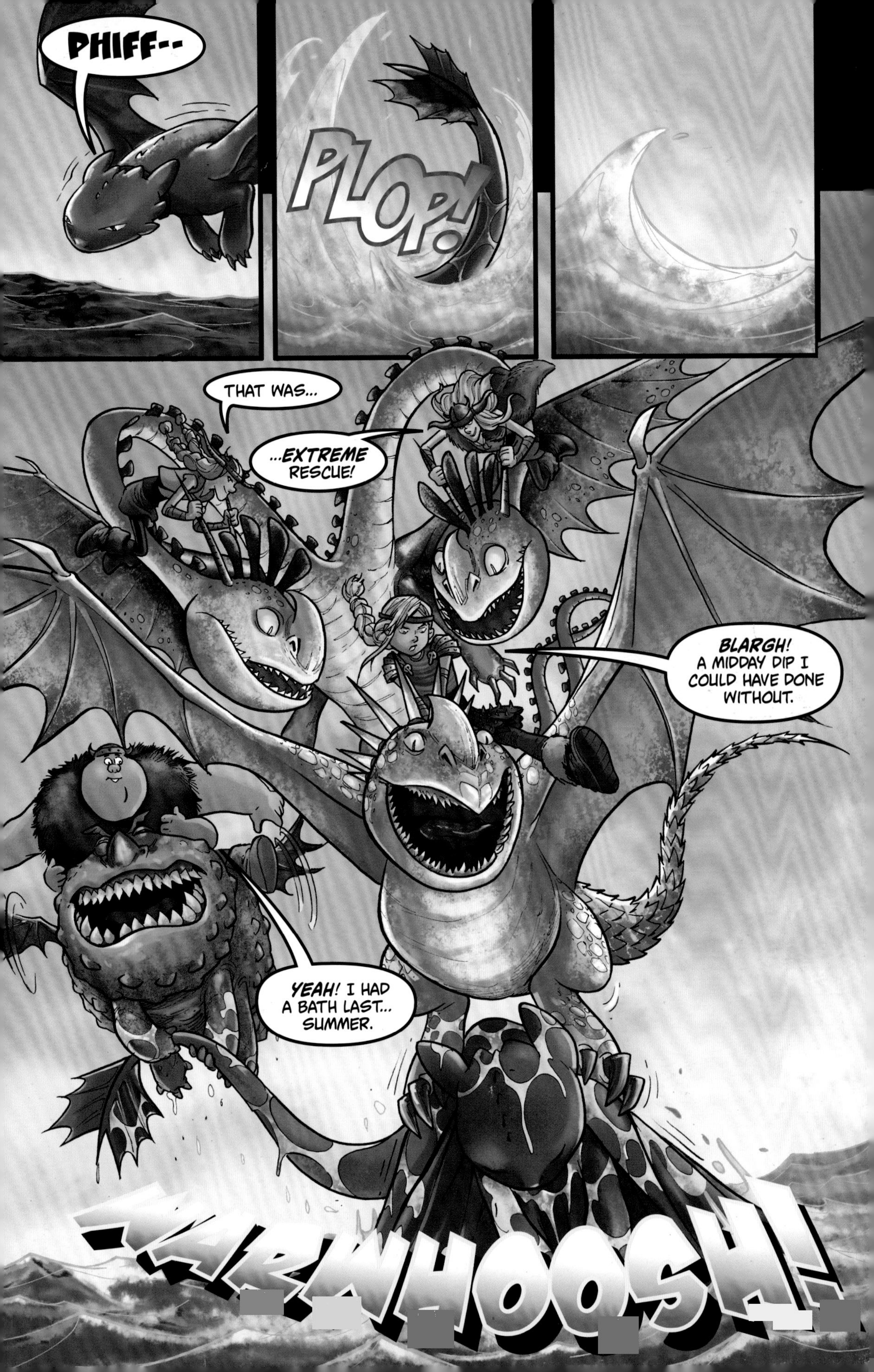
PHIFF--
PLOP!
THAT WAS...
...EXTREME RESCUE!
BLARGH! A MIDDAY DIP I COULD HAVE DONE WITHOUT.
YEAH! I HAD A BATH LAST... SUMMER.

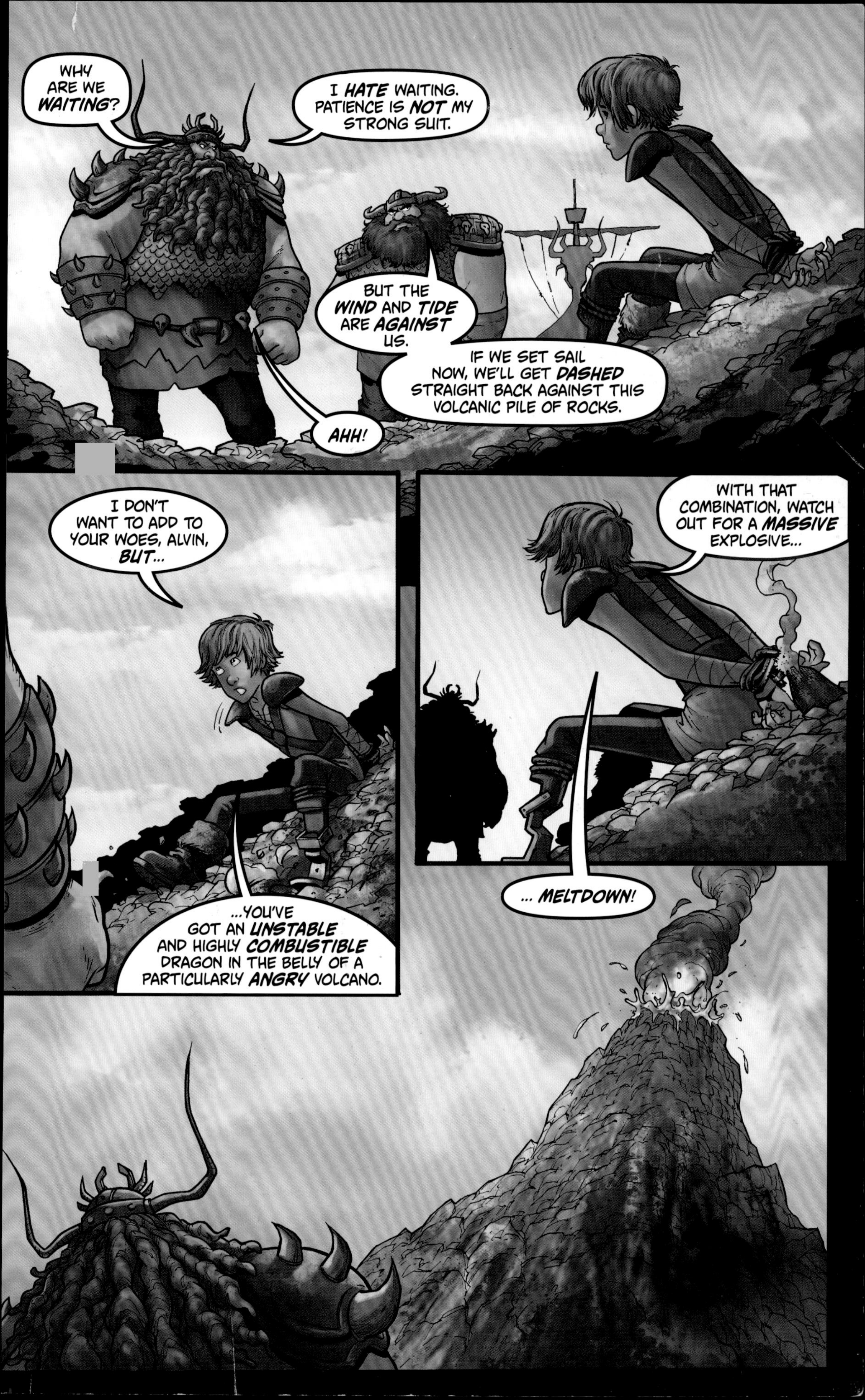
WHY ARE WE WAITING?
I HATE WAITING. PATIENCE IS NOT MY STRONG SUIT.
BUT THE WIND AND TIDE ARE AGAINST US.
IF WE SET SAIL NOW, WE'LL GET DASHED STRAIGHT BACK AGAINST THIS VOLCANIC PILE OF ROCKS.
AHH!
I DON'T WANT TO ADD TO YOUR WOES, ALVIN, BUT...
...YOU'VE GOT AN UNSTABLE AND HIGHLY COMBUSTIBLE DRAGON IN THE BELLY OF A PARTICULARLY ANGRY VOLCANO.
WITH THAT COMBINATION, WATCH OUT FOR A MASSIVE EXPLOSIVE...
... MELTDOWN!

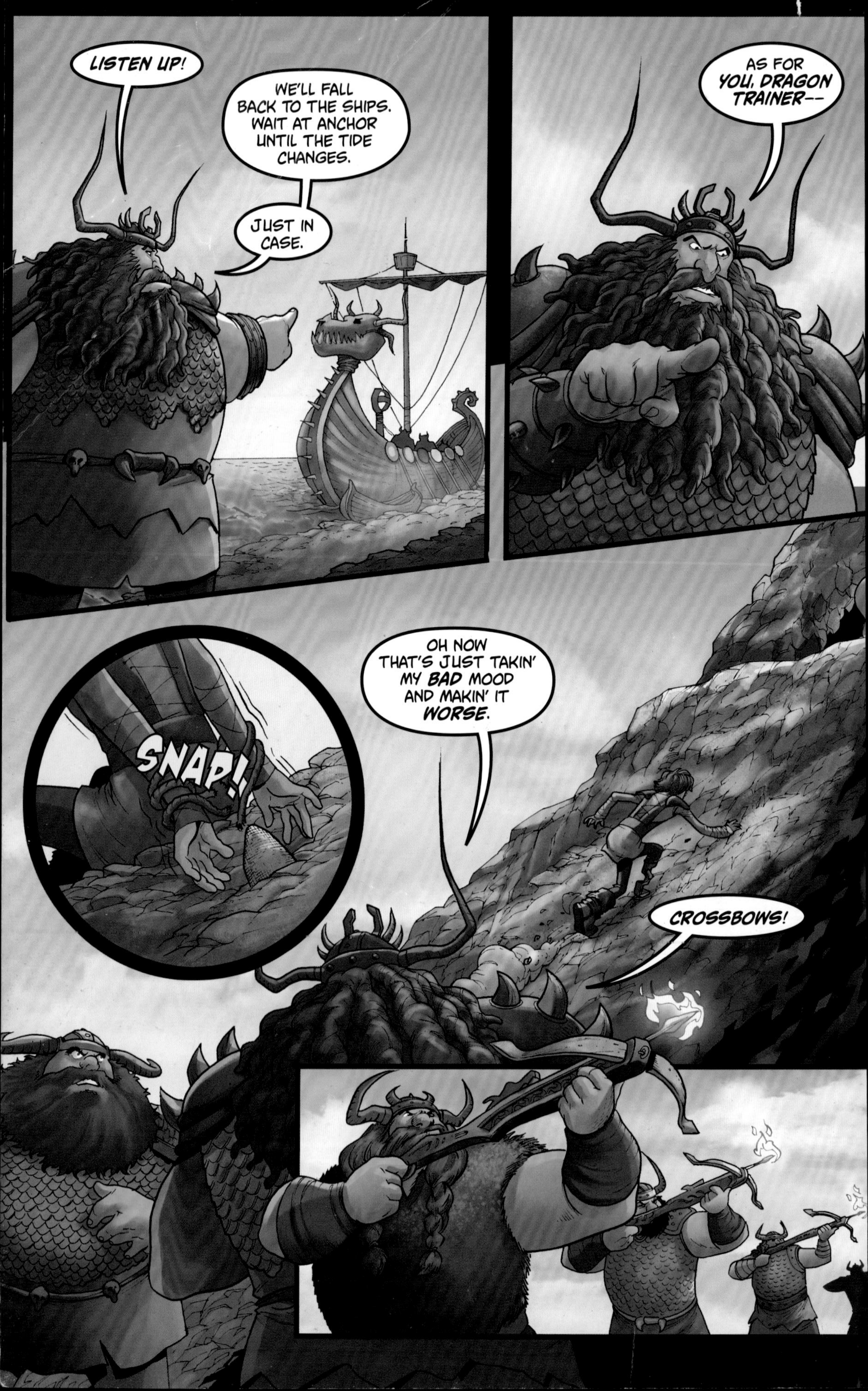
LISTEN UP!
WE'LL FALL BACK TO THE SHIPS. WAIT AT ANCHOR UNTIL THE TIDE CHANGES.
JUST IN CASE.
AS FOR YOU, DRAGON TRAINER--
SNAP!!
OH NOW THAT'S JUST TAKIN' MY BAD MOOD AND MAKIN' IT WORSE.
CROSSBOWS!

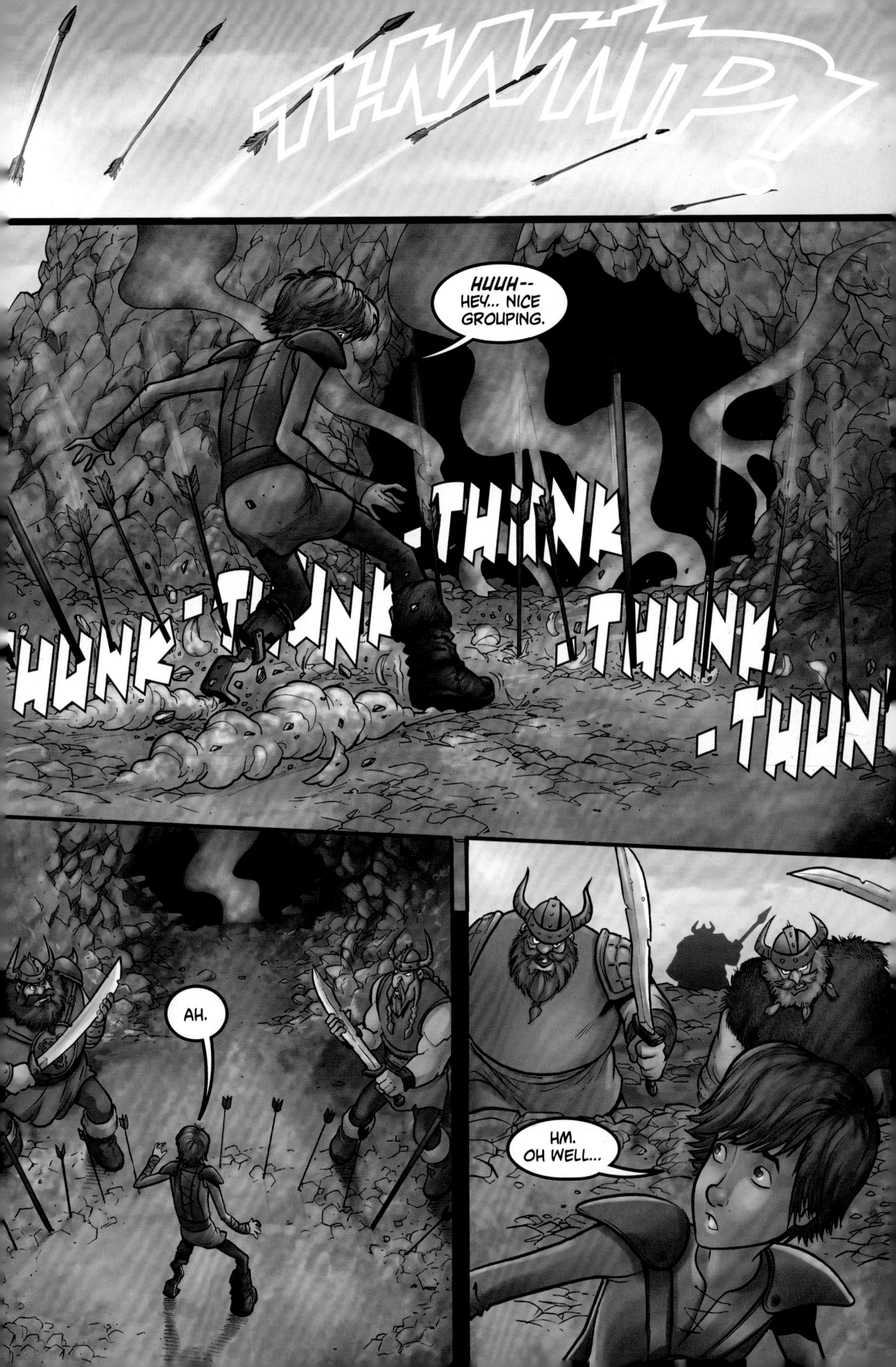
THWWIP
HUUH-- HEY... NICE GROUPING.
THUNK
THUNK
THUNK
THUNK
THUN
AH.
HM. OH WELL...

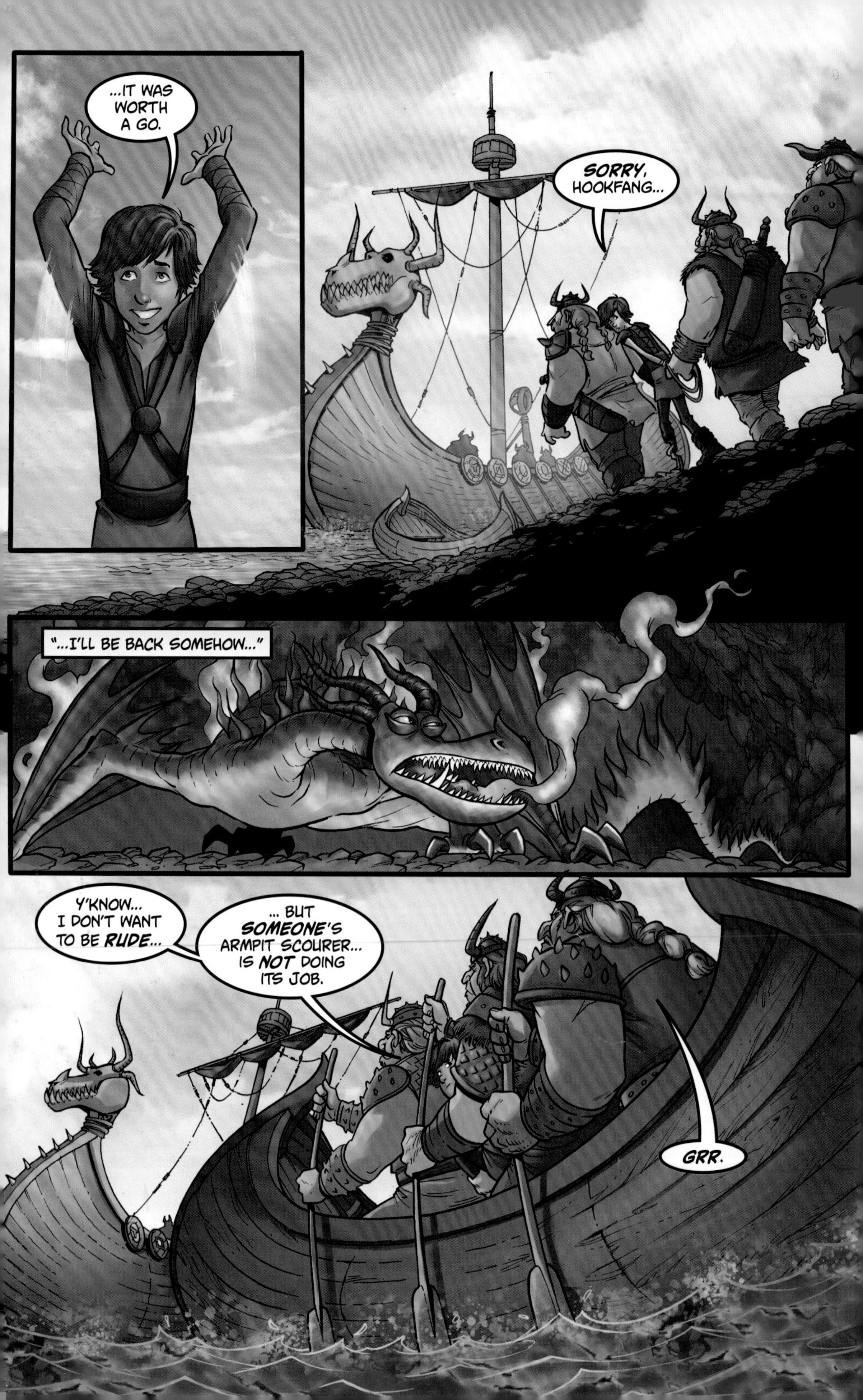
...IT WAS WORTH A GO.
SORRY, HOOKFANG...
"...I'LL BE BACK SOMEHOW..."
Y'KNOW... I DON'T WANT TO BE RUDE...
... BUT SOMEONE'S ARMPIT SCOURER... IS NOT DOING ITS JOB.
GRR.

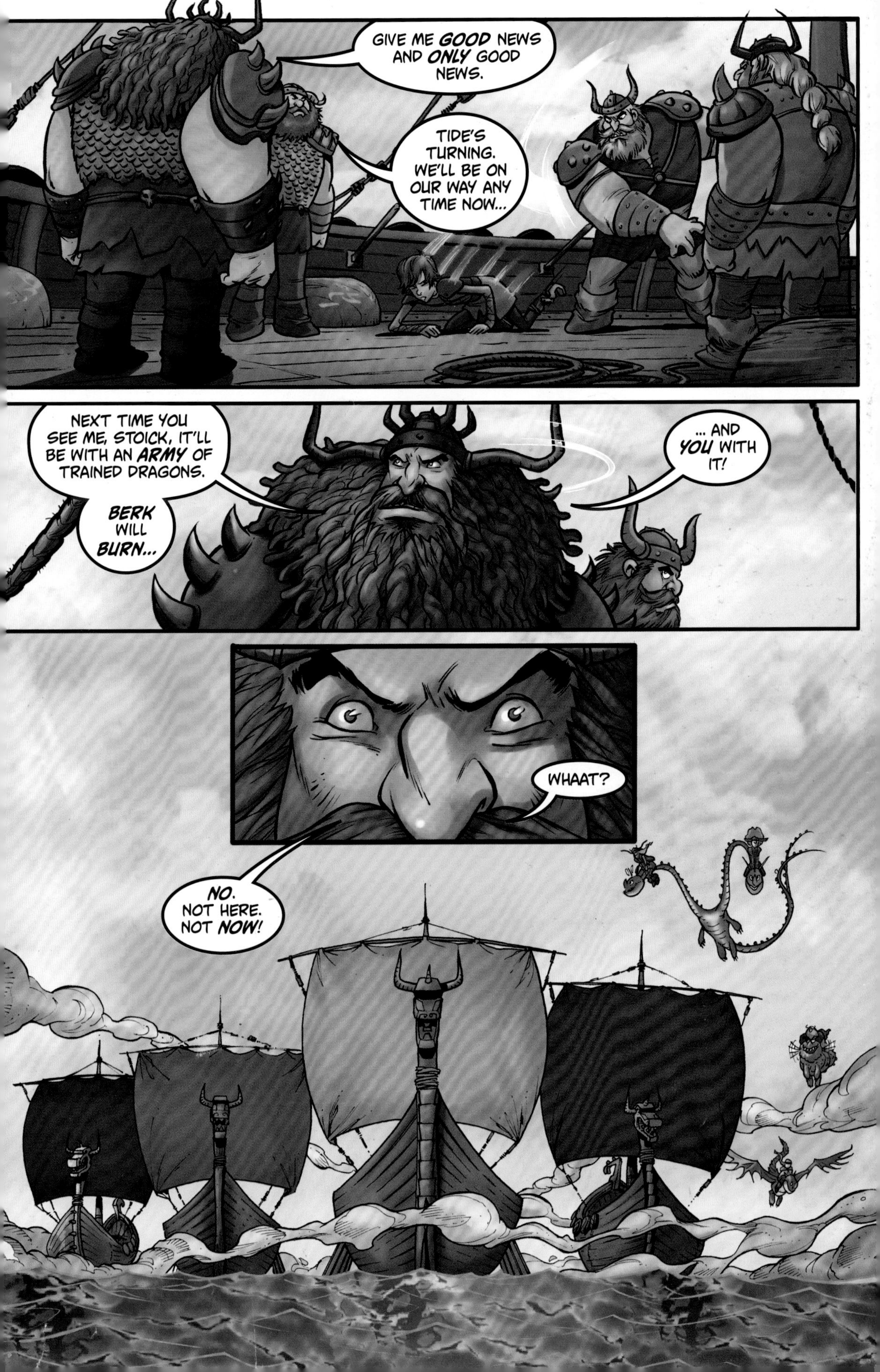
GIVE ME GOOD NEWS AND ONLY GOOD NEWS.
TIDE'S TURNING. WE'LL BE ON OUR WAY ANY TIME NOW...
NEXT TIME YOU SEE ME, STOICK, IT'LL BE WITH AN ARMY OF TRAINED DRAGONS.
BERK WILL BURN...
... AND YOU WITH IT!
WHAAT?
NO. NOT HERE. NOT NOW!

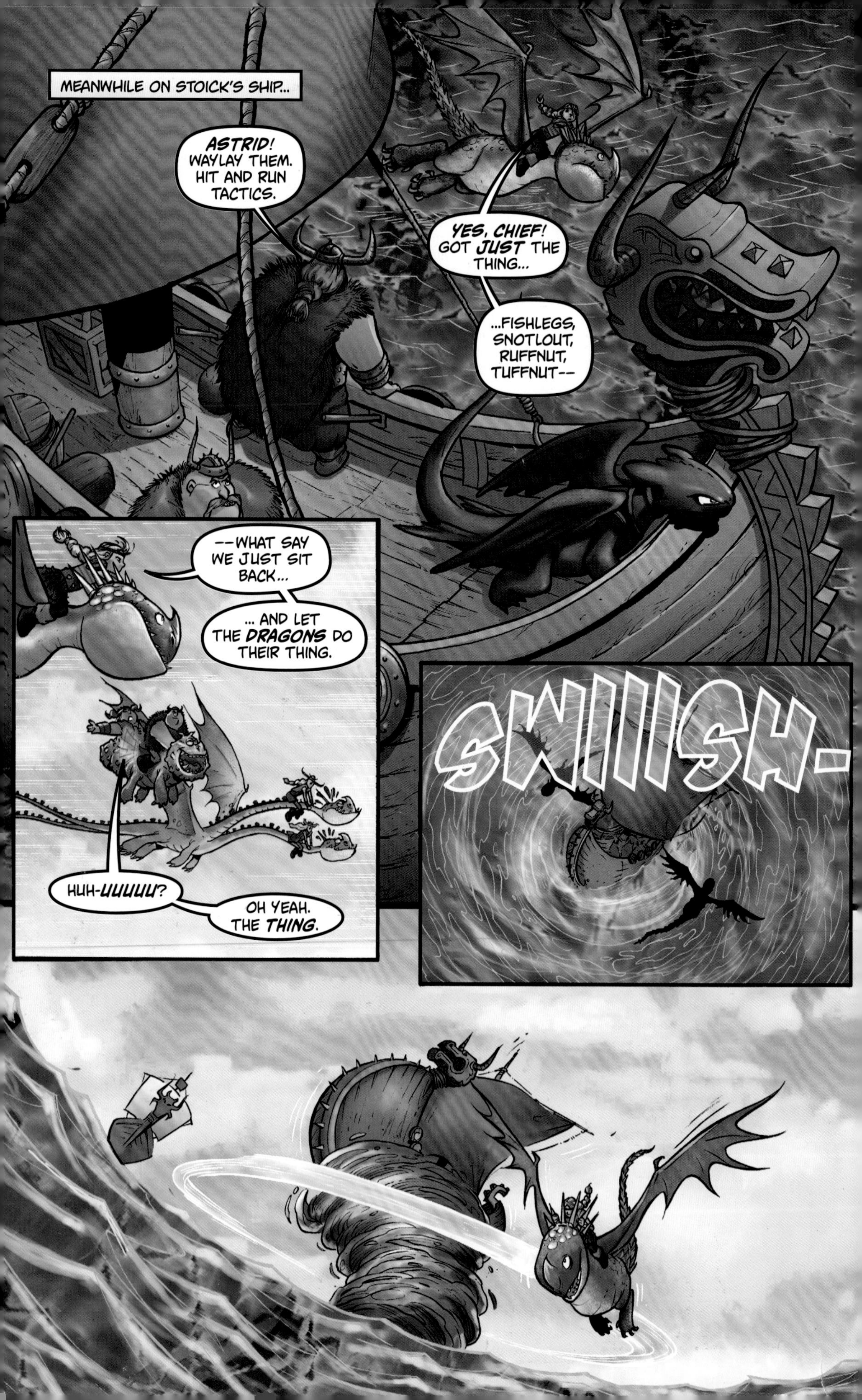
MEANWHILE ON STOICK'S SHIP...
ASTRID! WAYLAY THEM. HIT AND RUN TACTICS.
YES, CHIEF! GOT JUST THE THING...
...FISHLEGS, SNOTLOUT, RUFFNUT, TUFFNUT--
--WHAT SAY WE JUST SIT BACK...
... AND LET THE DRAGONS DO THEIR THING.
HUH-UUUUU?
OH YEAH. THE THING.
SWIIISH-

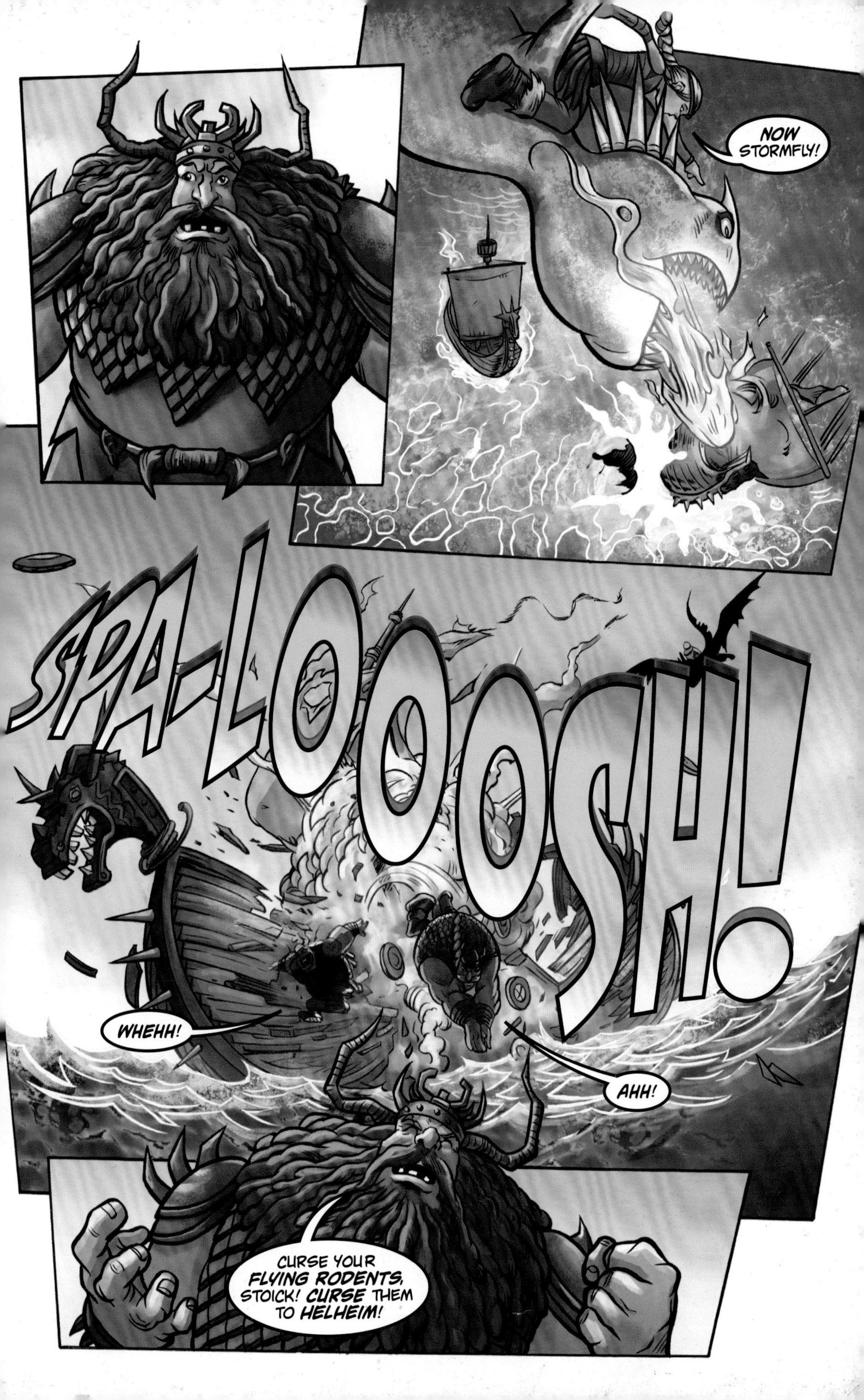
NOW STORMFLY!
SPA-LOOOSH!
WHEHH!
AHH!
CURSE YOUR FLYING RODENTS, STOICK! CURSE THEM TO HELHEIM!

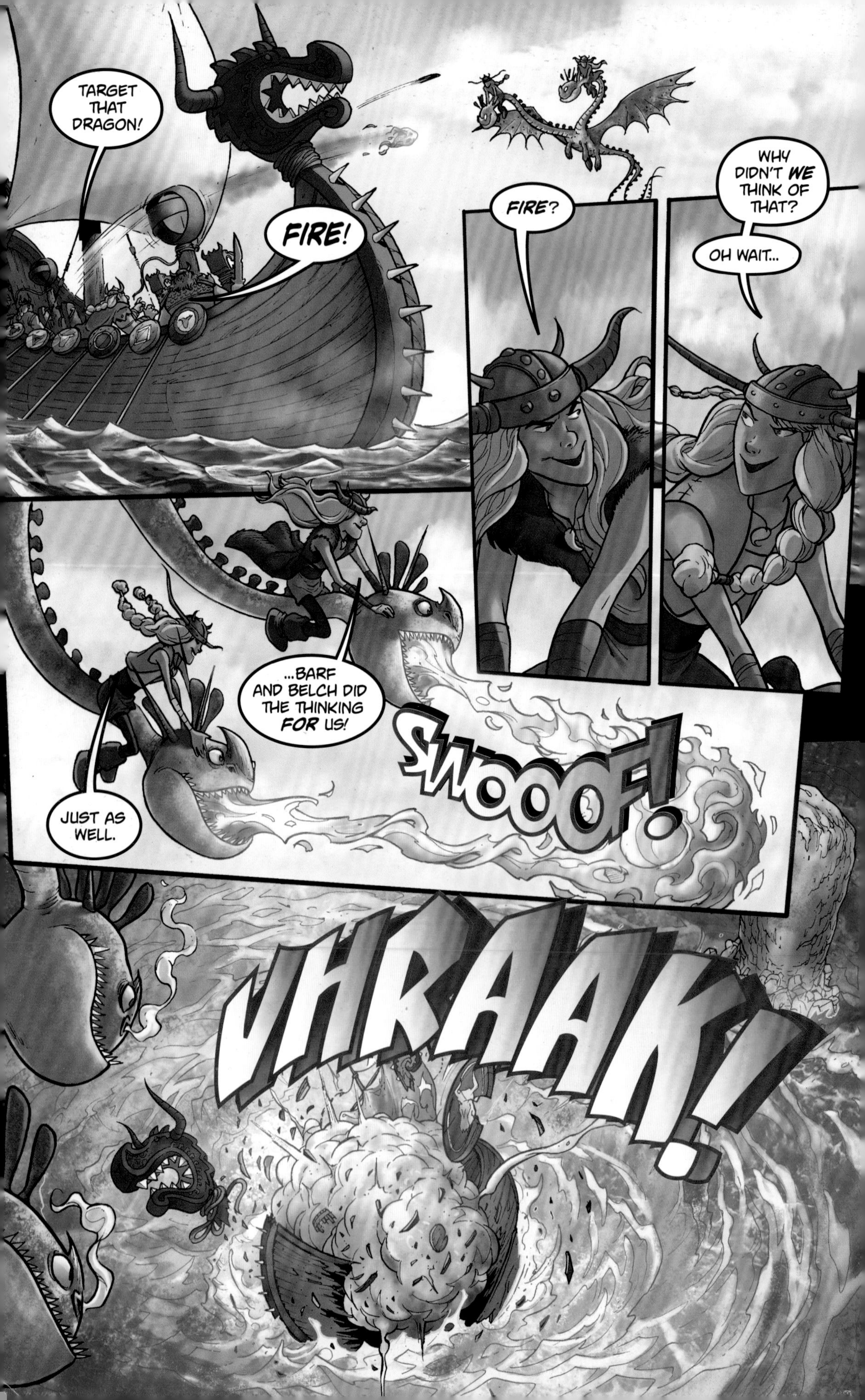
TARGET THAT DRAGON!
FIRE!
FIRE?
WHY DIDN'T WE THINK OF THAT?
OH WAIT...
...BARF AND BELCH DID THE THINKING FOR US!
JUST AS WELL.
SWOOOF!
SHRAAK!

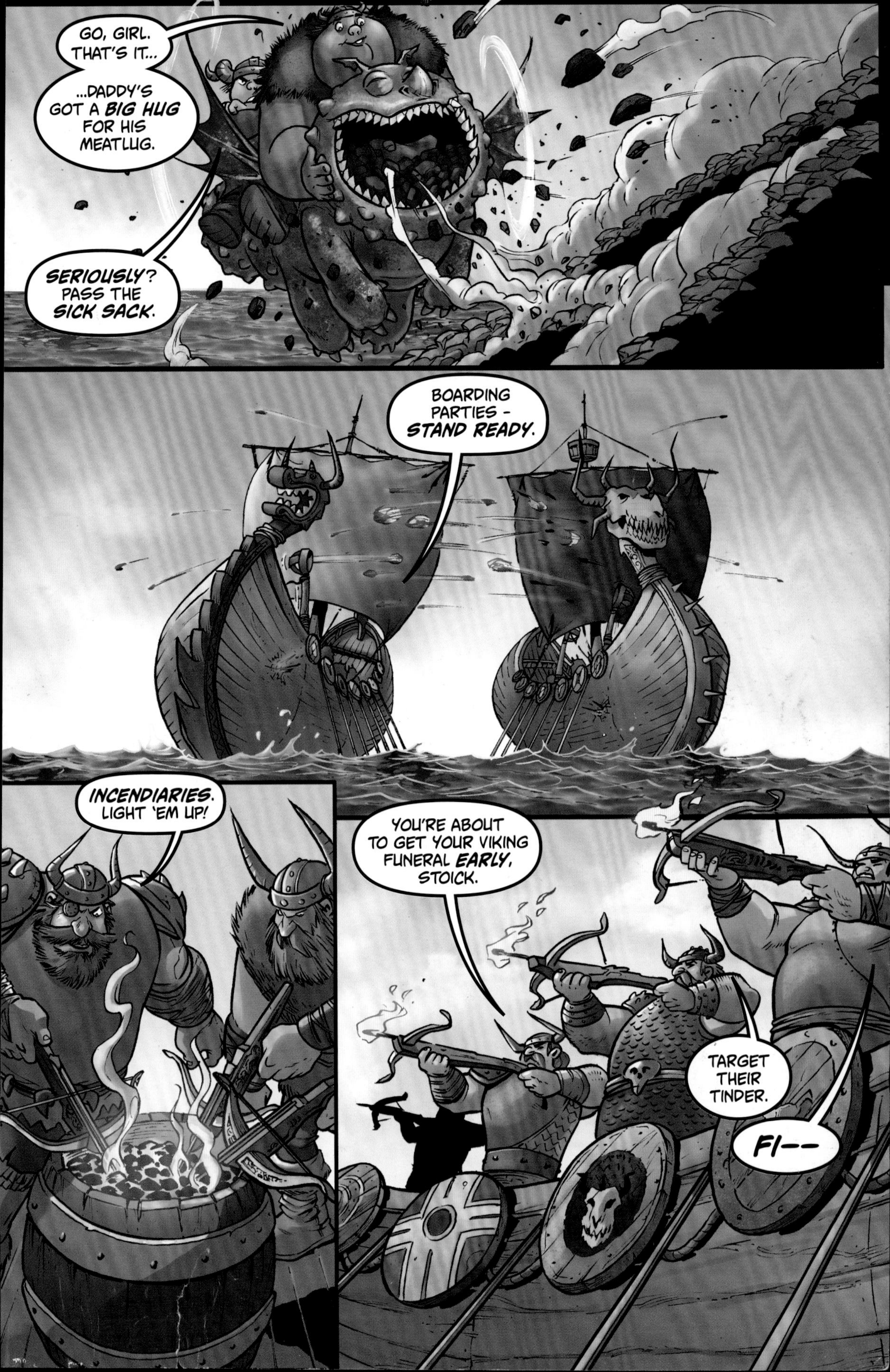
GO, GIRL. THAT'S IT...
...DADDY'S GOT A BIG HUG FOR HIS MEATLUG.
SERIOUSLY? PASS THE SICK SACK.
BOARDING PARTIES - STAND READY.
INCENDIARIES. LIGHT 'EM UP!
YOU'RE ABOUT TO GET YOUR VIKING FUNERAL EARLY, STOICK.
TARGET THEIR TINDER.
FI--

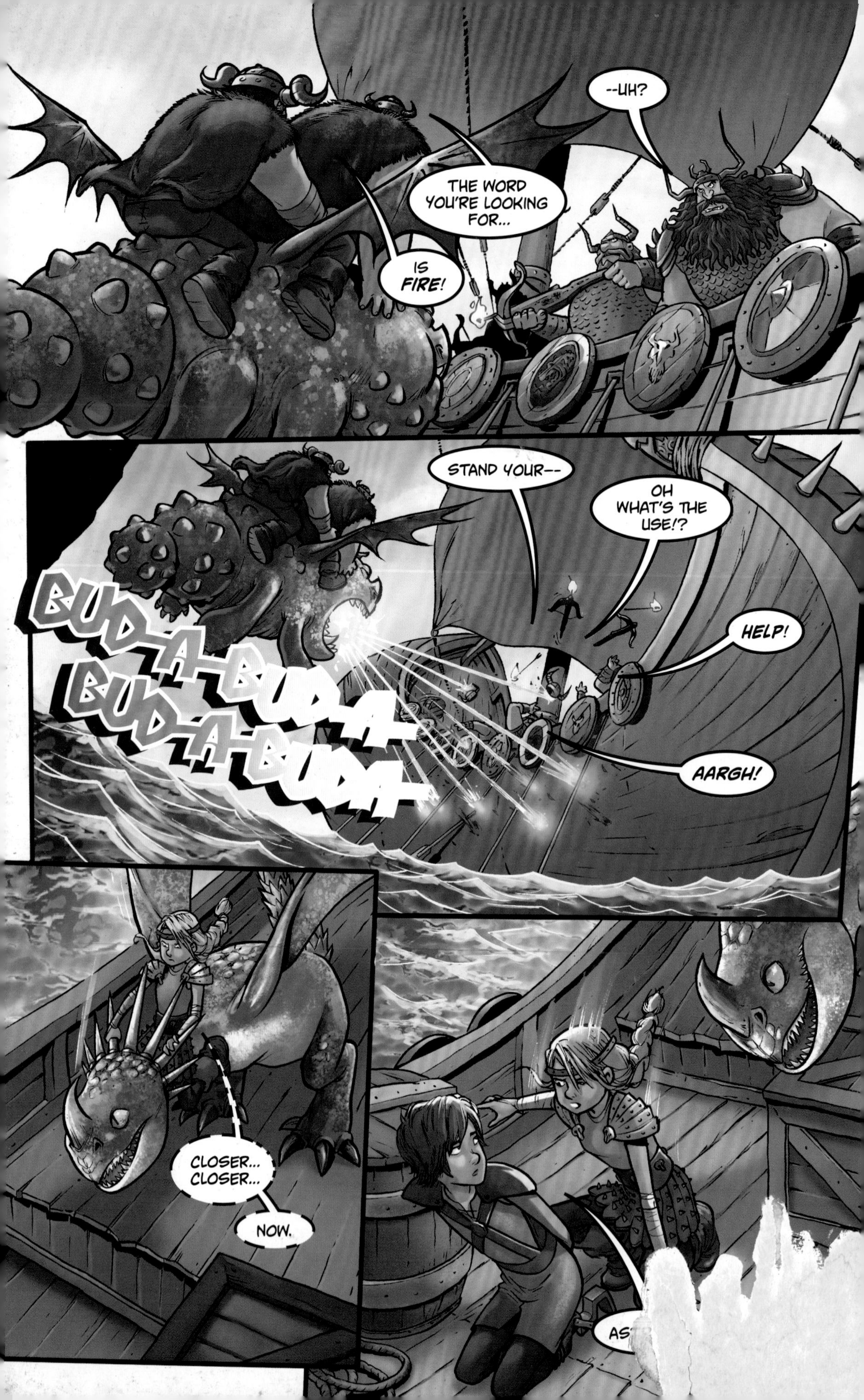
--UH?
THE WORD YOU'RE LOOKING FOR...
IS FIRE!
STAND YOUR--
OH WHAT'S THE USE!?
BUD-A-BUD-A-
BUD-A-BUDA
HELP!
AARGH!
CLOSER... CLOSER...
NOW.
AS

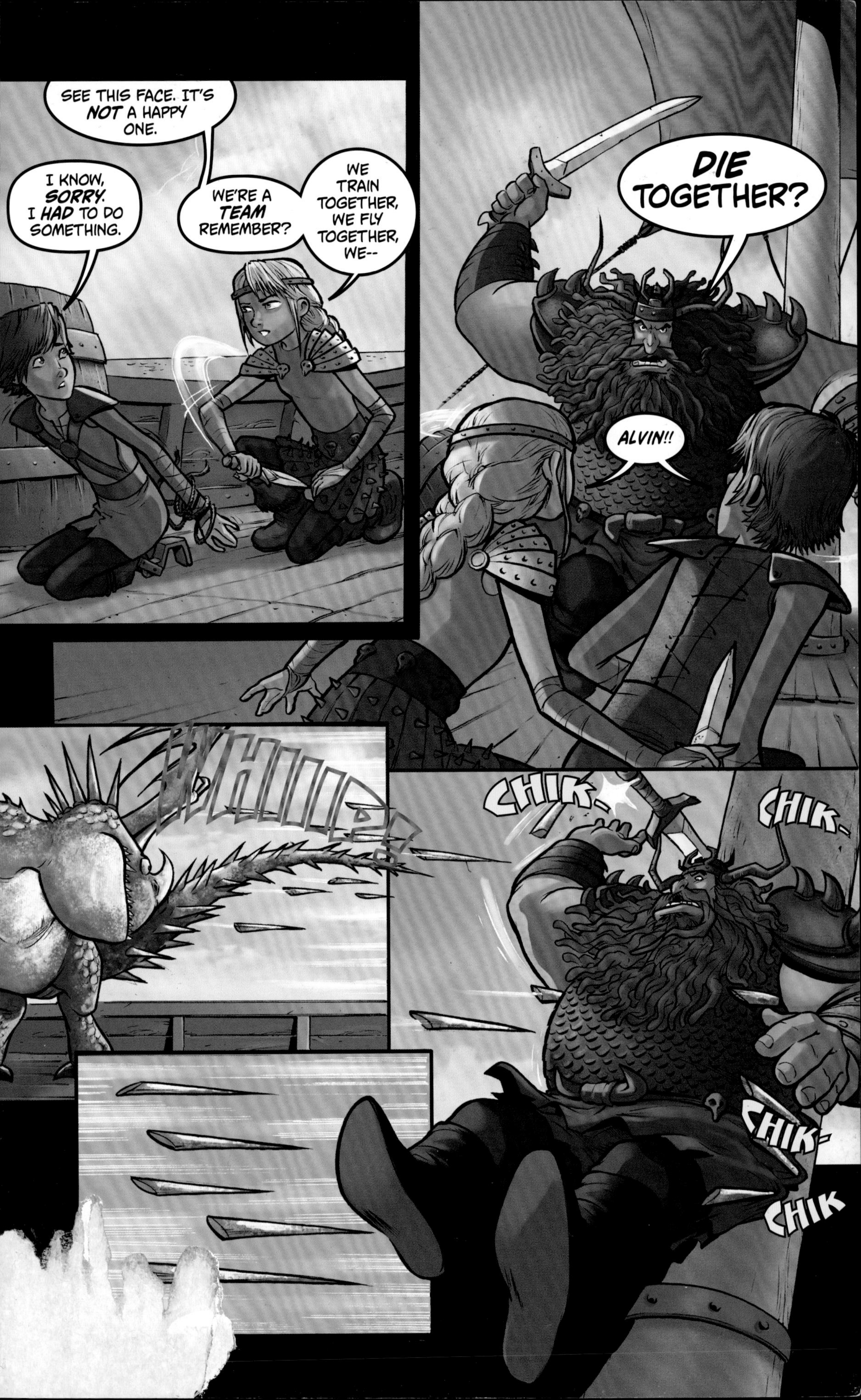
SEE THIS FACE. IT'S NOT A HAPPY ONE.
I KNOW, SORRY. I HAD TO DO SOMETHING.
WE'RE A TEAM REMEMBER?
WE TRAIN TOGETHER, WE FLY TOGETHER, WE--
DIE TOGETHER?
ALVIN!!
CHIK-
CHIK-
CHIK-
CHIK

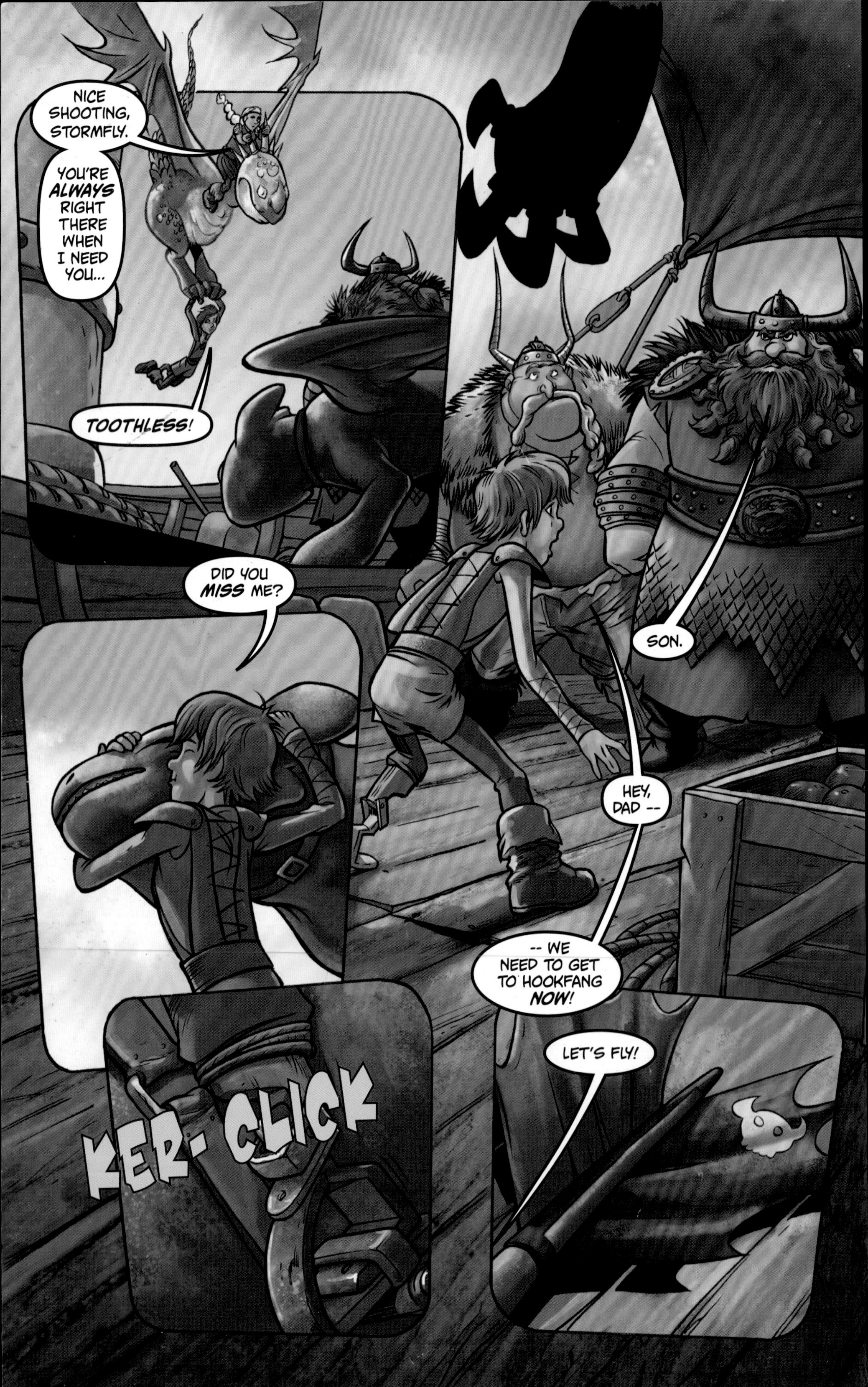
NICE SHOOTING, STORMFLY.
YOU'RE ALWAYS RIGHT THERE WHEN I NEED YOU...
TOOTHLESS!
SON.
HEY, DAD --
-- WE NEED TO GET TO HOOKFANG NOW!
DID YOU MISS ME?
KER-CLICK
LET'S FLY!

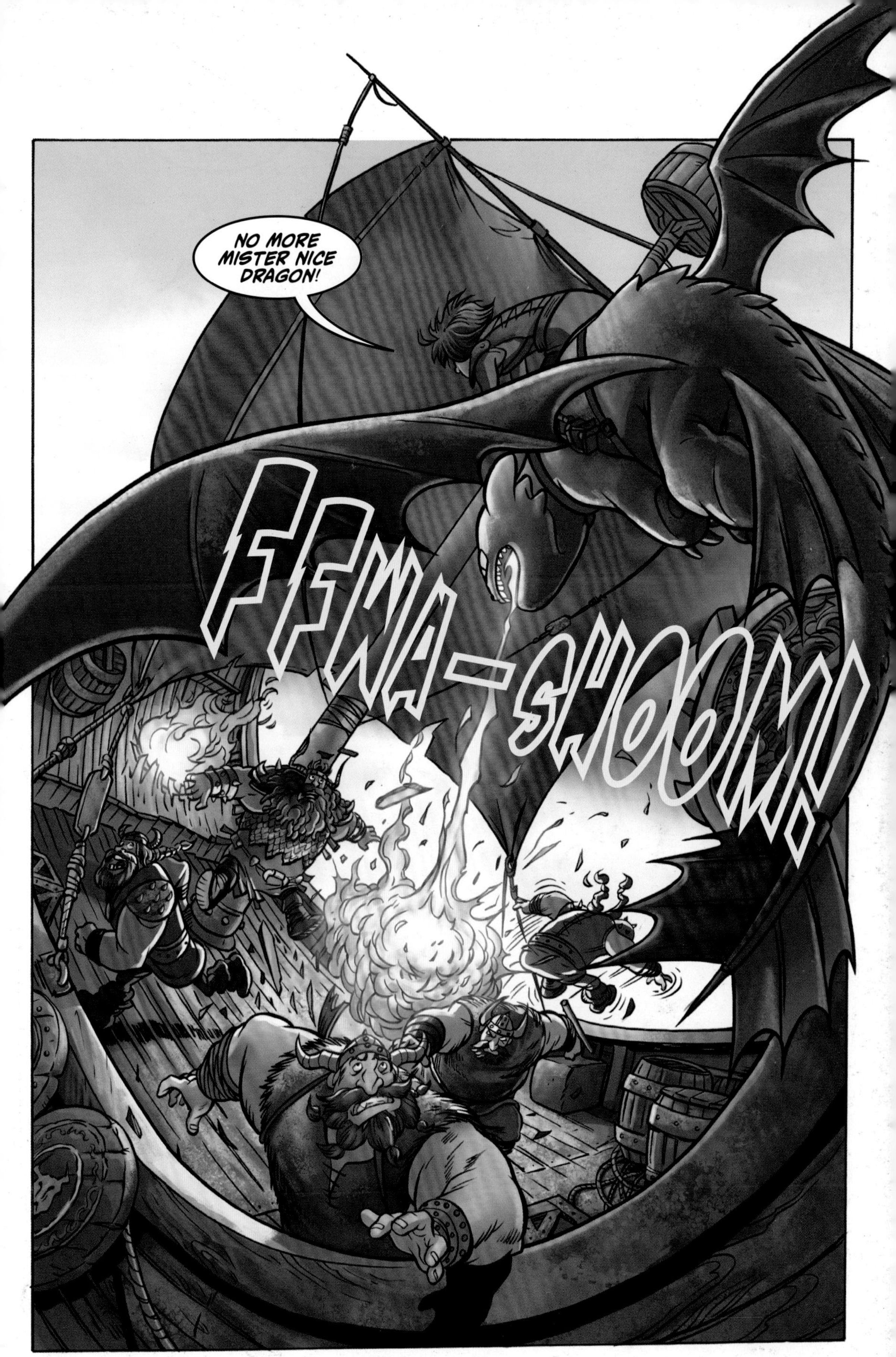
NO MORE MISTER NICE DRAGON!
FFWA-SHOOM!

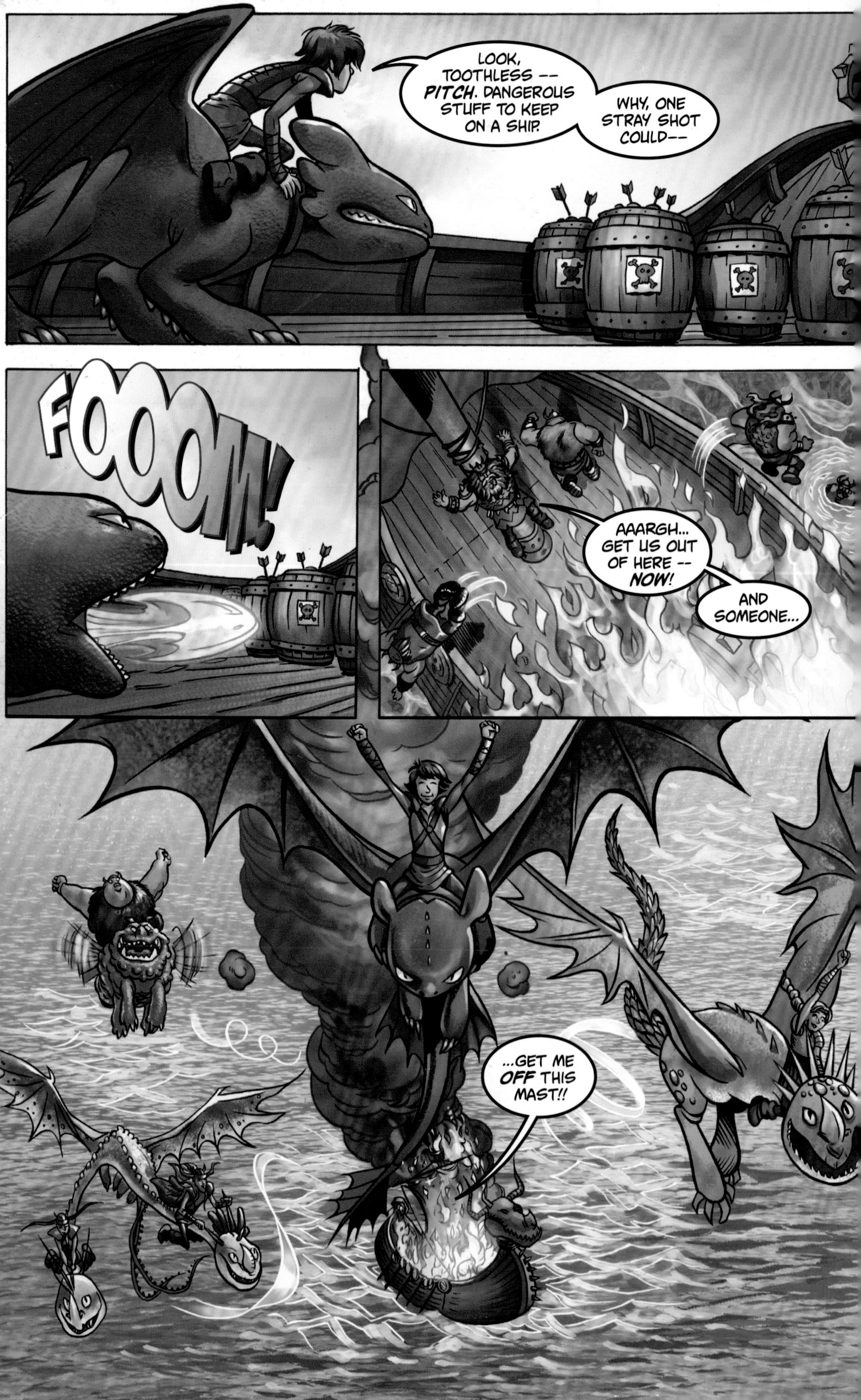
LOOK, TOOTHLESS -- PITCH. DANGEROUS STUFF TO KEEP ON A SHIP.
WHY, ONE STRAY SHOT COULD--
FOOOM!
AAARGH... GET US OUT OF HERE -- NOW!
AND SOMEONE...
...GET ME OFF THIS MAST!!

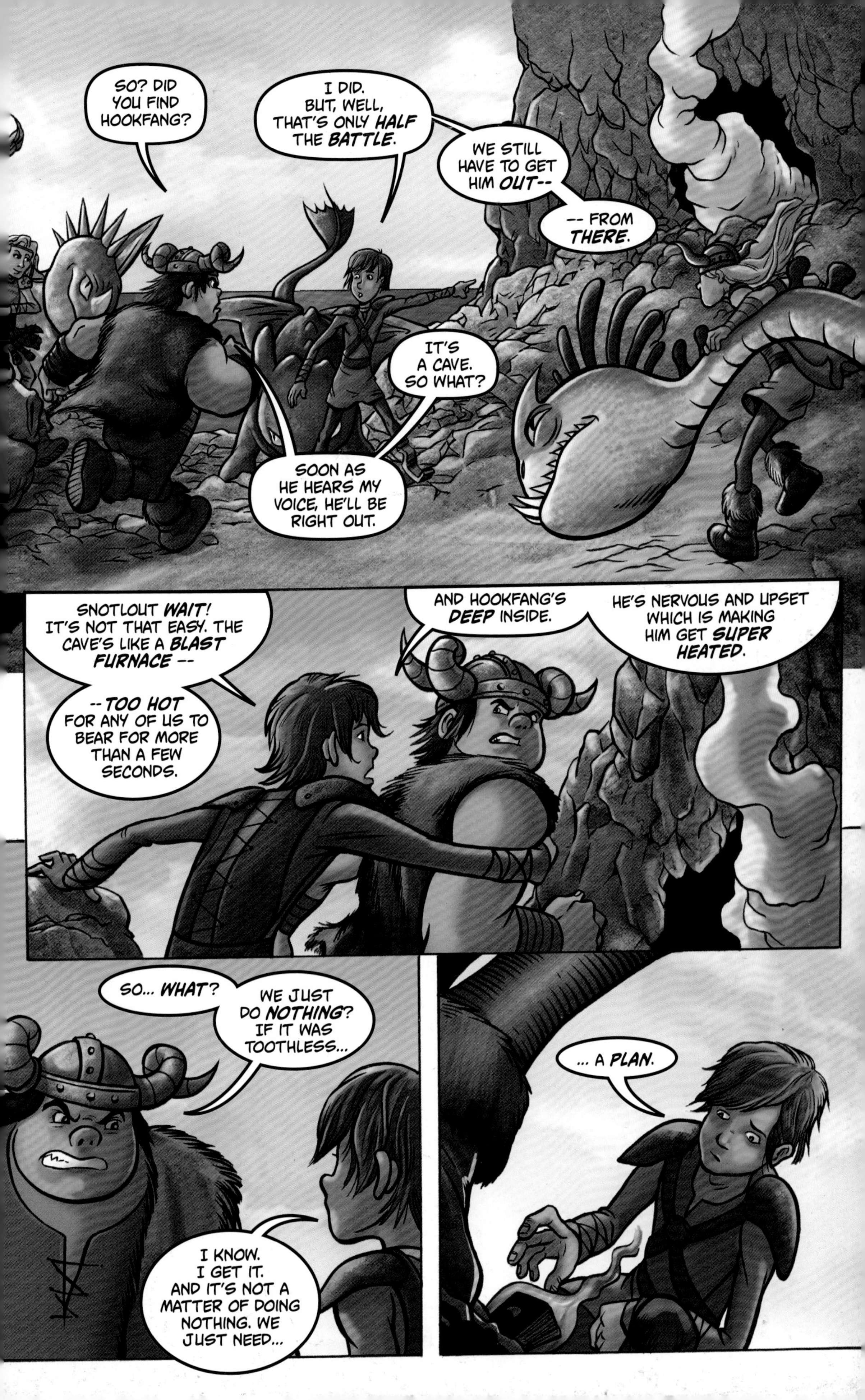
SO? DID YOU FIND HOOKFANG?
I DID. BUT, WELL, THAT'S ONLY HALF THE BATTLE.
WE STILL HAVE TO GET HIM OUT--
-- FROM THERE.
IT'S A CAVE. SO WHAT?
SOON AS HE HEARS MY VOICE, HE'LL BE RIGHT OUT.
SNOTLOUT WAIT! IT'S NOT THAT EASY. THE CAVE'S LIKE A BLAST FURNACE --
--TOO HOT FOR ANY OF US TO BEAR FOR MORE THAN A FEW SECONDS.
AND HOOKFANG'S DEEP INSIDE.
HE'S NERVOUS AND UPSET WHICH IS MAKING HIM GET SUPER HEATED.
SO... WHAT?
WE JUST DO NOTHING? IF IT WAS TOOTHLESS...
I KNOW. I GET IT. AND IT'S NOT A MATTER OF DOING NOTHING. WE JUST NEED...
... A PLAN.

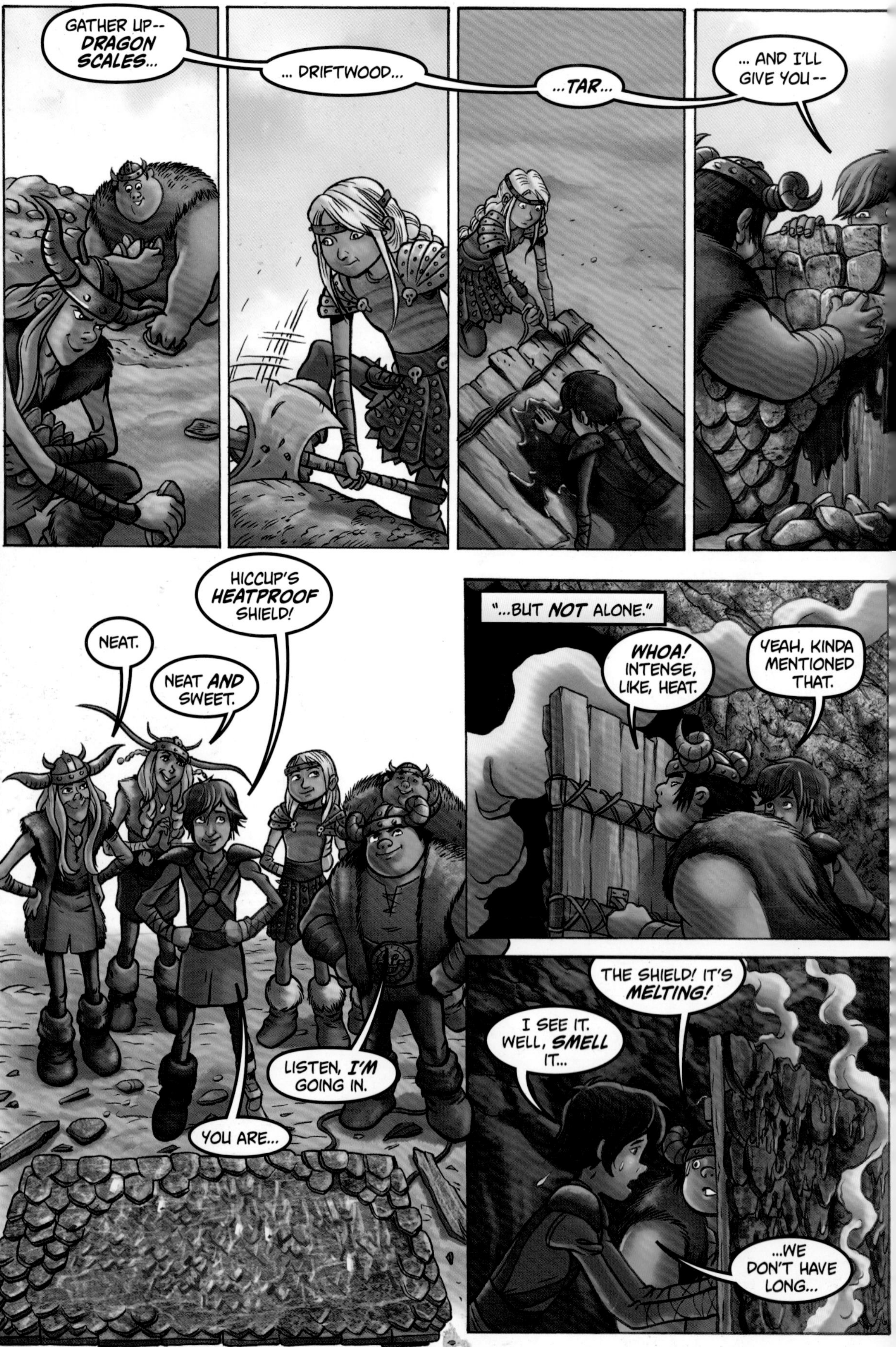
GATHER UP-- DRAGON SCALES...
... DRIFTWOOD...
...TAR...
... AND I'LL GIVE YOU --
HICCUP'S HEATPROOF SHIELD!
NEAT.
NEAT AND SWEET.
LISTEN, I'M GOING IN.
YOU ARE...
"...BUT NOT ALONE."
WHOA! INTENSE, LIKE, HEAT.
YEAH, KINDA MENTIONED THAT.
THE SHIELD! IT'S MELTING!
I SEE IT. WELL, SMELL IT...
...WE DON'T HAVE LONG...

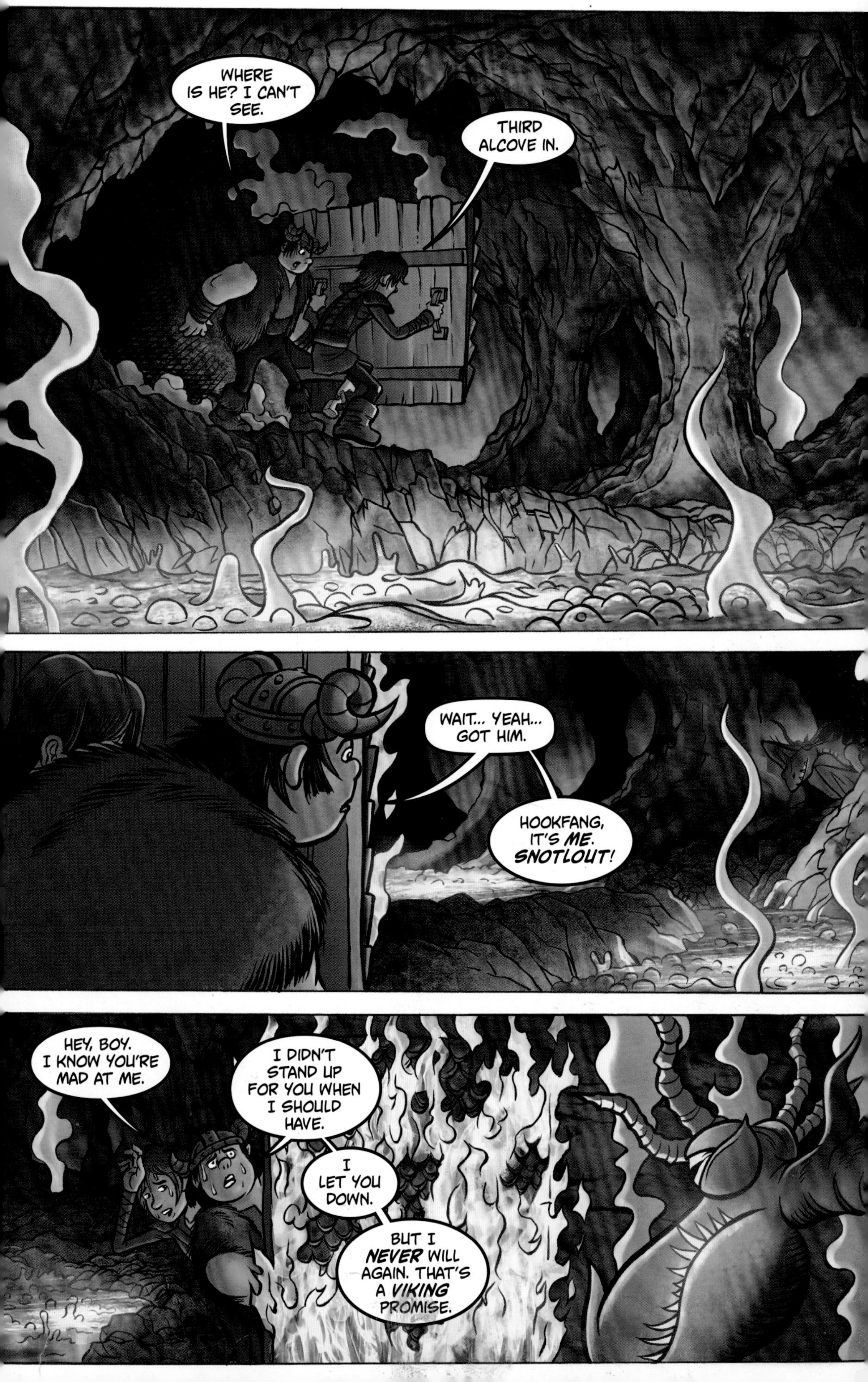

WHERE IS HE? I CAN'T SEE.
THIRD ALCOVE IN.
WAIT... YEAH... GOT HIM.
HOOKFANG, IT'S ME. SNOTLOUT!
HEY, BOY. I KNOW YOU'RE MAD AT ME.
I DIDN'T STAND UP FOR YOU WHEN I SHOULD HAVE.
I LET YOU DOWN.
BUT I NEVER WILL AGAIN. THAT'S A VIKING PROMISE.

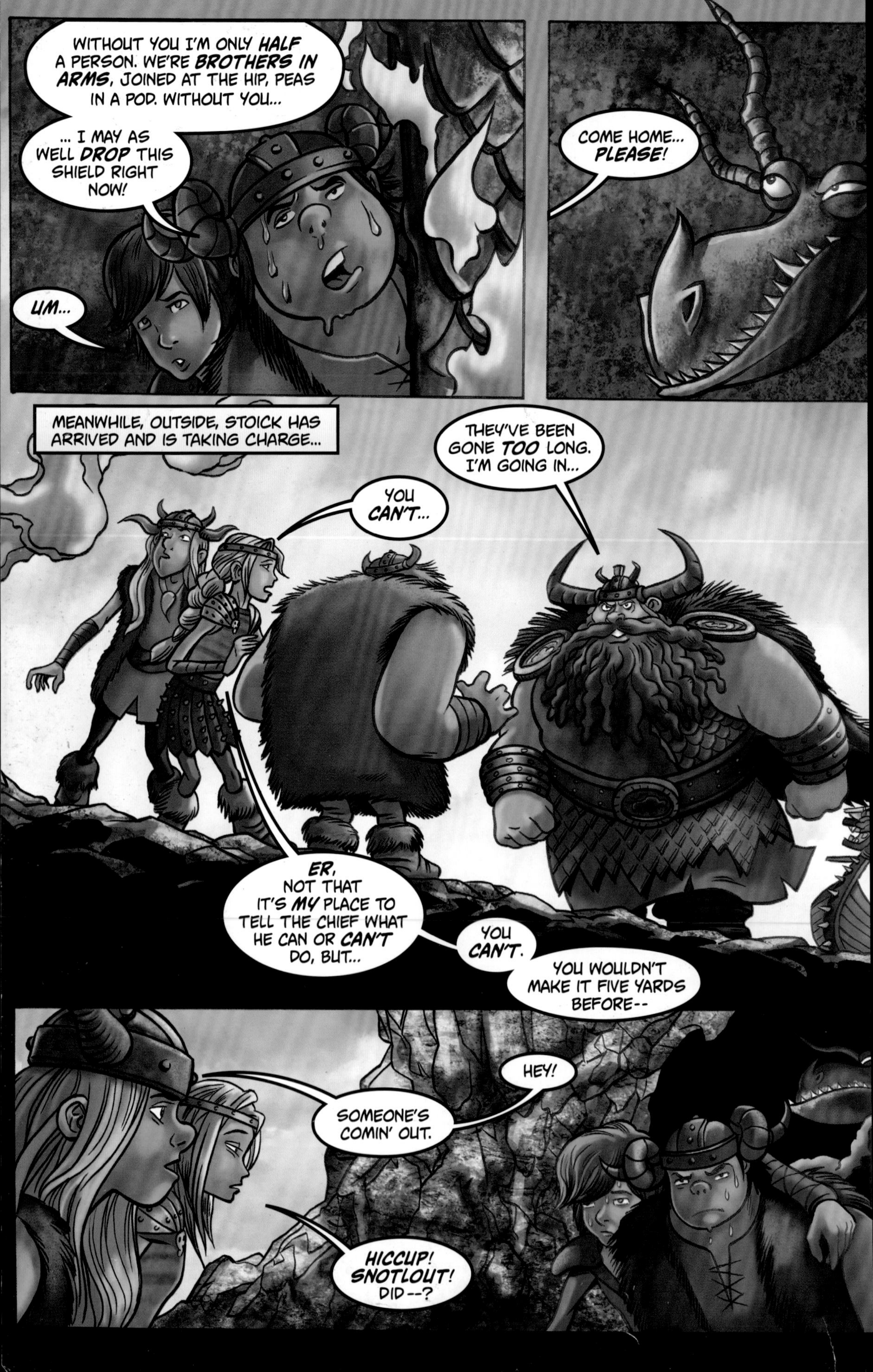
WITHOUT YOU I'M ONLY HALF A PERSON. WE'RE BROTHERS IN ARMS, JOINED AT THE HIP, PEAS IN A POD. WITHOUT YOU...
... I MAY AS WELL DROP THIS SHIELD RIGHT NOW!
UM...
COME HOME... PLEASE!
MEANWHILE, OUTSIDE, STOICK HAS ARRIVED AND IS TAKING CHARGE...
THEY'VE BEEN GONE TOO LONG. I'M GOING IN...
YOU CAN'T...
ER, NOT THAT IT'S MY PLACE TO TELL THE CHIEF WHAT HE CAN OR CAN'T DO, BUT...
YOU CAN'T.
YOU WOULDN'T MAKE IT FIVE YARDS BEFORE--
HEY!
SOMEONE'S COMIN' OUT.
HICCUP! SNOTLOUT! DID--?

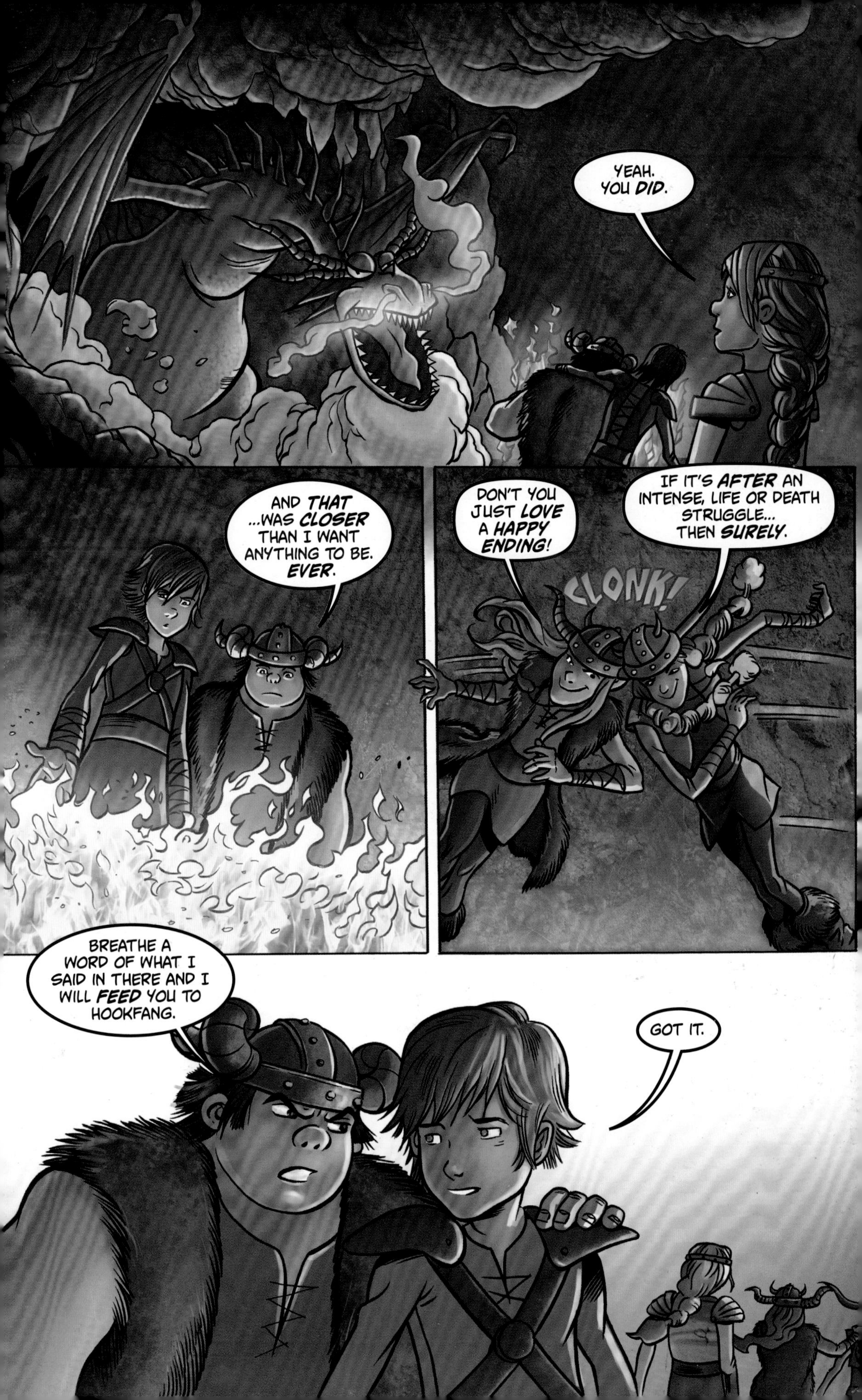
YEAH. YOU DID.
AND THAT ...WAS CLOSER THAN I WANT ANYTHING TO BE. EVER.
DON'T YOU JUST LOVE A HAPPY ENDING!
IF IT'S AFTER AN INTENSE, LIFE OR DEATH STRUGGLE... THEN SURELY.
CLONK!
BREATHE A WORD OF WHAT I SAID IN THERE AND I WILL FEED YOU TO HOOKFANG.
GOT IT.

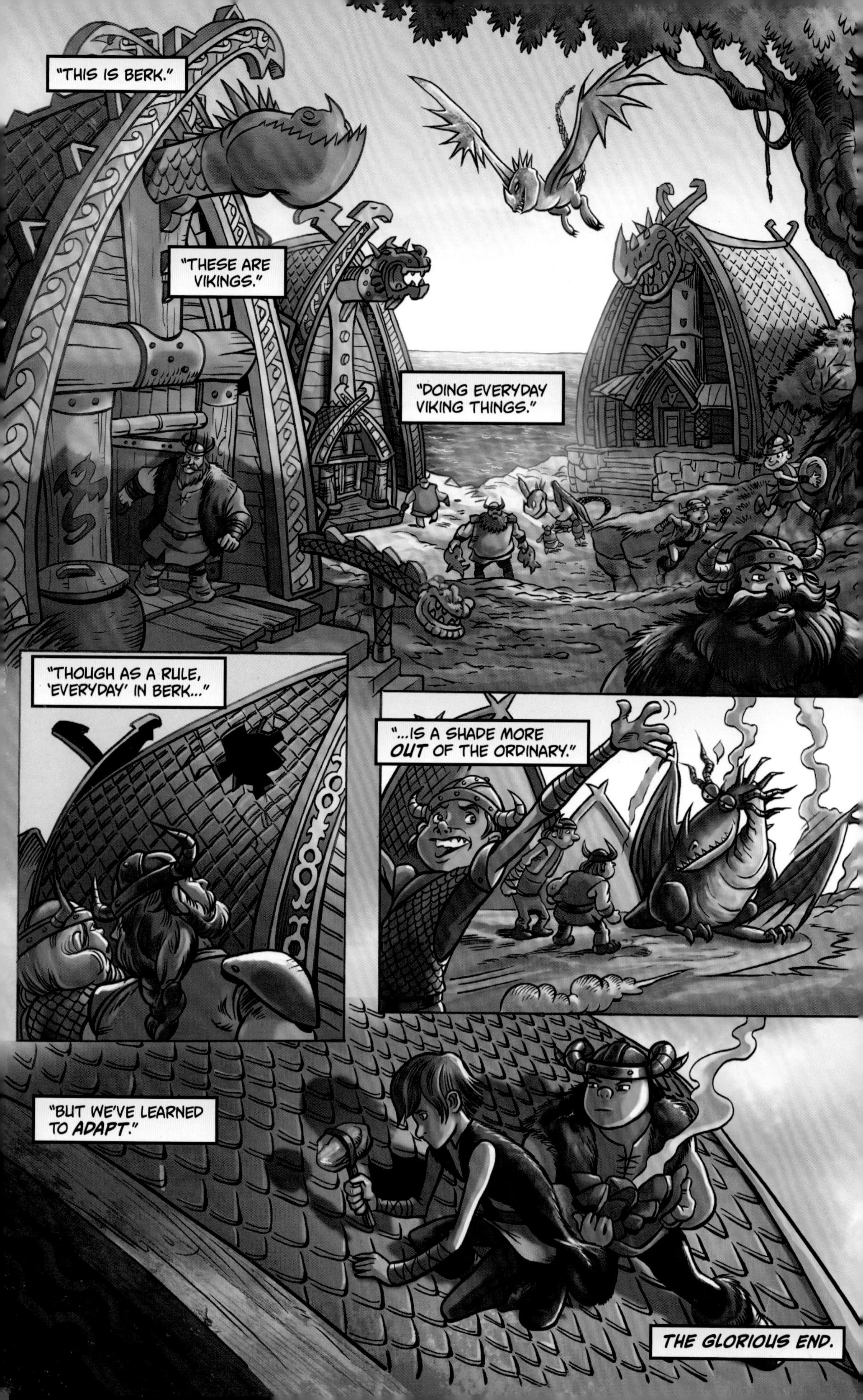
"THIS IS BERK."
"THESE ARE VIKINGS."
"DOING EVERYDAY VIKING THINGS."
"THOUGH AS A RULE, 'EVERYDAY' IN BERK..."
"...IS A SHADE MORE OUT OF THE ORDINARY."
"BUT WE'VE LEARNED TO ADAPT."
THE GLORIOUS END.

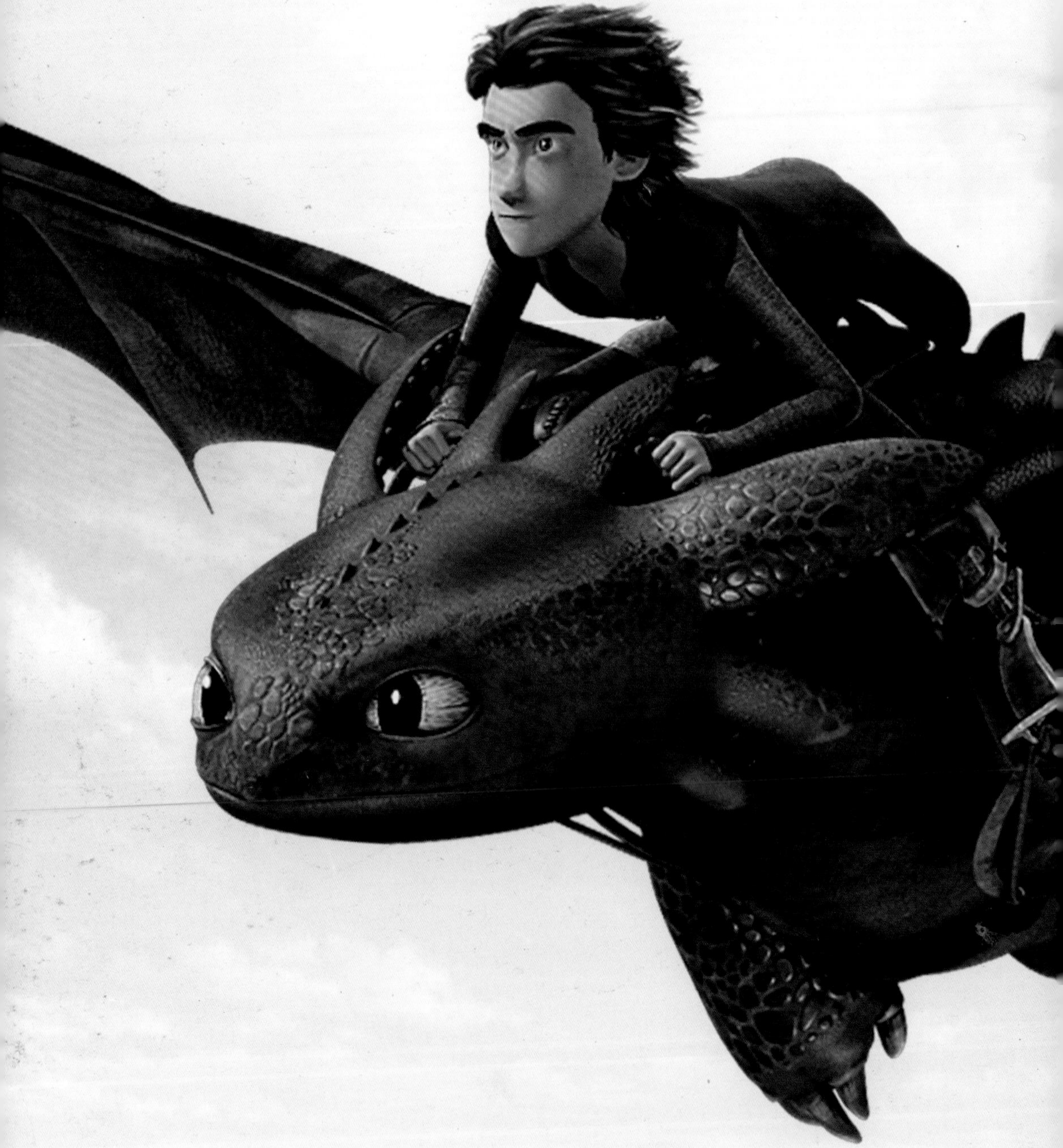

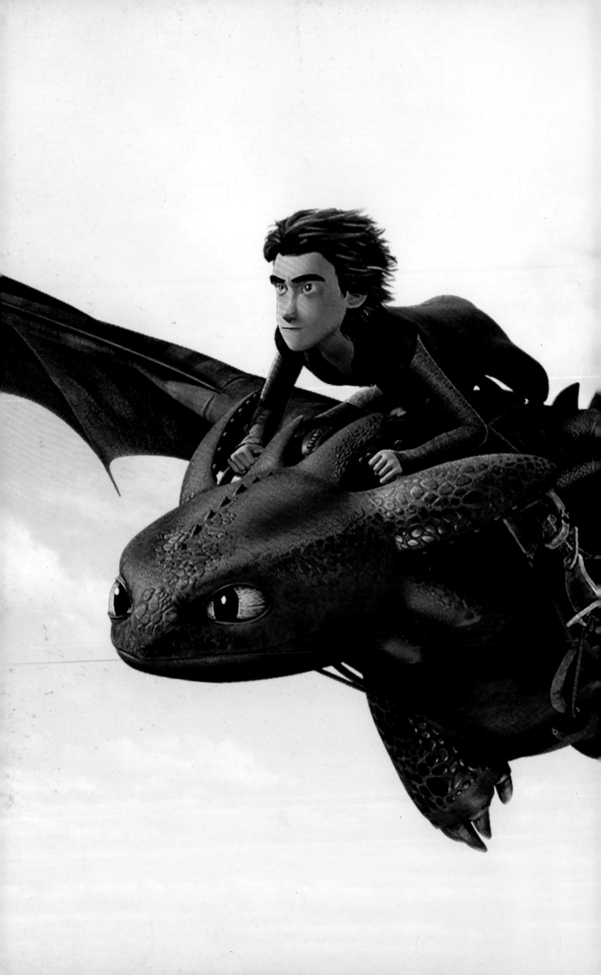

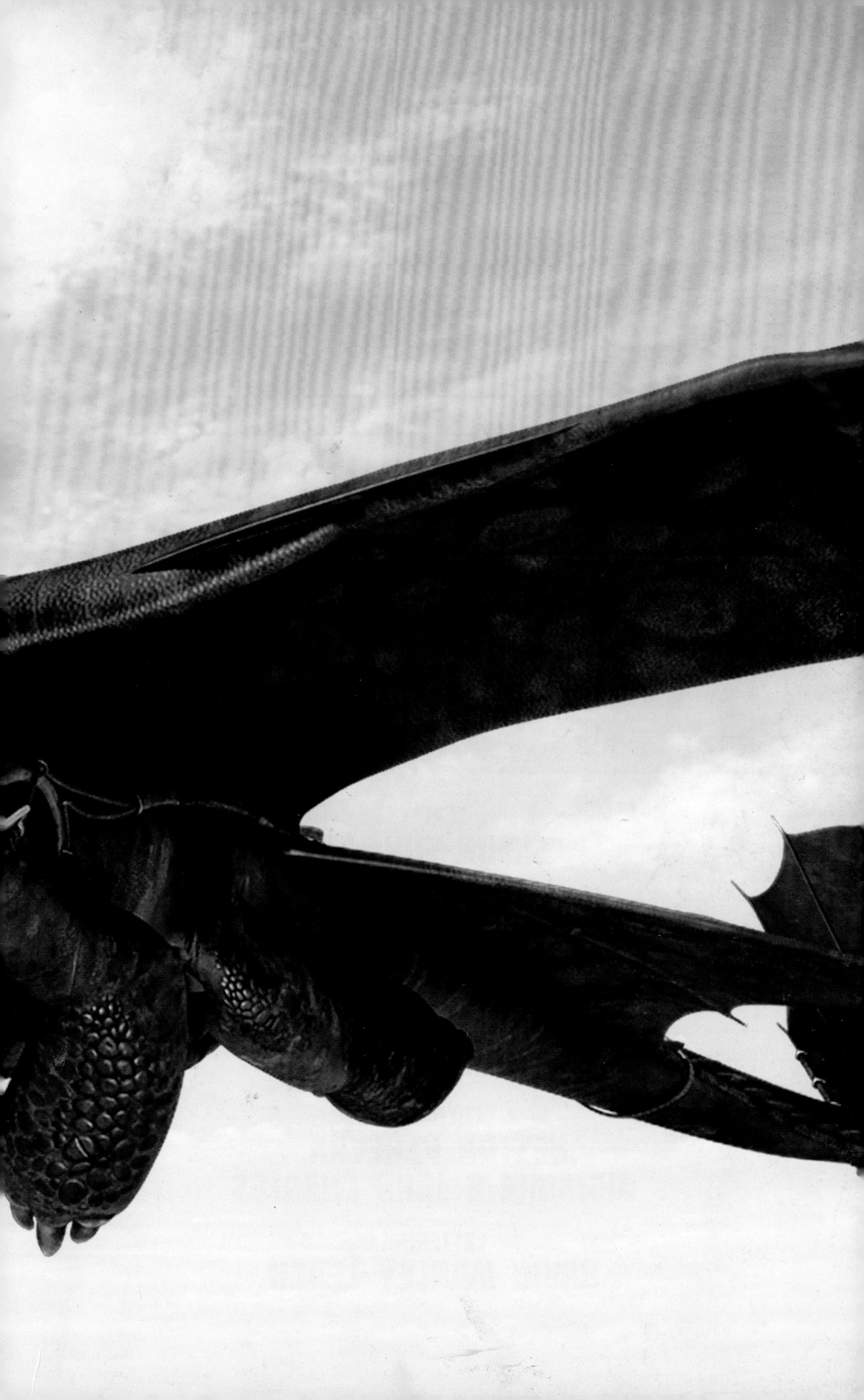

DANGERS OF THE DEEP

SCRIPT
SIMON FURMAN

PENCILS
IWAN NAZIF

INKS
IWAN NAZIF
WITH LEE TOWNSEND

COLORING
NESTOR PEREYRA,
DIGIKORE & JOHN CHARLES

LETTERING
DAVID MANLEY-LEACH

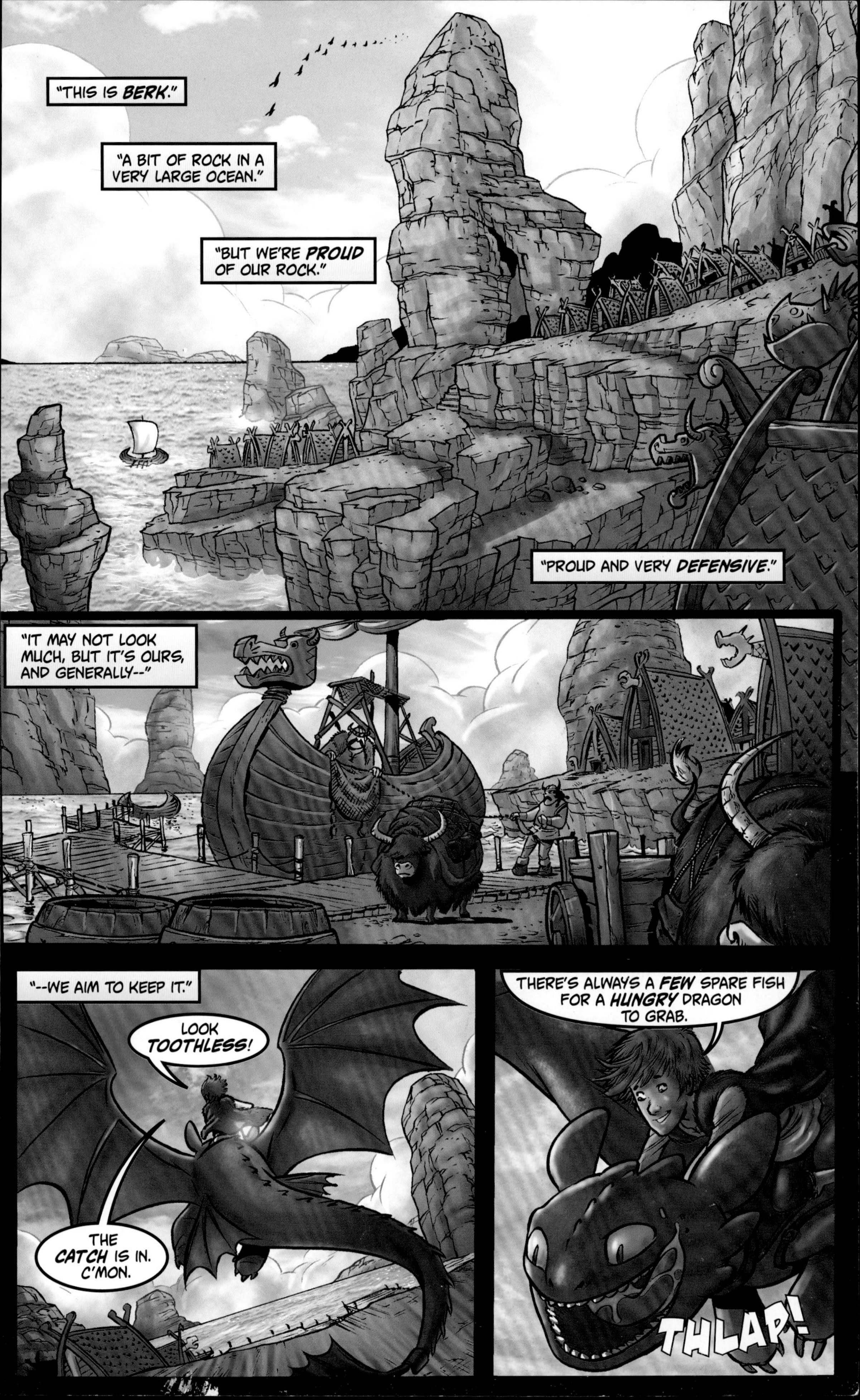
"THIS IS BERK."
"A BIT OF ROCK IN A VERY LARGE OCEAN."
"BUT WE'RE PROUD OF OUR ROCK."
"PROUD AND VERY DEFENSIVE."
"IT MAY NOT LOOK MUCH, BUT IT'S OURS, AND GENERALLY--"
"--WE AIM TO KEEP IT."
LOOK TOOTHLESS!
THE CATCH IS IN. C'MON.
THERE'S ALWAYS A FEW SPARE FISH FOR A HUNGRY DRAGON TO GRAB.
THLAP!

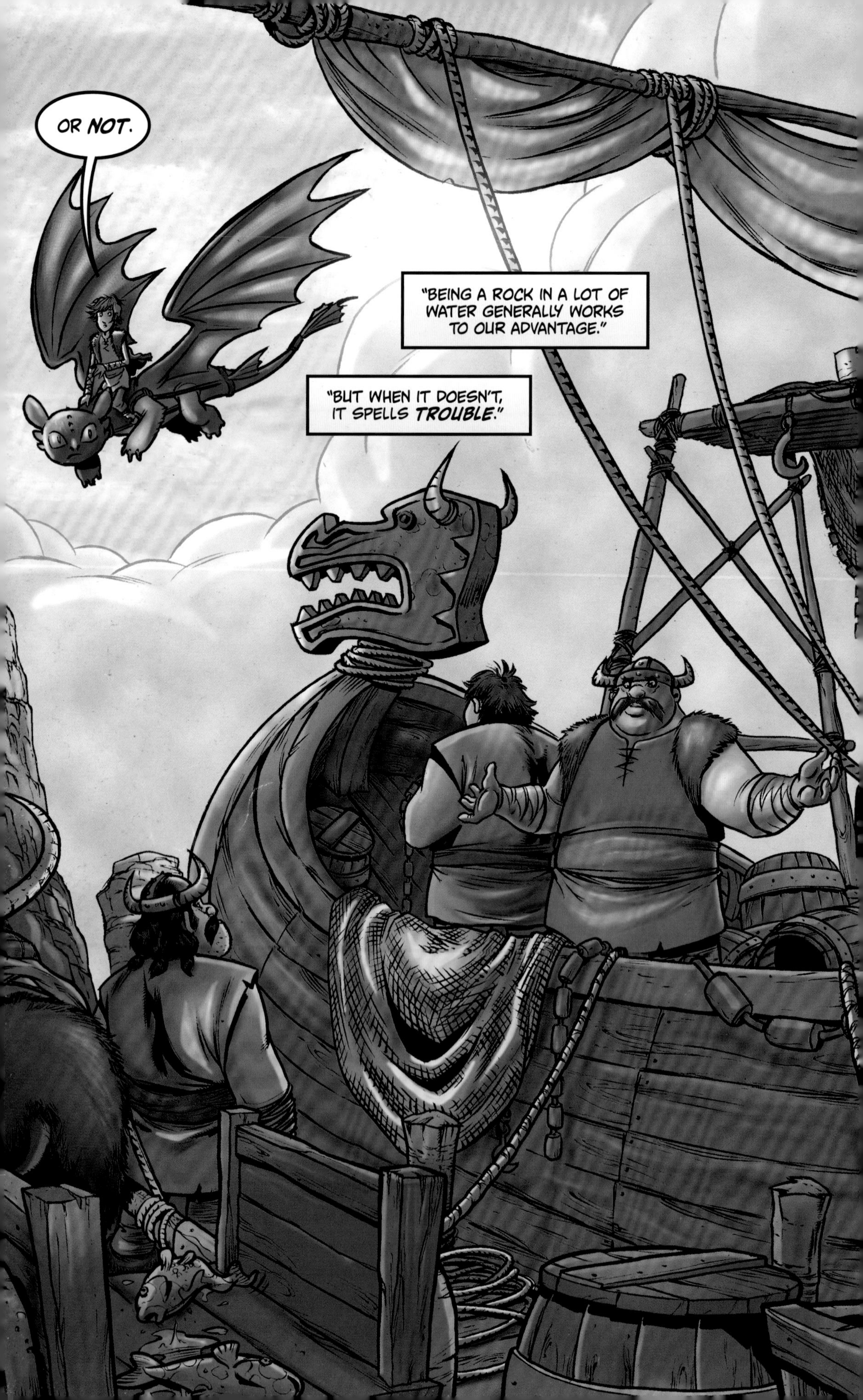
OR NOT.
"BEING A ROCK IN A LOT OF WATER GENERALLY WORKS TO OUR ADVANTAGE."
"BUT WHEN IT DOESN'T, IT SPELLS TROUBLE."

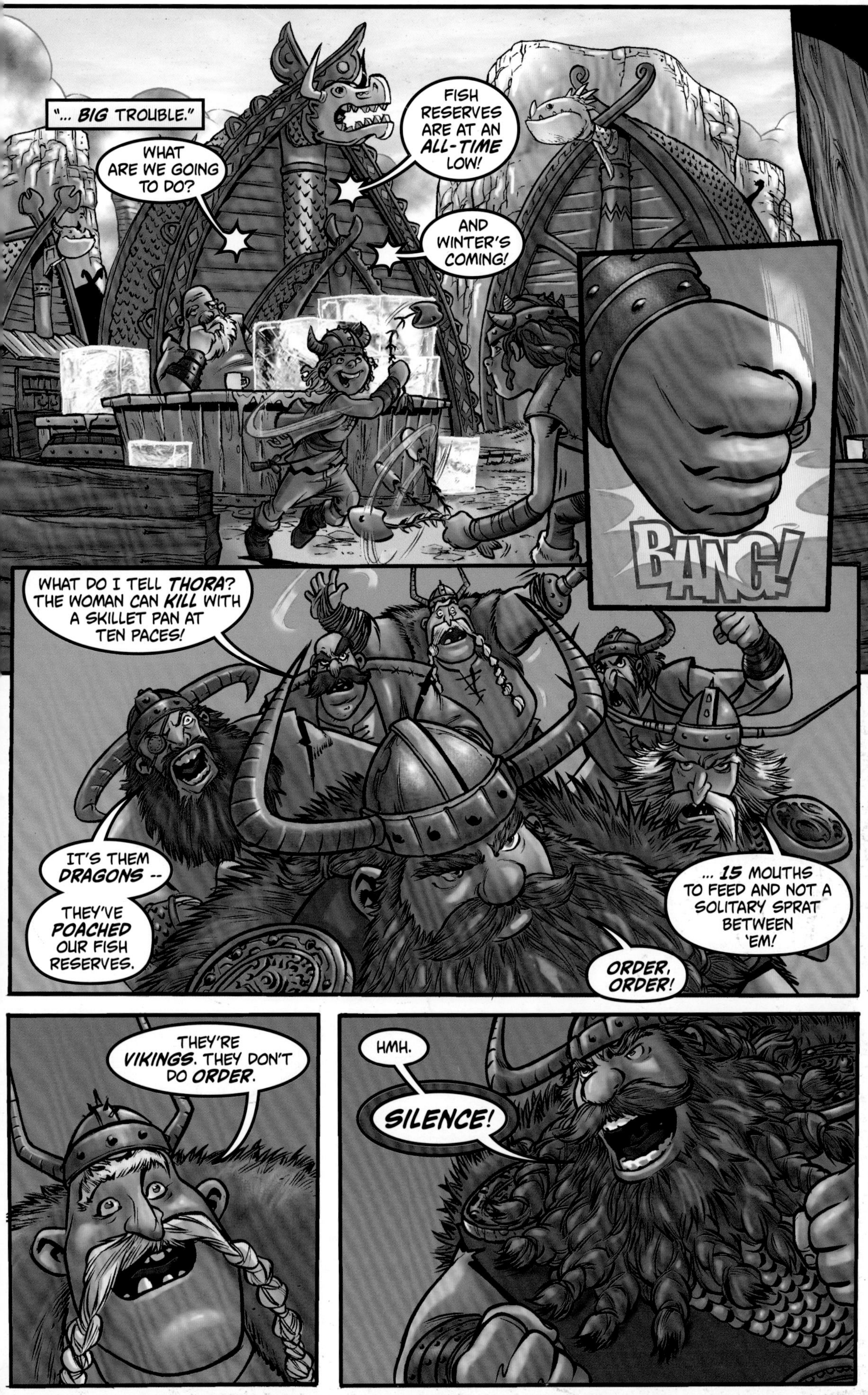
"... BIG TROUBLE."
WHAT ARE WE GOING TO DO?
FISH RESERVES ARE AT AN ALL-TIME LOW!
AND WINTER'S COMING!
BANG!
WHAT DO I TELL THORA? THE WOMAN CAN KILL WITH A SKILLET PAN AT TEN PACES!
IT'S THEM DRAGONS --
THEY'VE POACHED OUR FISH RESERVES.
... 15 MOUTHS TO FEED AND NOT A SOLITARY SPRAT BETWEEN 'EM!
ORDER, ORDER!
THEY'RE VIKINGS. THEY DON'T DO ORDER.
HMH.
SILENCE!

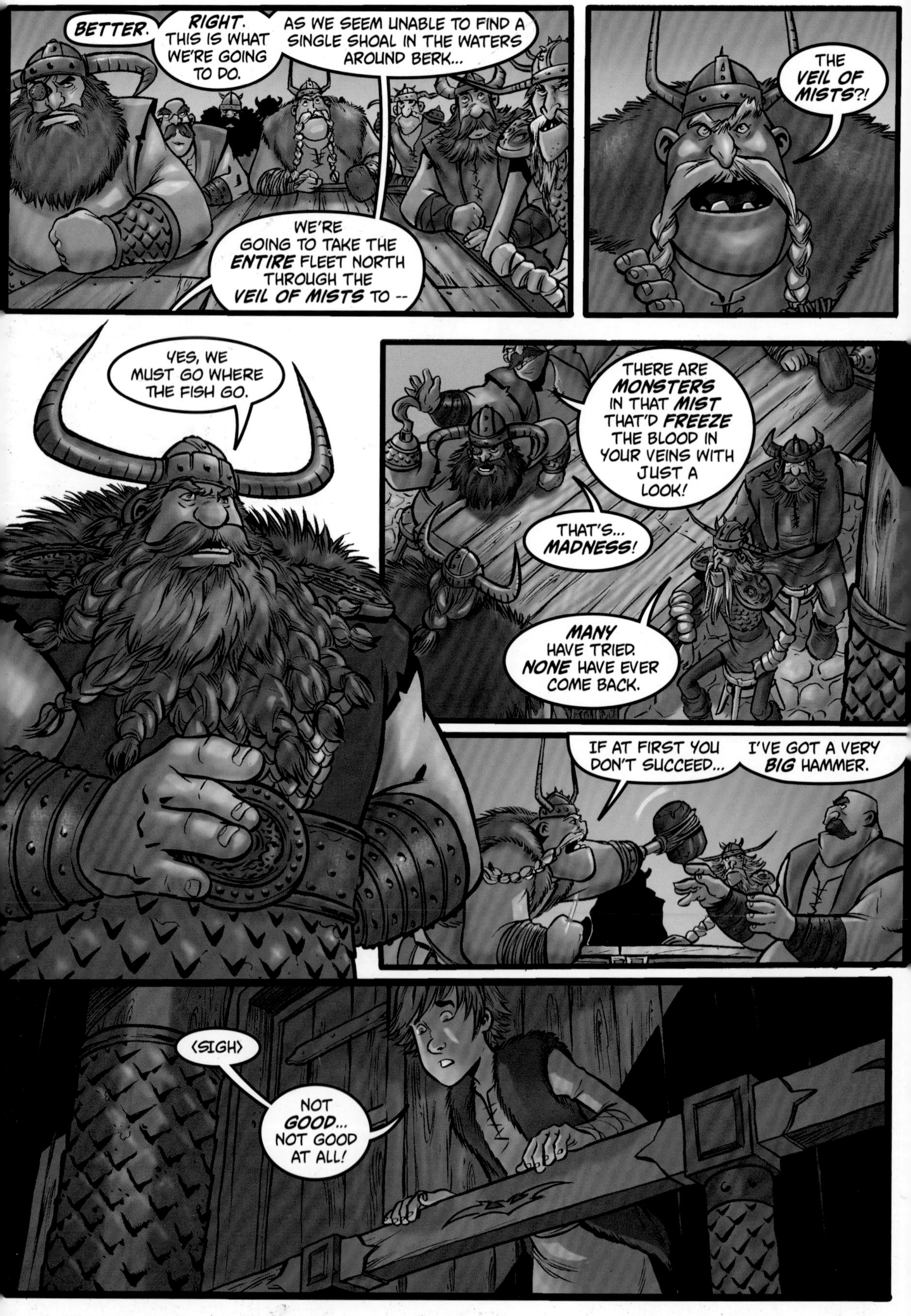
BETTER.
RIGHT. THIS IS WHAT WE'RE GOING TO DO.
AS WE SEEM UNABLE TO FIND A SINGLE SHOAL IN THE WATERS AROUND BERK...
WE'RE GOING TO TAKE THE ENTIRE FLEET NORTH THROUGH THE VEIL OF MISTS TO --
THE VEIL OF MISTS?!
YES, WE MUST GO WHERE THE FISH GO.
THERE ARE MONSTERS IN THAT MIST THAT'D FREEZE THE BLOOD IN YOUR VEINS WITH JUST A LOOK!
THAT'S... MADNESS!
MANY HAVE TRIED. NONE HAVE EVER COME BACK.
IF AT FIRST YOU DON'T SUCCEED...
I'VE GOT A VERY BIG HAMMER.
(SIGH)
NOT GOOD... NOT GOOD AT ALL!

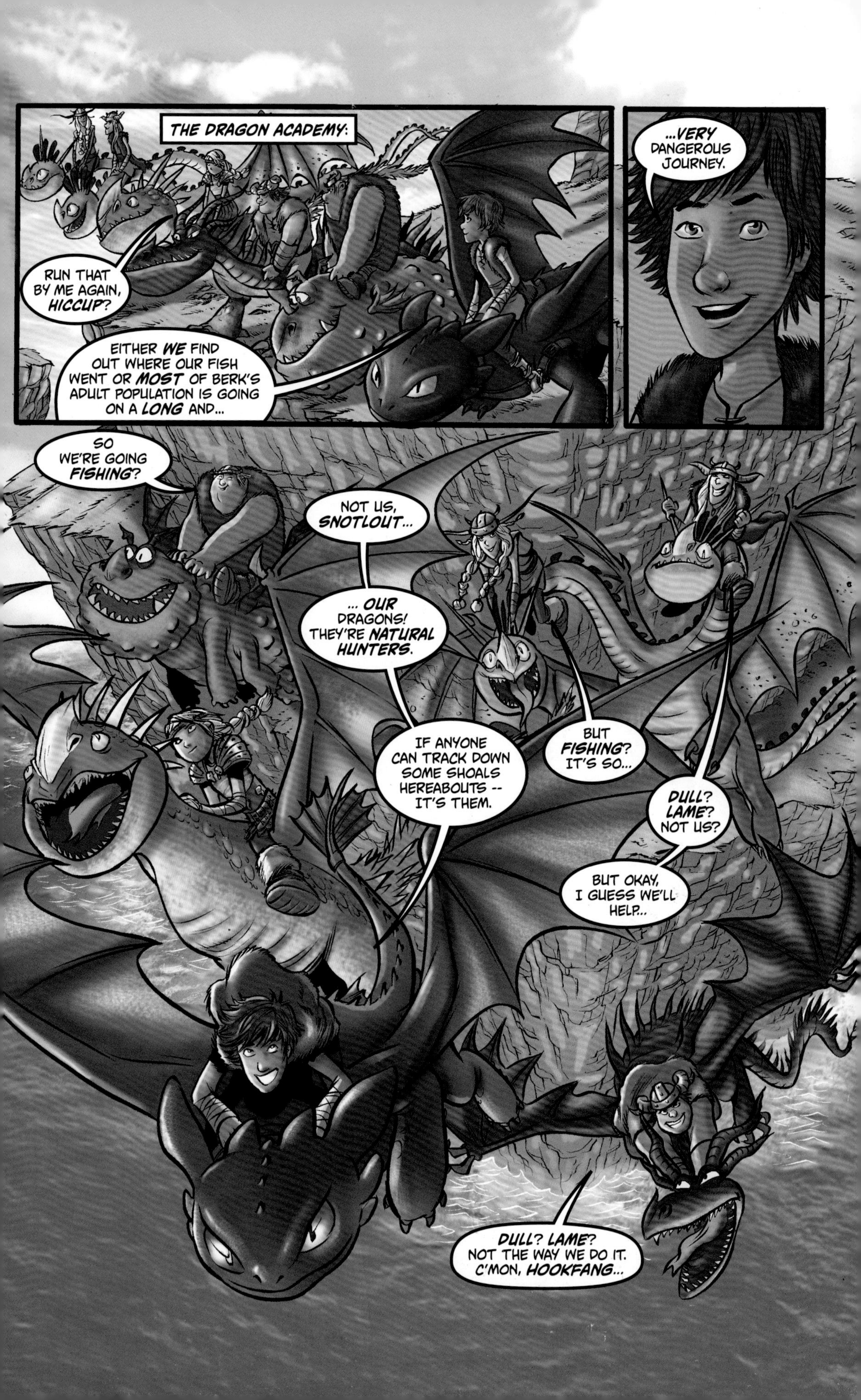
THE DRAGON ACADEMY:
RUN THAT BY ME AGAIN, HICCUP?
EITHER WE FIND OUT WHERE OUR FISH WENT OR MOST OF BERK'S ADULT POPULATION IS GOING ON A LONG AND...
...VERY DANGEROUS JOURNEY.
SO WE'RE GOING FISHING?
NOT US, SNOTLOUT...
... OUR DRAGONS! THEY'RE NATURAL HUNTERS.
IF ANYONE CAN TRACK DOWN SOME SHOALS HEREABOUTS -- IT'S THEM.
BUT FISHING? IT'S SO...
DULL? LAME? NOT US?
BUT OKAY, I GUESS WE'LL HELP...
DULL? LAME? NOT THE WAY WE DO IT. C'MON, HOOKFANG...

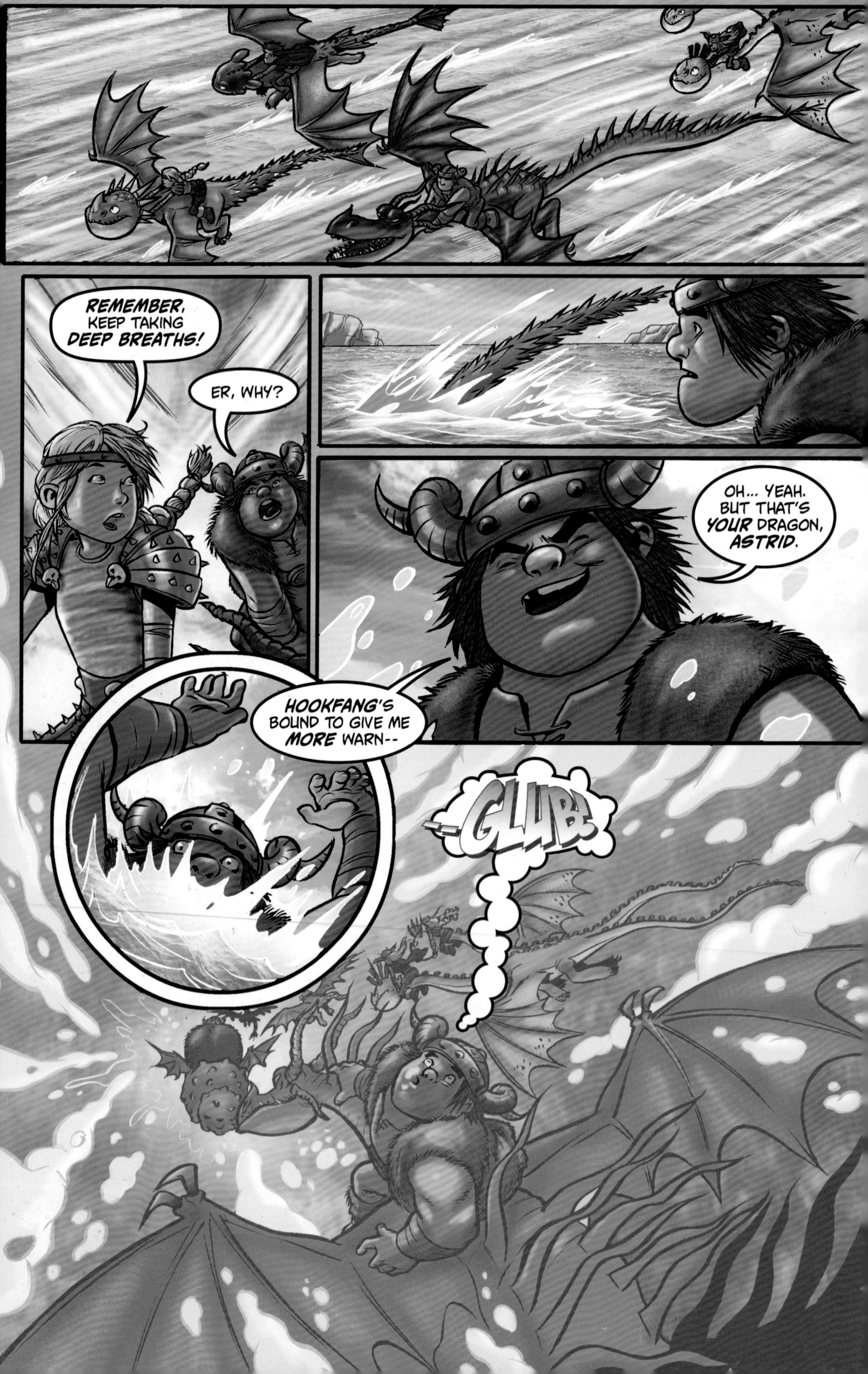
REMEMBER, KEEP TAKING DEEP BREATHS!
ER, WHY?
OH... YEAH. BUT THAT'S YOUR DRAGON, ASTRID.
HOOKFANG'S BOUND TO GIVE ME MORE WARN--
--GLUB!

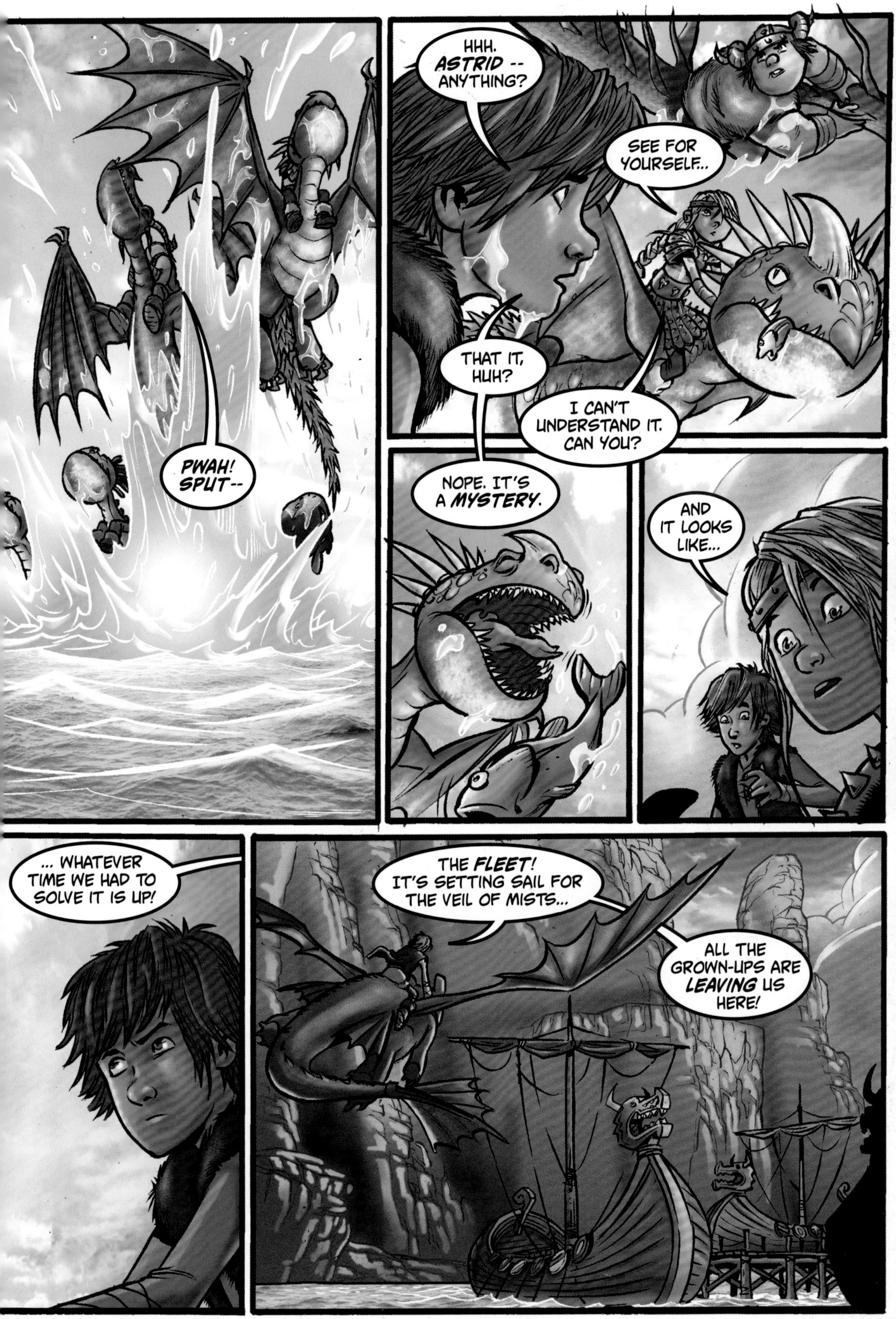
PWAH! SPUT--
HHH. ASTRID -- ANYTHING?
SEE FOR YOURSELF...
THAT IT, HUH?
I CAN'T UNDERSTAND IT. CAN YOU?
NOPE. IT'S A MYSTERY.
AND IT LOOKS LIKE...
... WHATEVER TIME WE HAD TO SOLVE IT IS UP!
THE FLEET! IT'S SETTING SAIL FOR THE VEIL OF MISTS...
ALL THE GROWN-UPS ARE LEAVING US HERE!

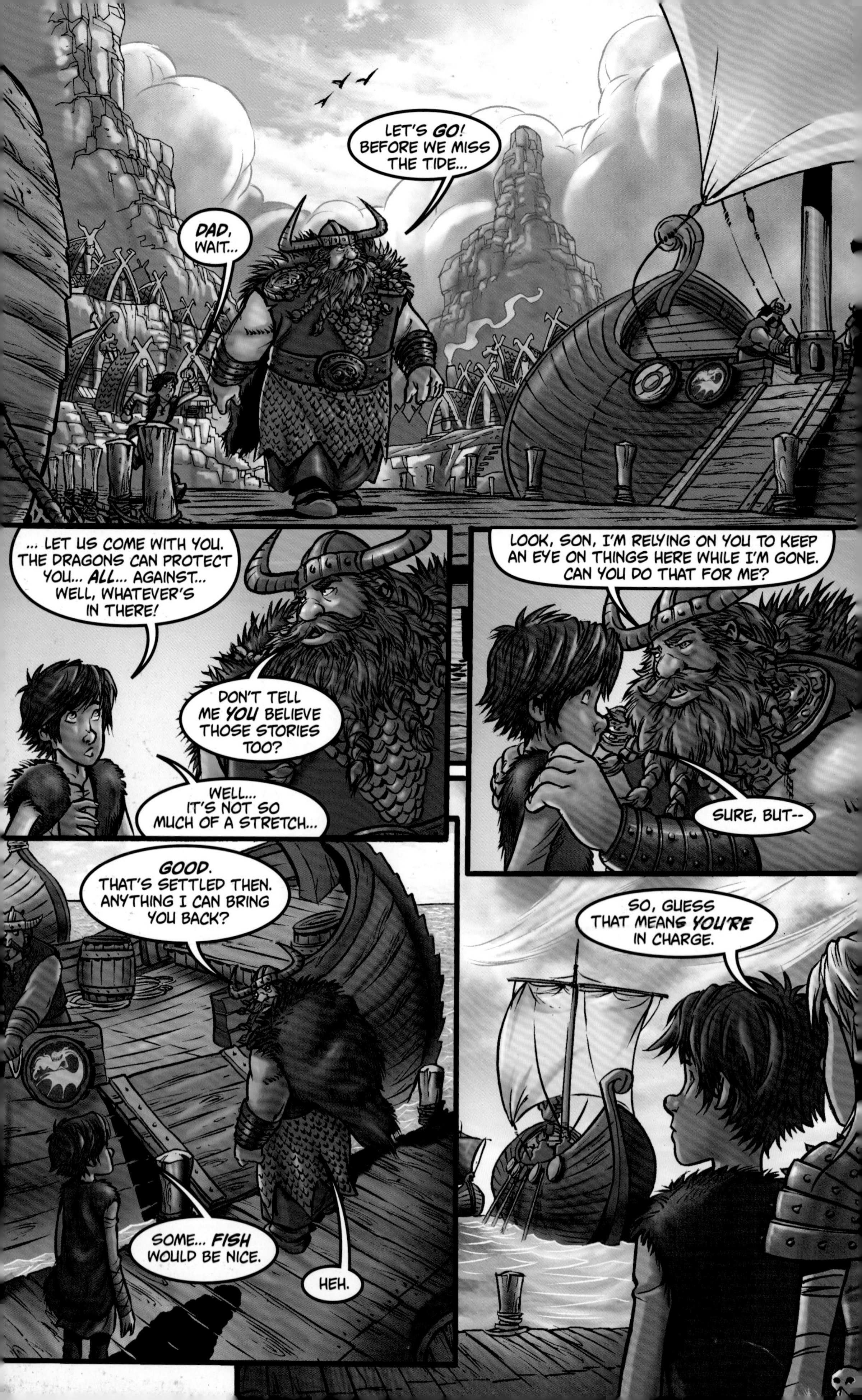
LET'S GO! BEFORE WE MISS THE TIDE...
DAD, WAIT...
... LET US COME WITH YOU. THE DRAGONS CAN PROTECT YOU... ALL... AGAINST... WELL, WHATEVER'S IN THERE!
DON'T TELL ME YOU BELIEVE THOSE STORIES TOO?
WELL... IT'S NOT SO MUCH OF A STRETCH...
LOOK, SON, I'M RELYING ON YOU TO KEEP AN EYE ON THINGS HERE WHILE I'M GONE. CAN YOU DO THAT FOR ME?
SURE, BUT--
GOOD. THAT'S SETTLED THEN. ANYTHING I CAN BRING YOU BACK?
SOME... FISH WOULD BE NICE.
HEH.
SO, GUESS THAT MEANS YOU'RE IN CHARGE.

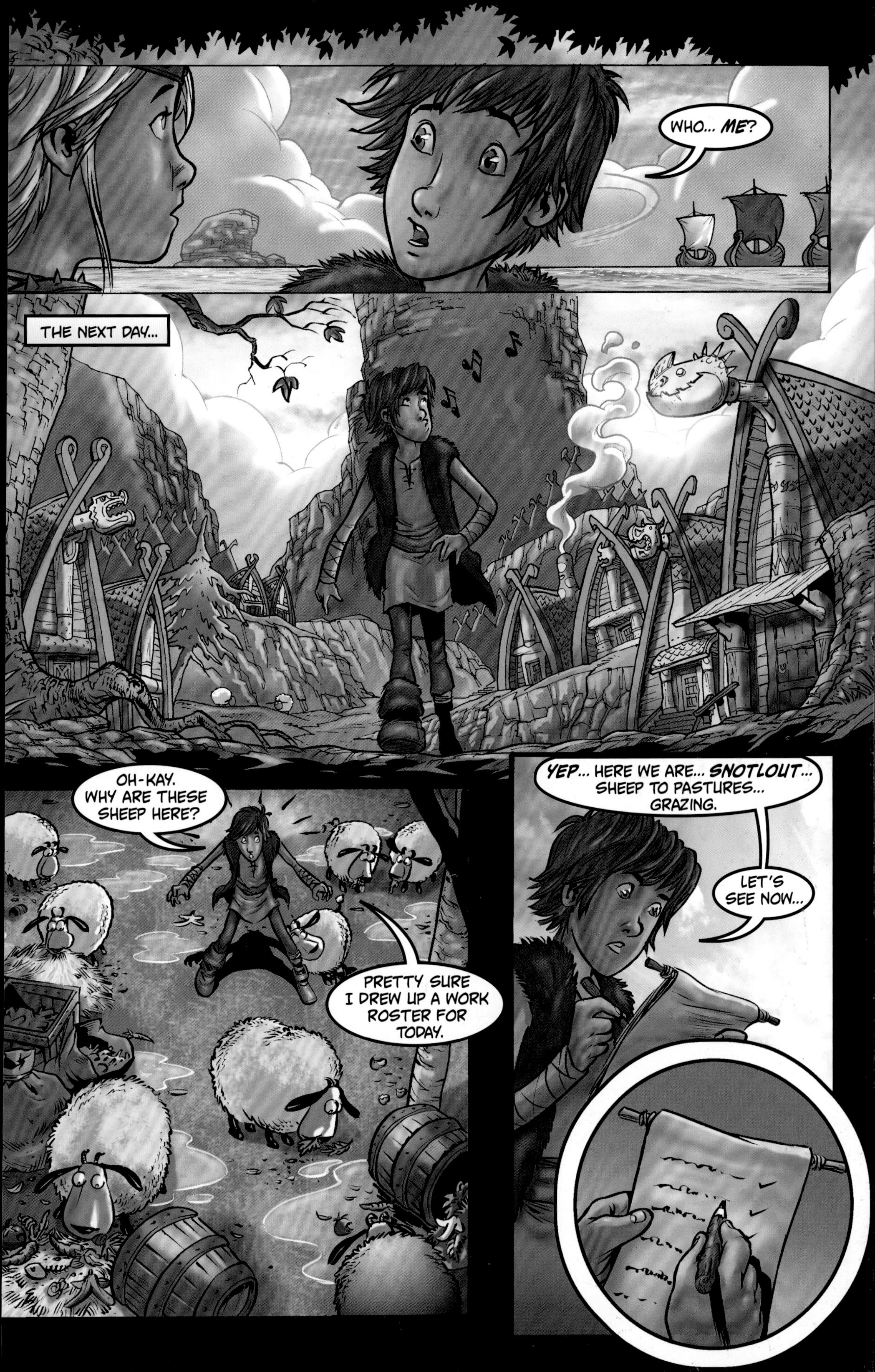
WHO... ME?
THE NEXT DAY...
OH-KAY. WHY ARE THESE SHEEP HERE?
PRETTY SURE I DREW UP A WORK ROSTER FOR TODAY.
YEP... HERE WE ARE... SNOTLOUT... SHEEP TO PASTURES... GRAZING.
LET'S SEE NOW...

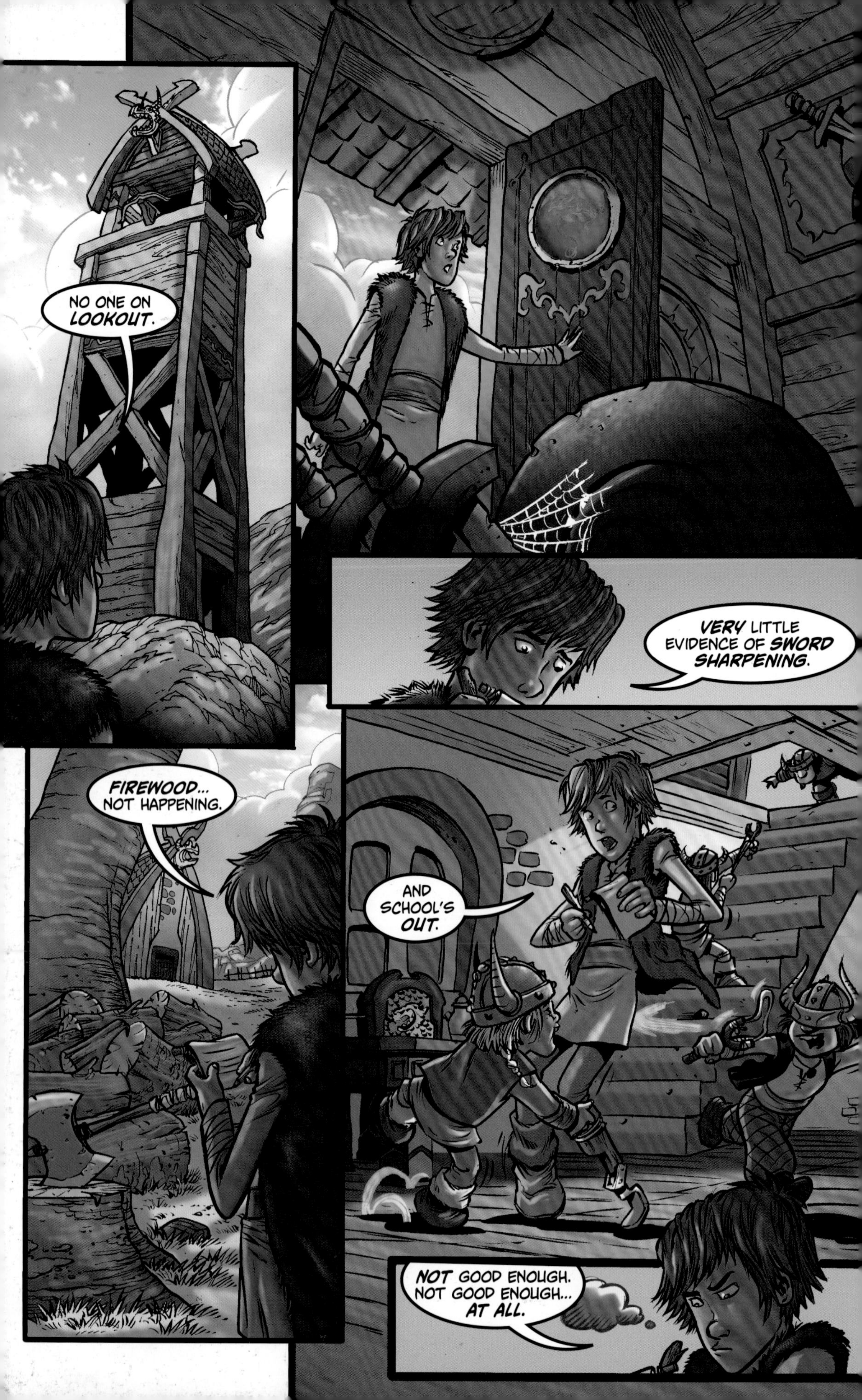
NO ONE ON LOOKOUT.
VERY LITTLE EVIDENCE OF SWORD SHARPENING.
FIREWOOD... NOT HAPPENING.
AND SCHOOL'S OUT.
NOT GOOD ENOUGH. NOT GOOD ENOUGH... AT ALL.

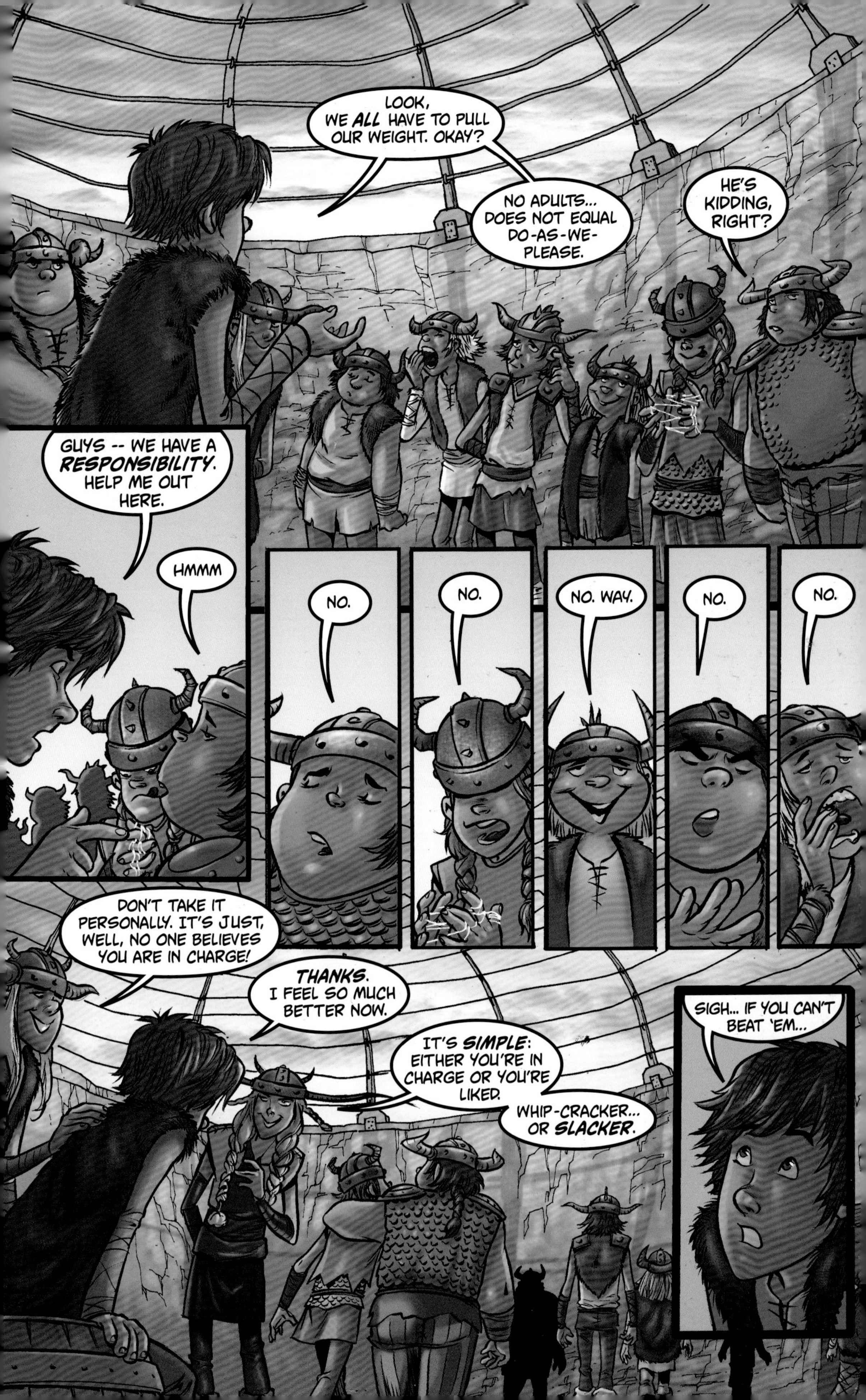
LOOK, WE ALL HAVE TO PULL OUR WEIGHT. OKAY?
NO ADULTS... DOES NOT EQUAL DO-AS-WE-PLEASE.
HE'S KIDDING, RIGHT?
GUYS -- WE HAVE A RESPONSIBILITY. HELP ME OUT HERE.
HMMM
NO.
NO.
NO. WAY.
NO.
NO.
DON'T TAKE IT PERSONALLY. IT'S JUST, WELL, NO ONE BELIEVES YOU ARE IN CHARGE!
THANKS. I FEEL SO MUCH BETTER NOW.
IT'S SIMPLE: EITHER YOU'RE IN CHARGE OR YOU'RE LIKED.
WHIP-CRACKER... OR SLACKER.
SIGH... IF YOU CAN'T BEAT 'EM...

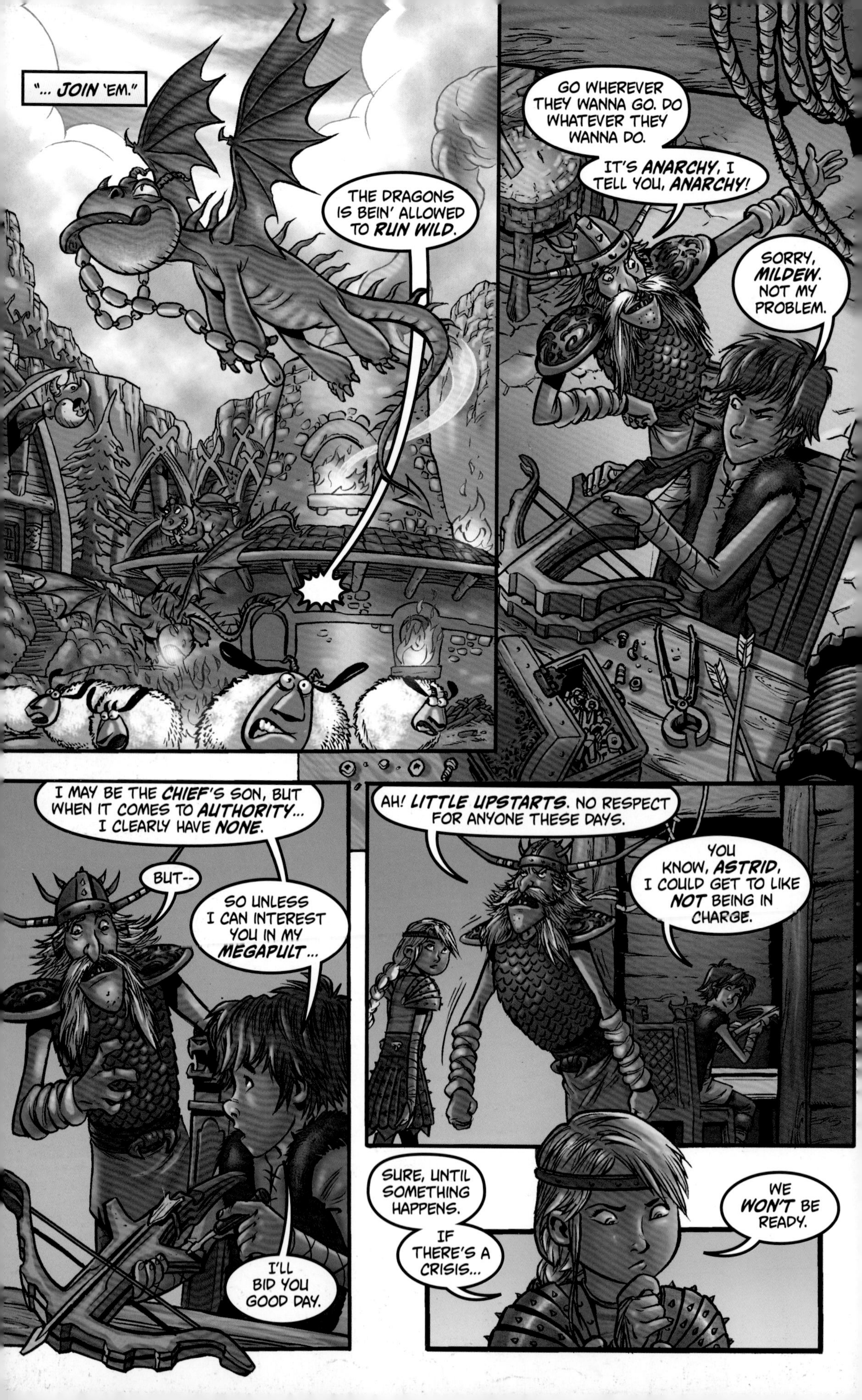
"... JOIN 'EM."
THE DRAGONS IS BEIN' ALLOWED TO RUN WILD.
GO WHEREVER THEY WANNA GO. DO WHATEVER THEY WANNA DO.
IT'S ANARCHY, I TELL YOU, ANARCHY!
SORRY, MILDEW. NOT MY PROBLEM.
I MAY BE THE CHIEF'S SON, BUT WHEN IT COMES TO AUTHORITY... I CLEARLY HAVE NONE.
BUT--
SO UNLESS I CAN INTEREST YOU IN MY MEGAPULT...
I'LL BID YOU GOOD DAY.
AH! LITTLE UPSTARTS. NO RESPECT FOR ANYONE THESE DAYS.
YOU KNOW, ASTRID, I COULD GET TO LIKE NOT BEING IN CHARGE.
SURE, UNTIL SOMETHING HAPPENS.
IF THERE'S A CRISIS...
WE WON'T BE READY.

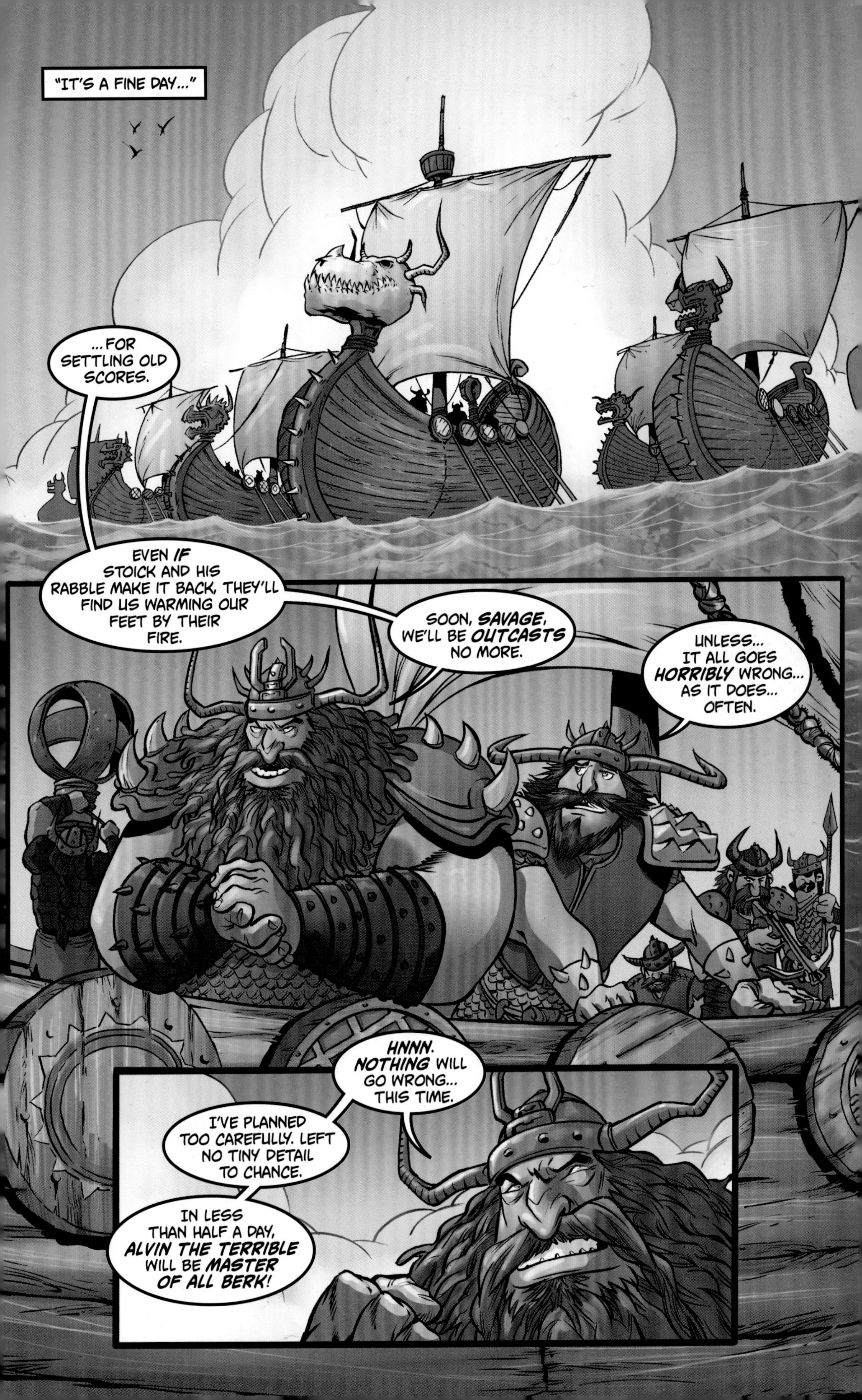
"IT'S A FINE DAY..."
...FOR SETTLING OLD SCORES.
EVEN *IF* STOICK AND HIS RABBLE MAKE IT BACK, THEY'LL FIND US WARMING OUR FEET BY THEIR FIRE.
SOON, *SAVAGE*, WE'LL BE *OUTCASTS* NO MORE.
UNLESS... IT ALL GOES *HORRIBLY* WRONG... AS IT DOES... OFTEN.
HNNN. *NOTHING* WILL GO WRONG... THIS TIME.
I'VE PLANNED TOO CAREFULLY. LEFT NO TINY DETAIL TO CHANCE.
IN LESS THAN HALF A DAY, *ALVIN THE TERRIBLE* WILL BE *MASTER OF ALL BERK*!

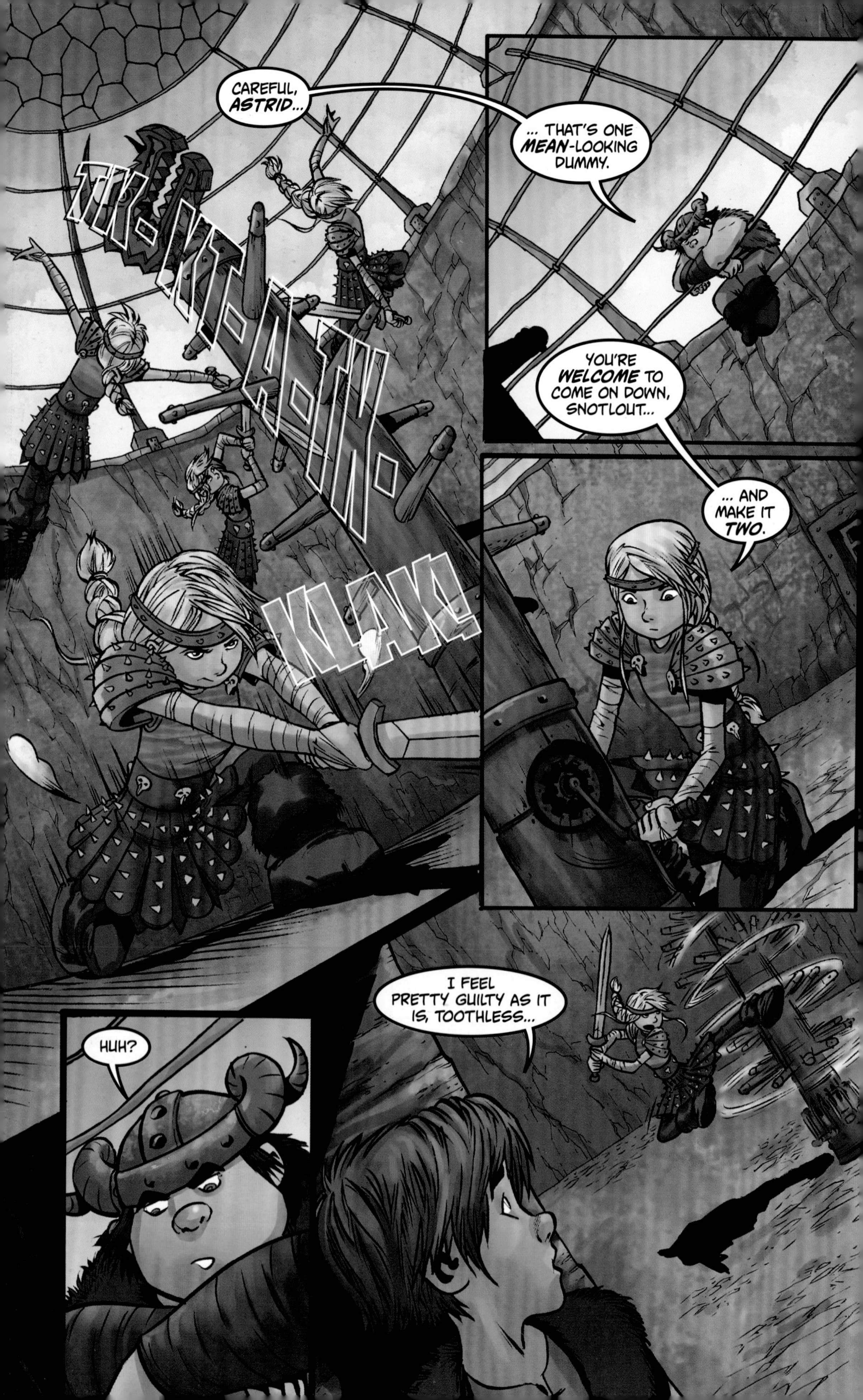
CAREFUL, ASTRID...
... THAT'S ONE MEAN-LOOKING DUMMY.
TK-KT-A-TK-
KLAK!
YOU'RE WELCOME TO COME ON DOWN, SNOTLOUT...
... AND MAKE IT TWO.
I FEEL PRETTY GUILTY AS IT IS, TOOTHLESS...
HUH?

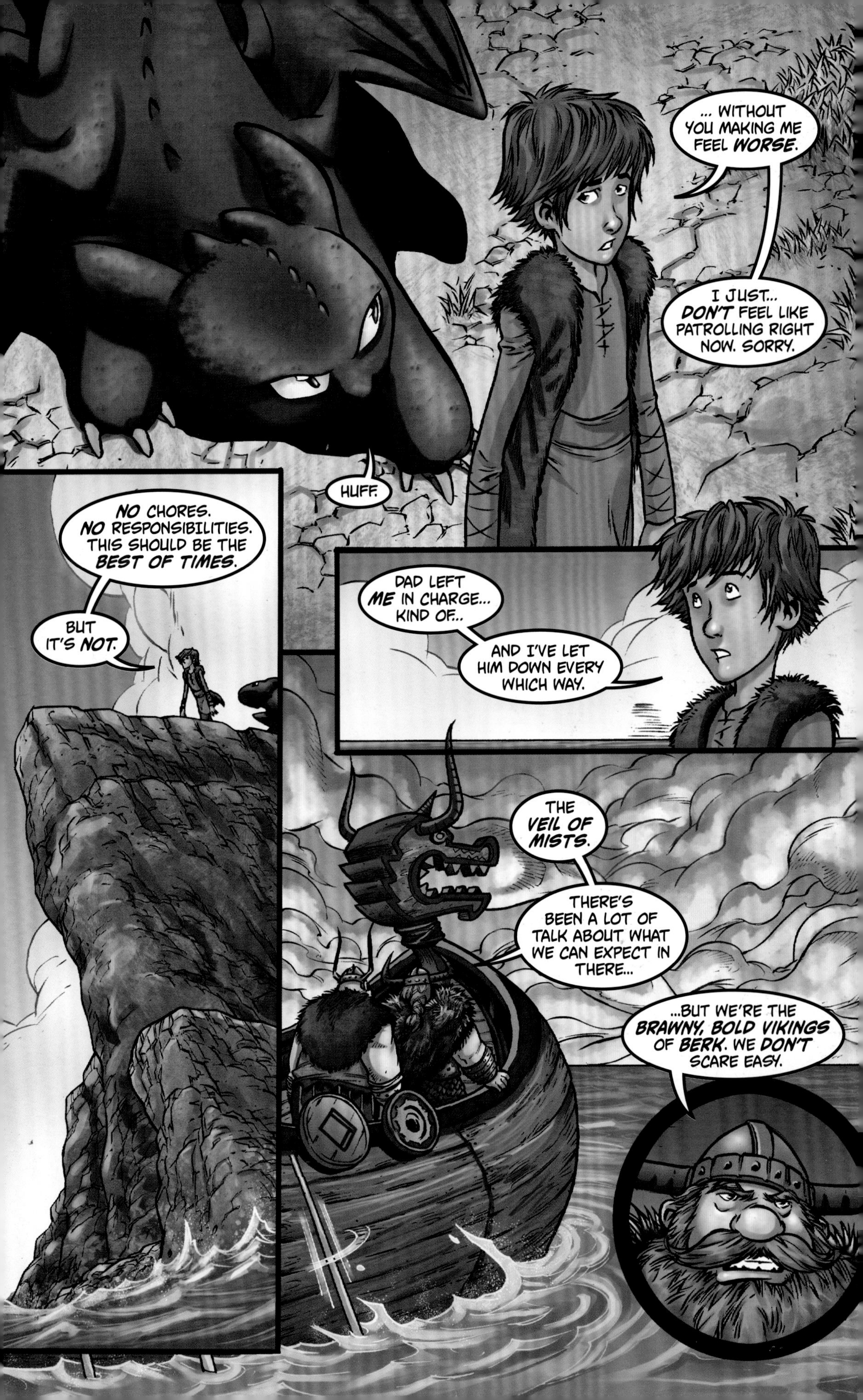
... WITHOUT YOU MAKING ME FEEL WORSE.
I JUST... DON'T FEEL LIKE PATROLLING RIGHT NOW. SORRY.
HUFF.
NO CHORES. NO RESPONSIBILITIES. THIS SHOULD BE THE BEST OF TIMES.
BUT IT'S NOT.
DAD LEFT ME IN CHARGE... KIND OF...
AND I'VE LET HIM DOWN EVERY WHICH WAY.
THE VEIL OF MISTS.
THERE'S BEEN A LOT OF TALK ABOUT WHAT WE CAN EXPECT IN THERE...
...BUT WE'RE THE BRAWNY, BOLD VIKINGS OF BERK. WE DON'T SCARE EASY.

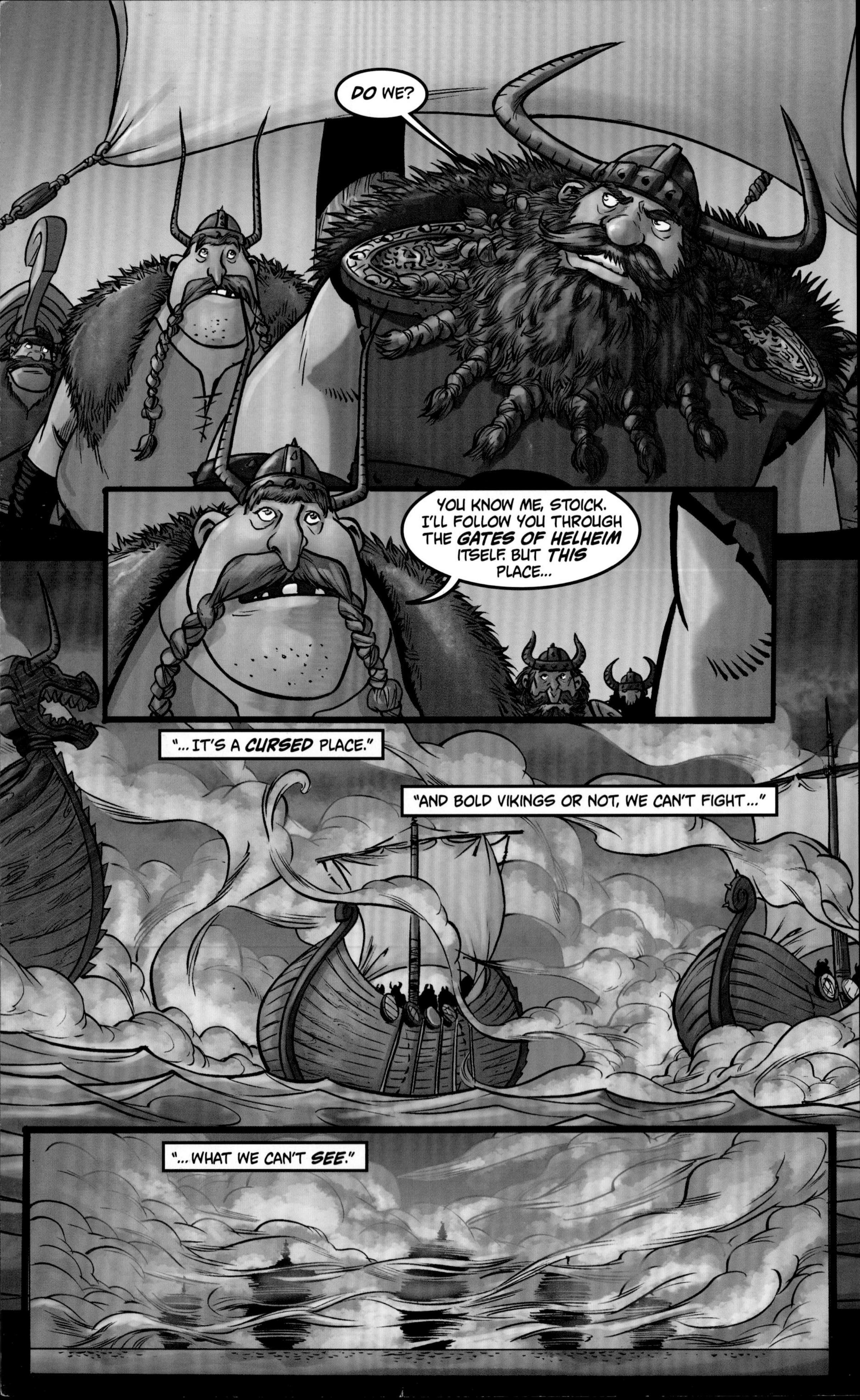
DO WE?
YOU KNOW ME, STOICK. I'LL FOLLOW YOU THROUGH THE GATES OF HELHEIM ITSELF. BUT THIS PLACE...
"...IT'S A CURSED PLACE."
"AND BOLD VIKINGS OR NOT, WE CAN'T FIGHT..."
"...WHAT WE CAN'T SEE."

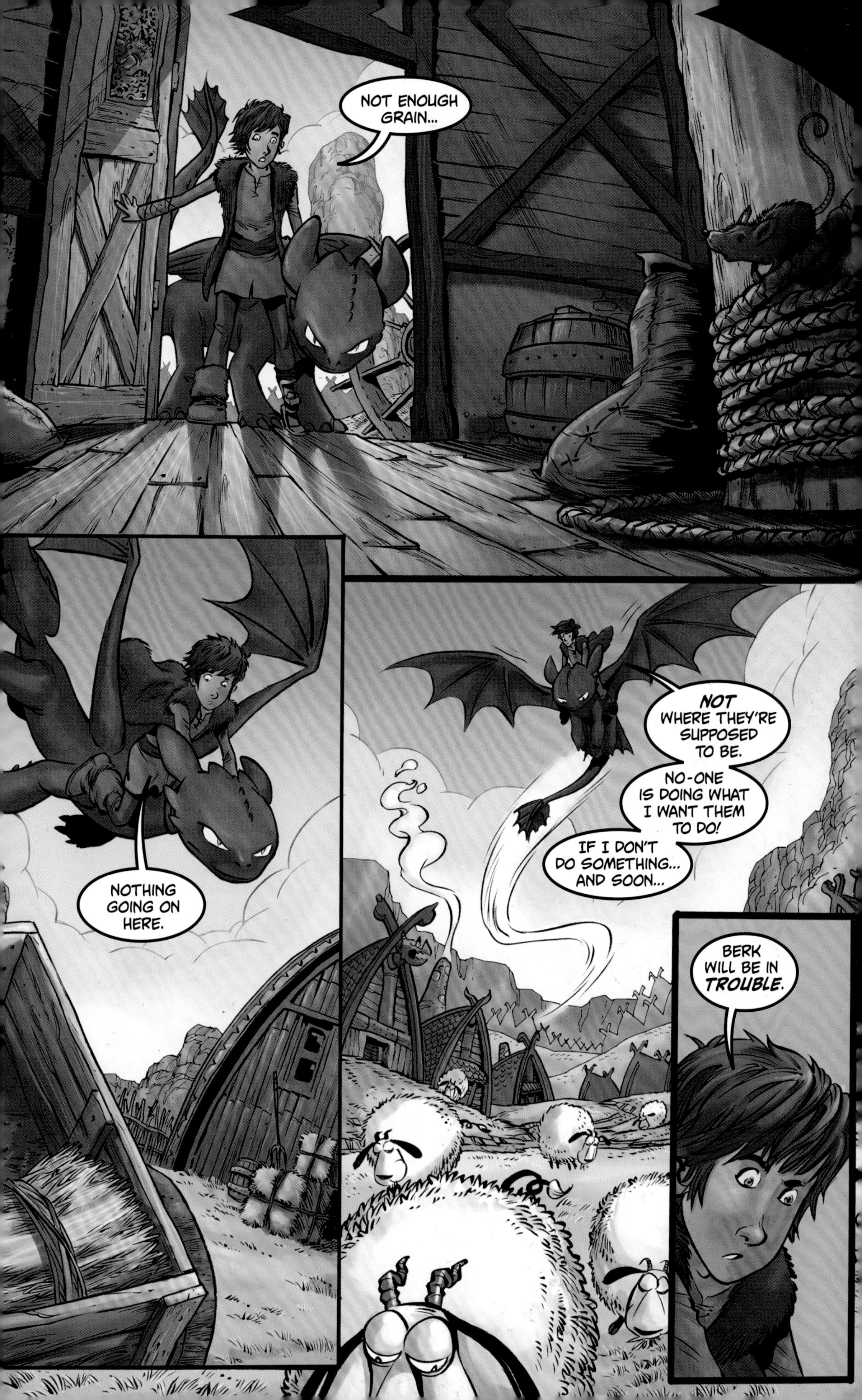
NOT ENOUGH GRAIN...
NOTHING GOING ON HERE.
NOT WHERE THEY'RE SUPPOSED TO BE.
NO-ONE IS DOING WHAT I WANT THEM TO DO!
IF I DON'T DO SOMETHING... AND SOON...
BERK WILL BE IN TROUBLE.

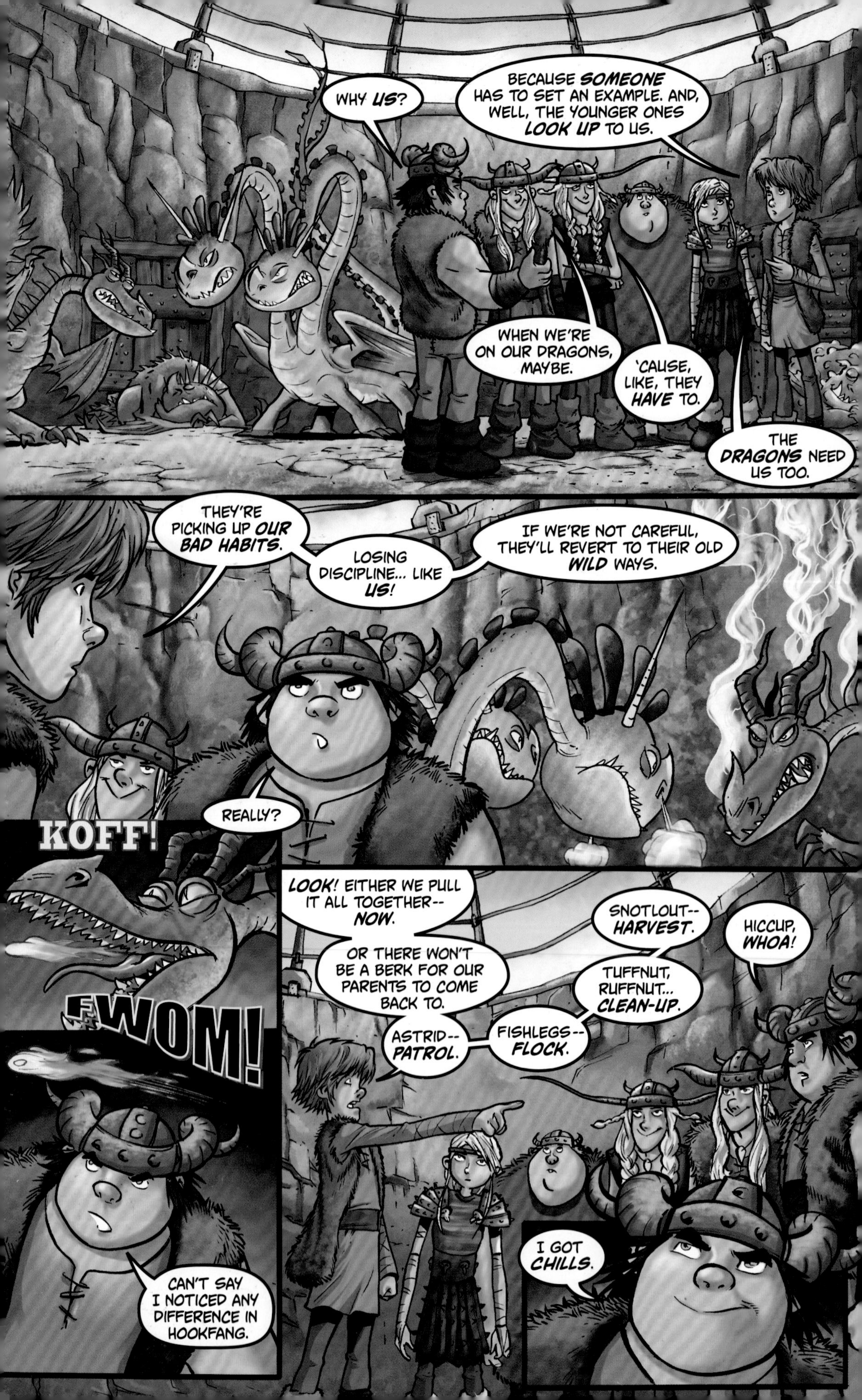
WHY US?
BECAUSE SOMEONE HAS TO SET AN EXAMPLE. AND, WELL, THE YOUNGER ONES LOOK UP TO US.
WHEN WE'RE ON OUR DRAGONS, MAYBE.
'CAUSE, LIKE, THEY HAVE TO.
THE DRAGONS NEED US TOO.
THEY'RE PICKING UP OUR BAD HABITS.
LOSING DISCIPLINE... LIKE US!
IF WE'RE NOT CAREFUL, THEY'LL REVERT TO THEIR OLD WILD WAYS.
REALLY?
KOFF!
FWOM!
CAN'T SAY I NOTICED ANY DIFFERENCE IN HOOKFANG.
LOOK! EITHER WE PULL IT ALL TOGETHER-- NOW.
OR THERE WON'T BE A BERK FOR OUR PARENTS TO COME BACK TO.
SNOTLOUT-- HARVEST.
TUFFNUT, RUFFNUT... CLEAN-UP.
FISHLEGS-- FLOCK.
ASTRID-- PATROL.
HICCUP, WHOA!
I GOT CHILLS.

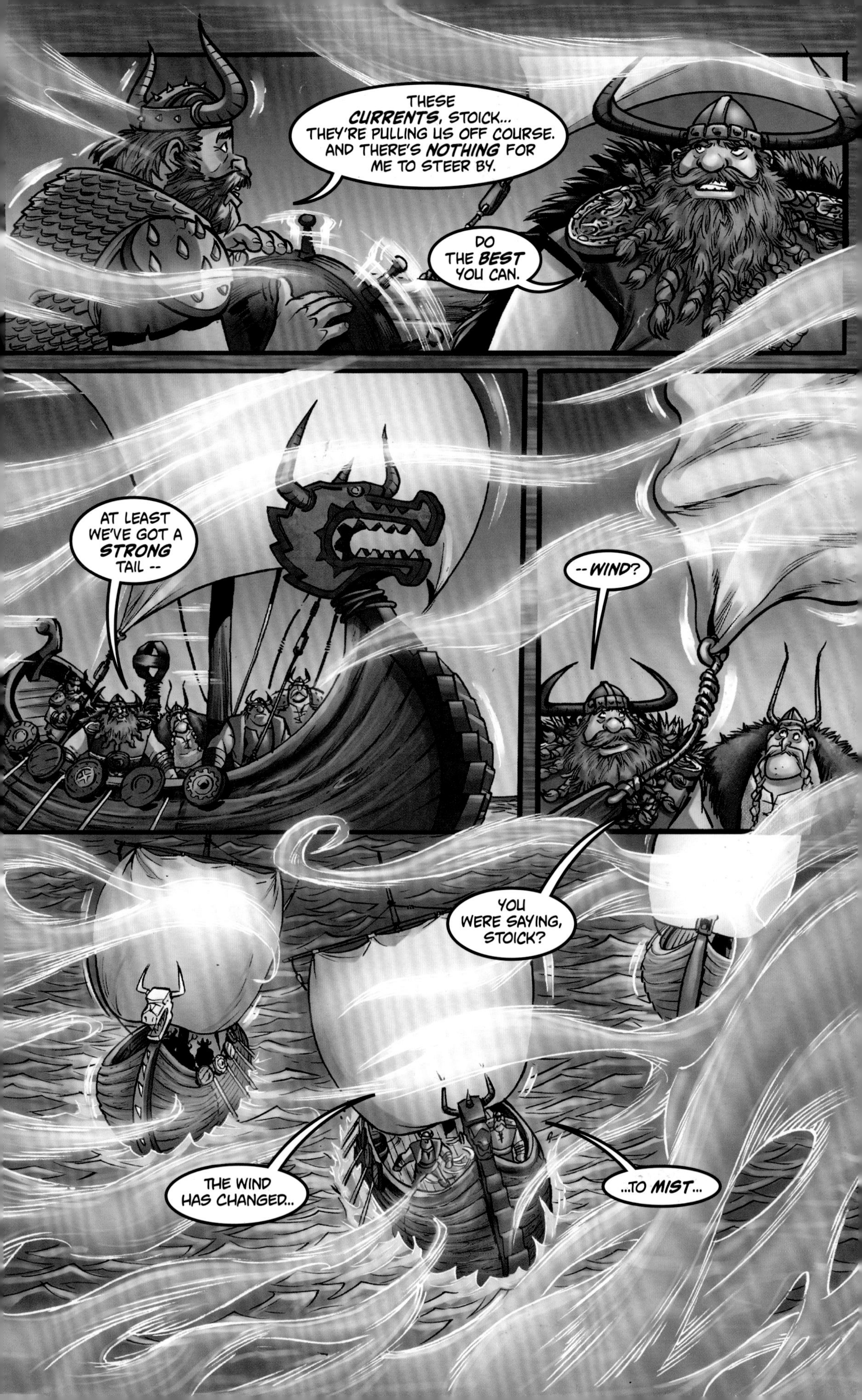
THESE CURRENTS, STOICK... THEY'RE PULLING US OFF COURSE. AND THERE'S NOTHING FOR ME TO STEER BY.
DO THE BEST YOU CAN.
AT LEAST WE'VE GOT A STRONG TAIL --
-- WIND?
YOU WERE SAYING, STOICK?
THE WIND HAS CHANGED...
...TO MIST...

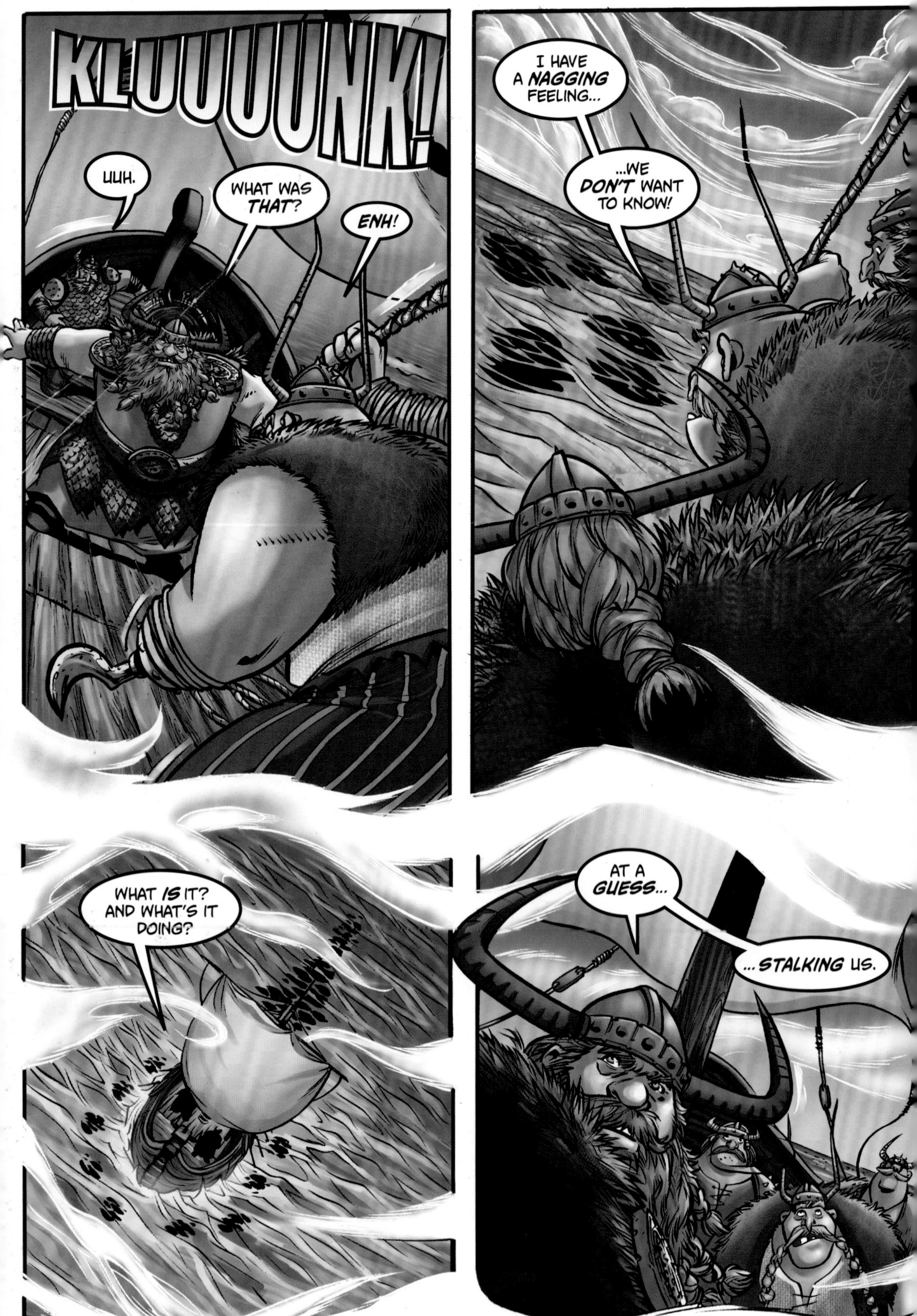
KLUUUUUNK!
UUH.
WHAT WAS THAT?
ENH!
I HAVE A NAGGING FEELING...
...WE DON'T WANT TO KNOW!
WHAT IS IT? AND WHAT'S IT DOING?
AT A GUESS...
...STALKING US.

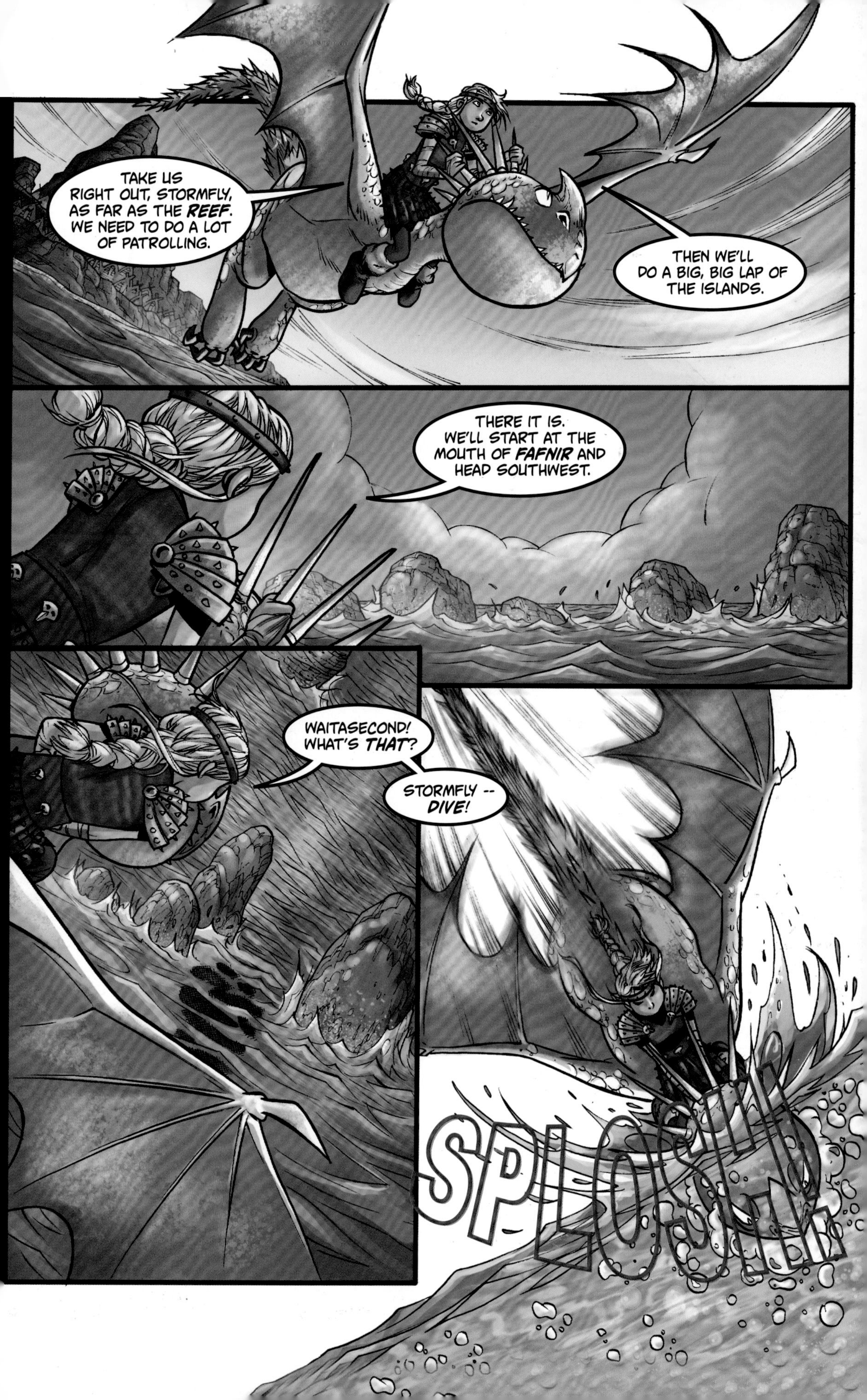
TAKE US RIGHT OUT, STORMFLY, AS FAR AS THE **REEF**. WE NEED TO DO A LOT OF PATROLLING.
THEN WE'LL DO A BIG, BIG LAP OF THE ISLANDS.
THERE IT IS. WE'LL START AT THE MOUTH OF **FAFNIR** AND HEAD SOUTHWEST.
WAITASECOND! WHAT'S **THAT**?
STORMFLY -- **DIVE**!
SPLOSH!

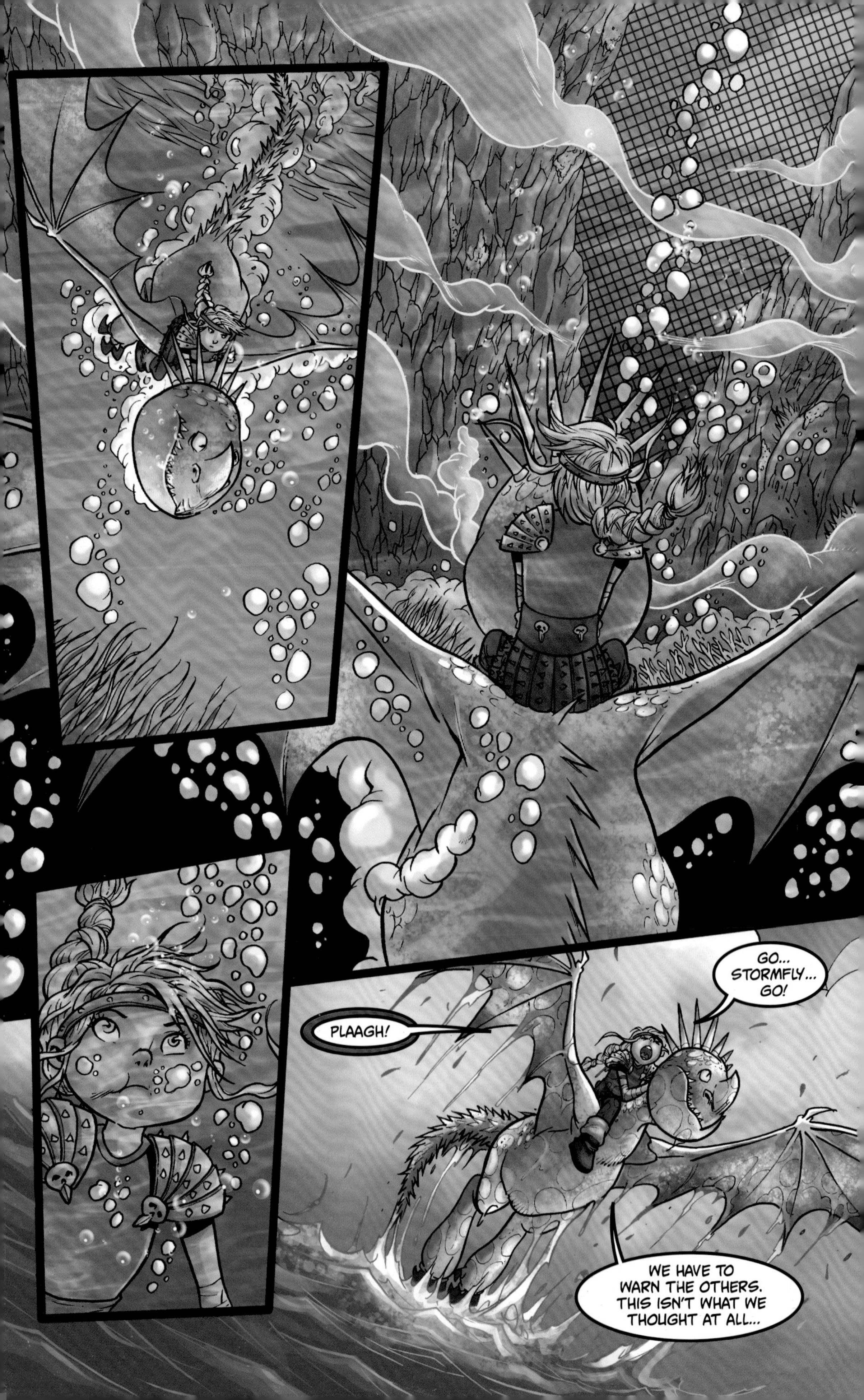
GO... STORMFLY... GO!
PLAAGH!
WE HAVE TO WARN THE OTHERS. THIS ISN'T WHAT WE THOUGHT AT ALL...

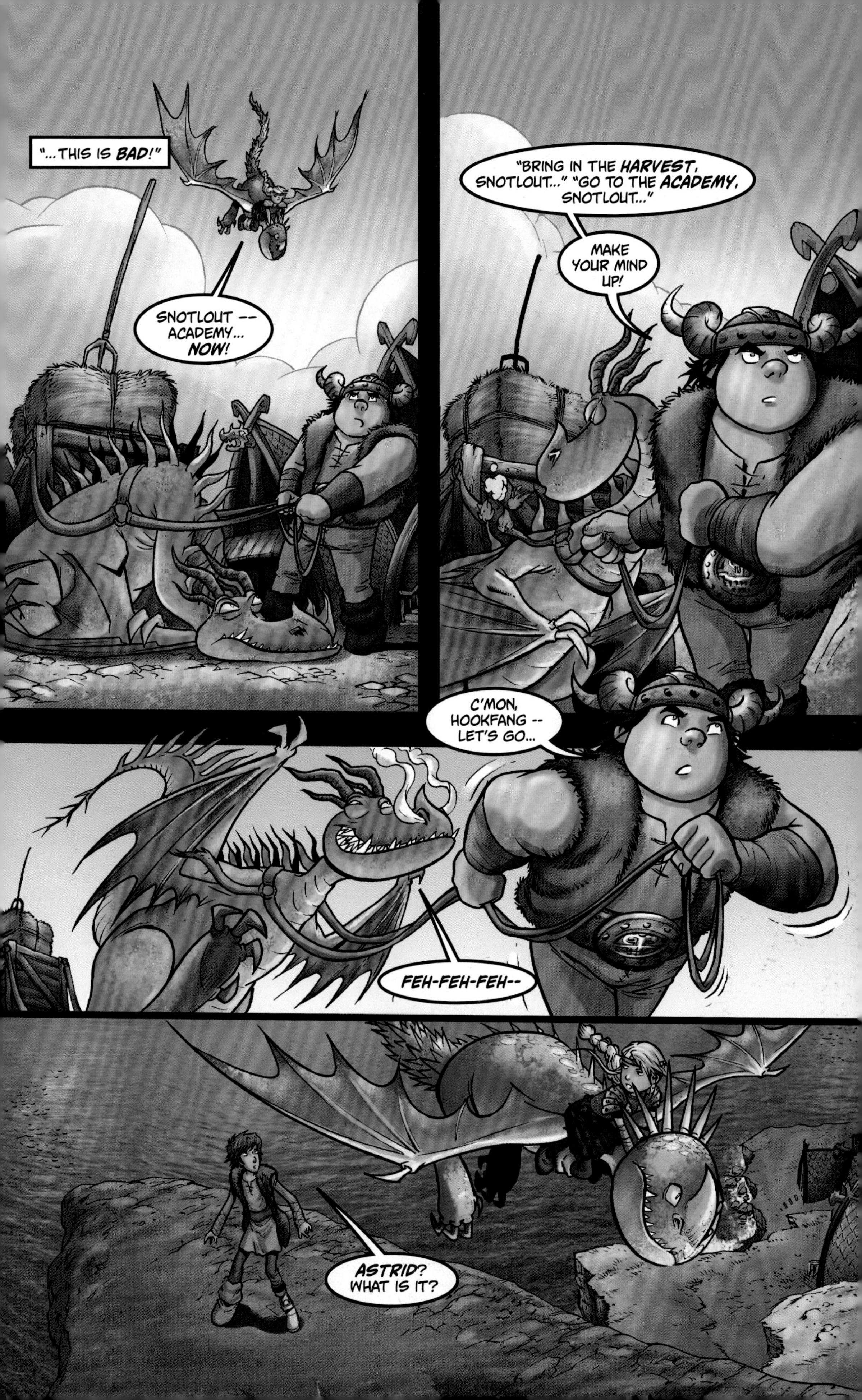
"...THIS IS BAD!"
SNOTLOUT -- ACADEMY... NOW!
"BRING IN THE HARVEST, SNOTLOUT..." "GO TO THE ACADEMY, SNOTLOUT..."
MAKE YOUR MIND UP!
C'MON, HOOKFANG -- LET'S GO...
FEH-FEH-FEH--
ASTRID? WHAT IS IT?

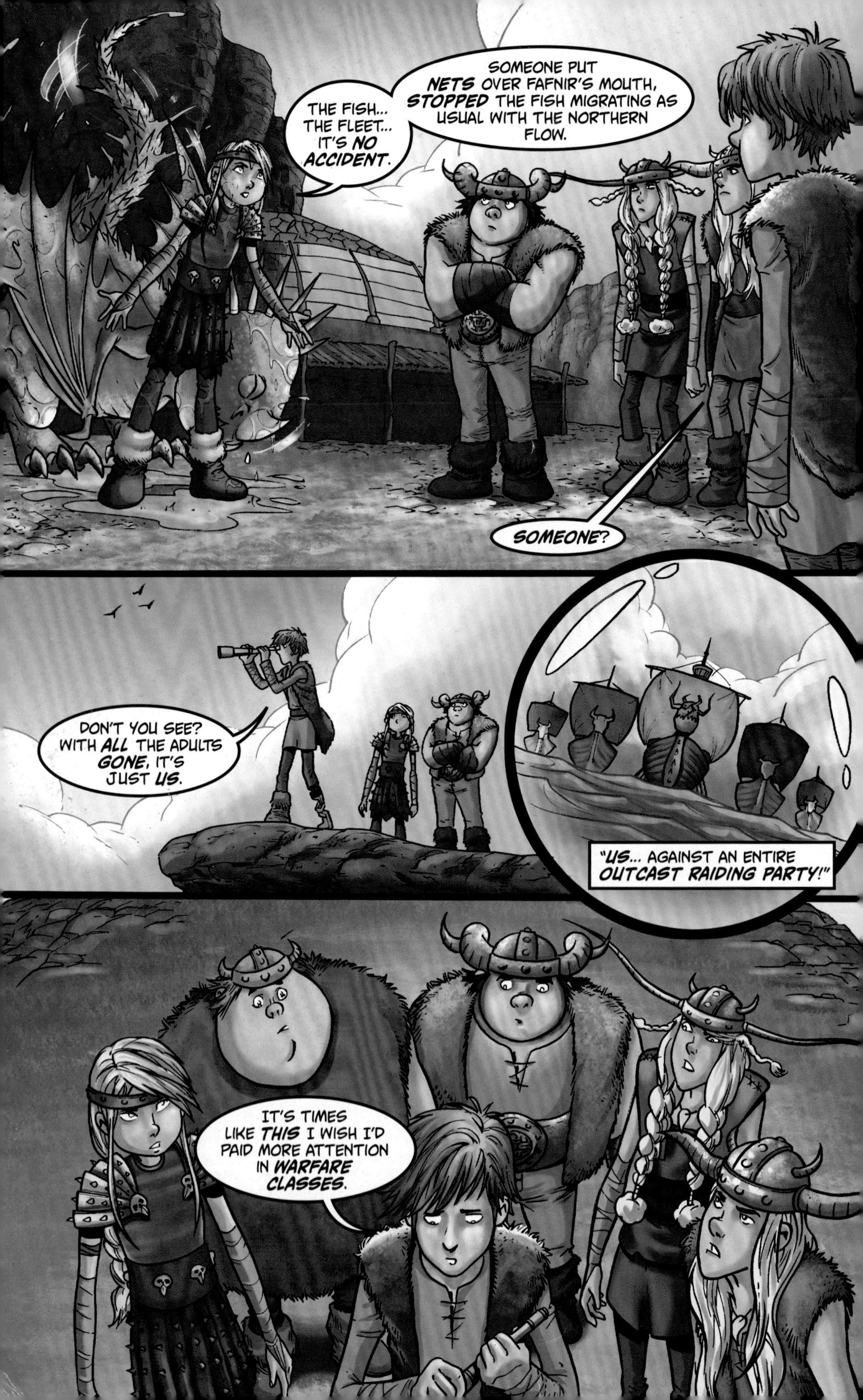
THE FISH... THE FLEET... IT'S NO ACCIDENT.
SOMEONE PUT NETS OVER FAFNIR'S MOUTH, STOPPED THE FISH MIGRATING AS USUAL WITH THE NORTHERN FLOW.
SOMEONE?
DON'T YOU SEE? WITH ALL THE ADULTS GONE, IT'S JUST US.
"US... AGAINST AN ENTIRE OUTCAST RAIDING PARTY!"
IT'S TIMES LIKE THIS I WISH I'D PAID MORE ATTENTION IN WARFARE CLASSES.

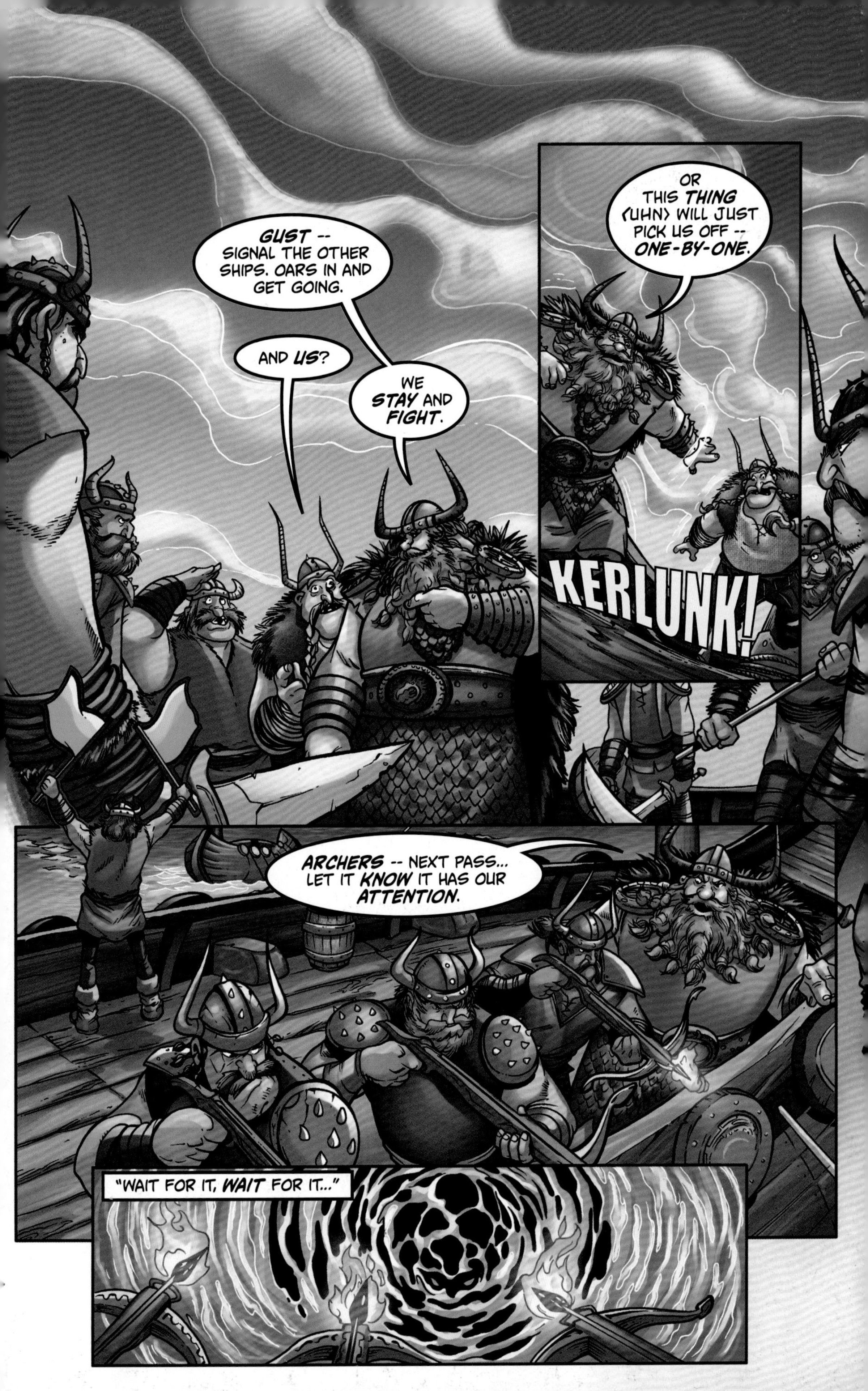
GUST -- SIGNAL THE OTHER SHIPS. OARS IN AND GET GOING.
AND US?
WE STAY AND FIGHT.
OR THIS THING (UHN) WILL JUST PICK US OFF -- ONE-BY-ONE.
KERLUNK!
ARCHERS -- NEXT PASS... LET IT KNOW IT HAS OUR ATTENTION.
"WAIT FOR IT, WAIT FOR IT..."

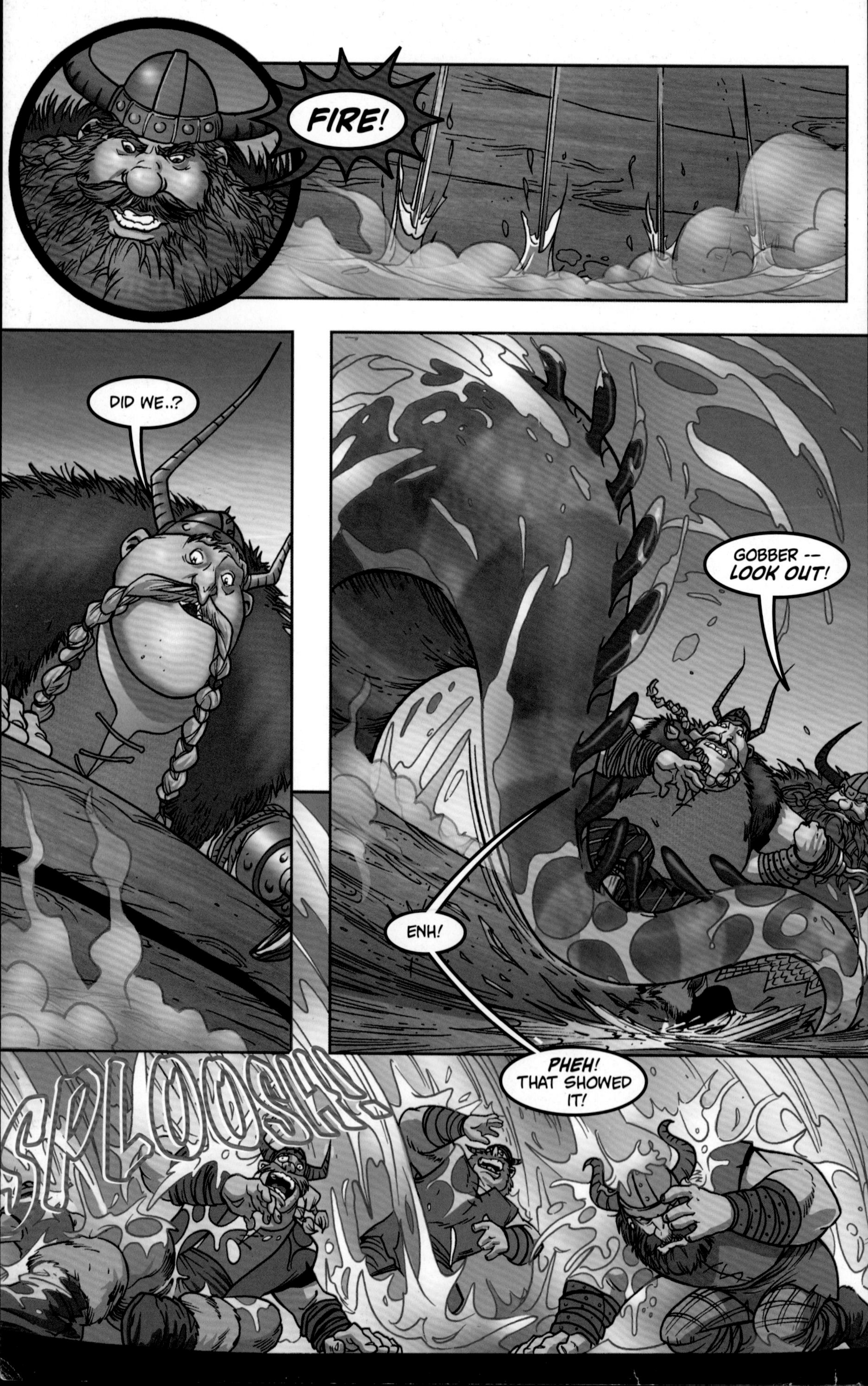
FIRE!
DID WE..?
GOBBER -- LOOK OUT!
ENH!
PHEH! THAT SHOWED IT!
SPLOOSH!

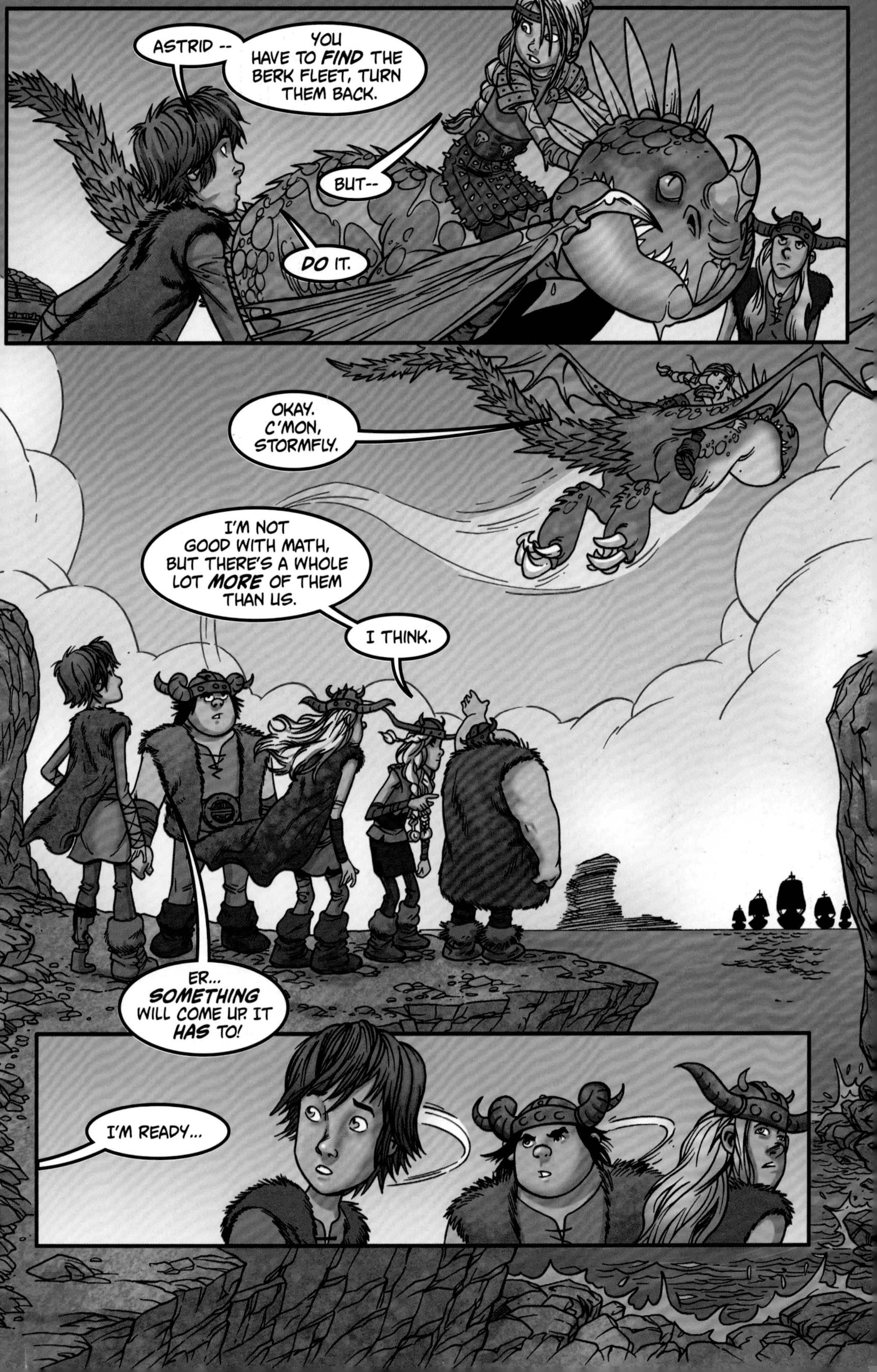
ASTRID --
YOU HAVE TO FIND THE BERK FLEET, TURN THEM BACK.
BUT--
DO IT.
OKAY. C'MON, STORMFLY.
I'M NOT GOOD WITH MATH, BUT THERE'S A WHOLE LOT MORE OF THEM THAN US.
I THINK.
ER... SOMETHING WILL COME UP. IT HAS TO!
I'M READY...

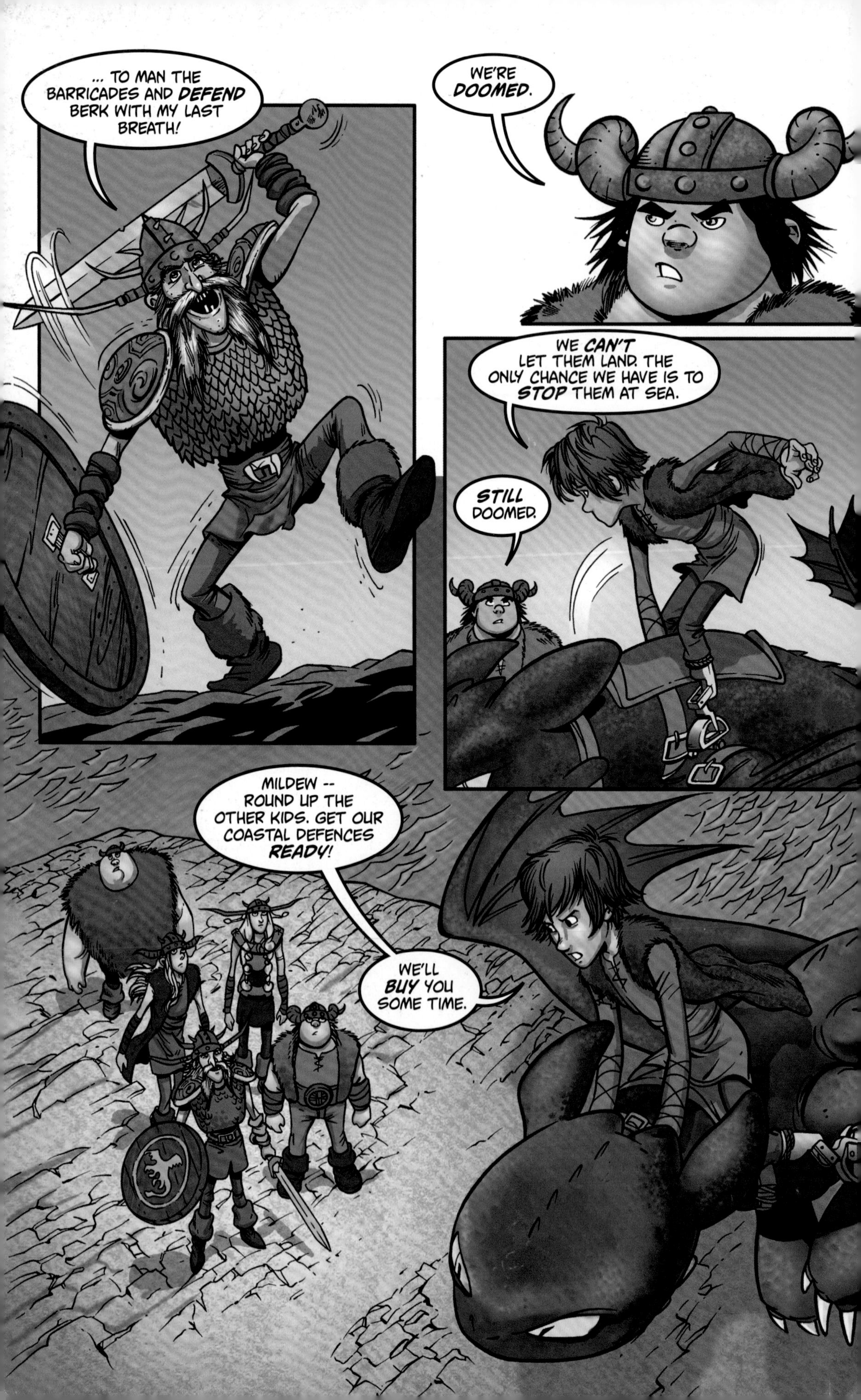
... TO MAN THE BARRICADES AND DEFEND BERK WITH MY LAST BREATH!
WE'RE DOOMED.
WE CAN'T LET THEM LAND. THE ONLY CHANCE WE HAVE IS TO STOP THEM AT SEA.
STILL DOOMED.
MILDEW -- ROUND UP THE OTHER KIDS. GET OUR COASTAL DEFENCES READY!
WE'LL BUY YOU SOME TIME.

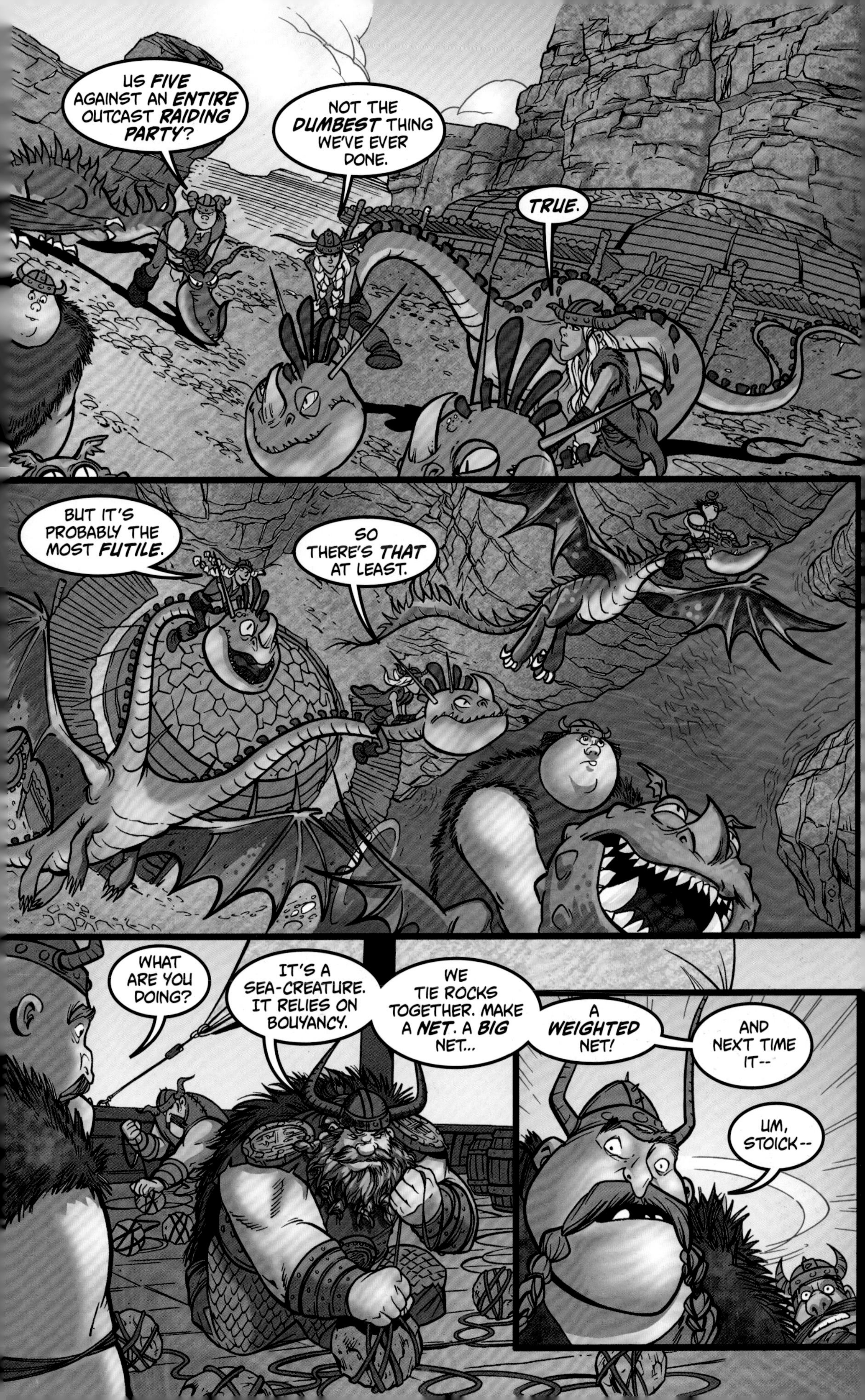

US FIVE AGAINST AN ENTIRE OUTCAST RAIDING PARTY?
NOT THE DUMBEST THING WE'VE EVER DONE.
TRUE.
BUT IT'S PROBABLY THE MOST FUTILE.
SO THERE'S THAT AT LEAST.
WHAT ARE YOU DOING?
IT'S A SEA-CREATURE. IT RELIES ON BOUYANCY.
WE TIE ROCKS TOGETHER. MAKE A NET. A BIG NET...
A WEIGHTED NET!
AND NEXT TIME IT--
UM, STOICK--

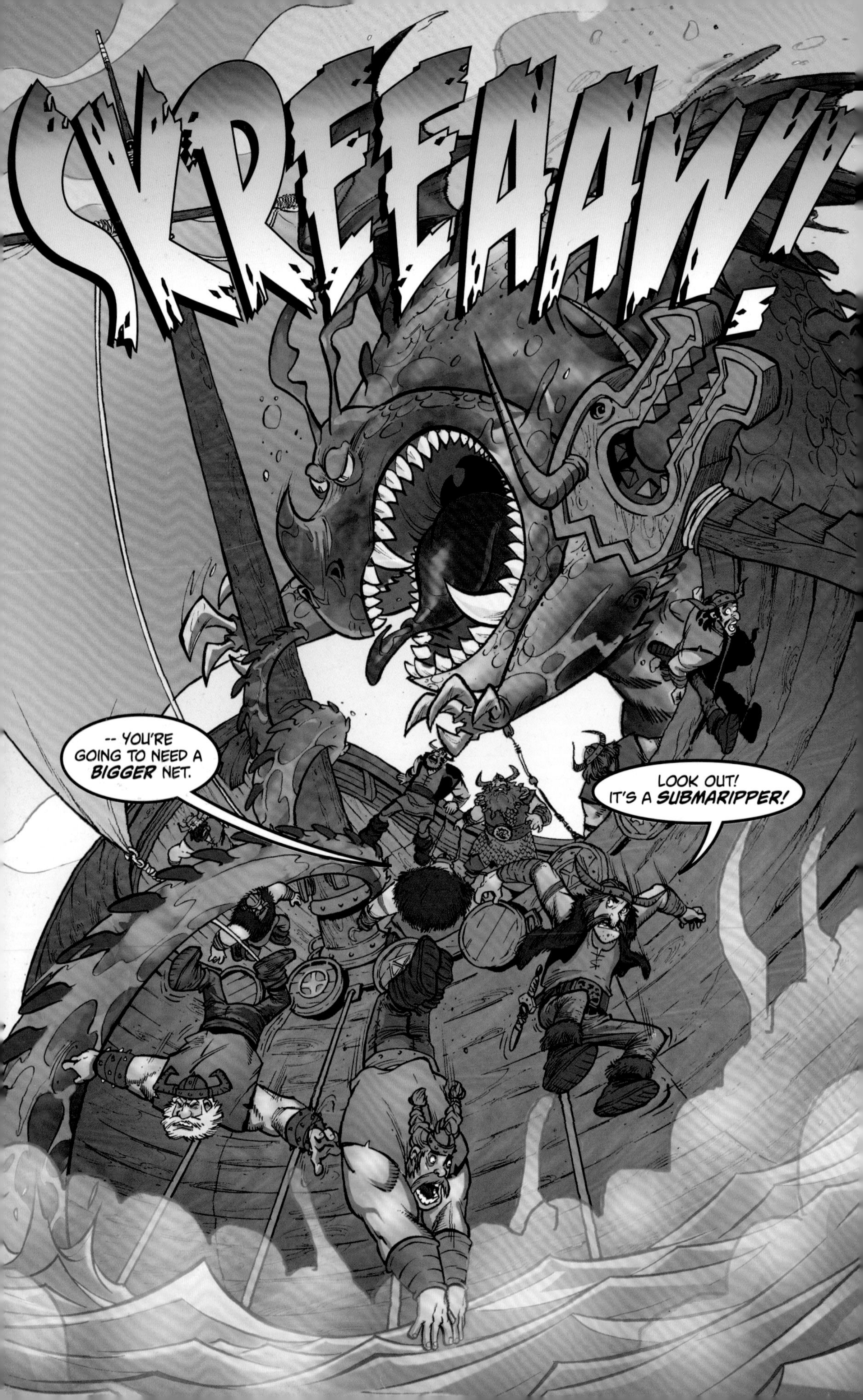
SKREEAAW!
-- YOU'RE GOING TO NEED A BIGGER NET.
LOOK OUT! IT'S A SUBMARIPPER!

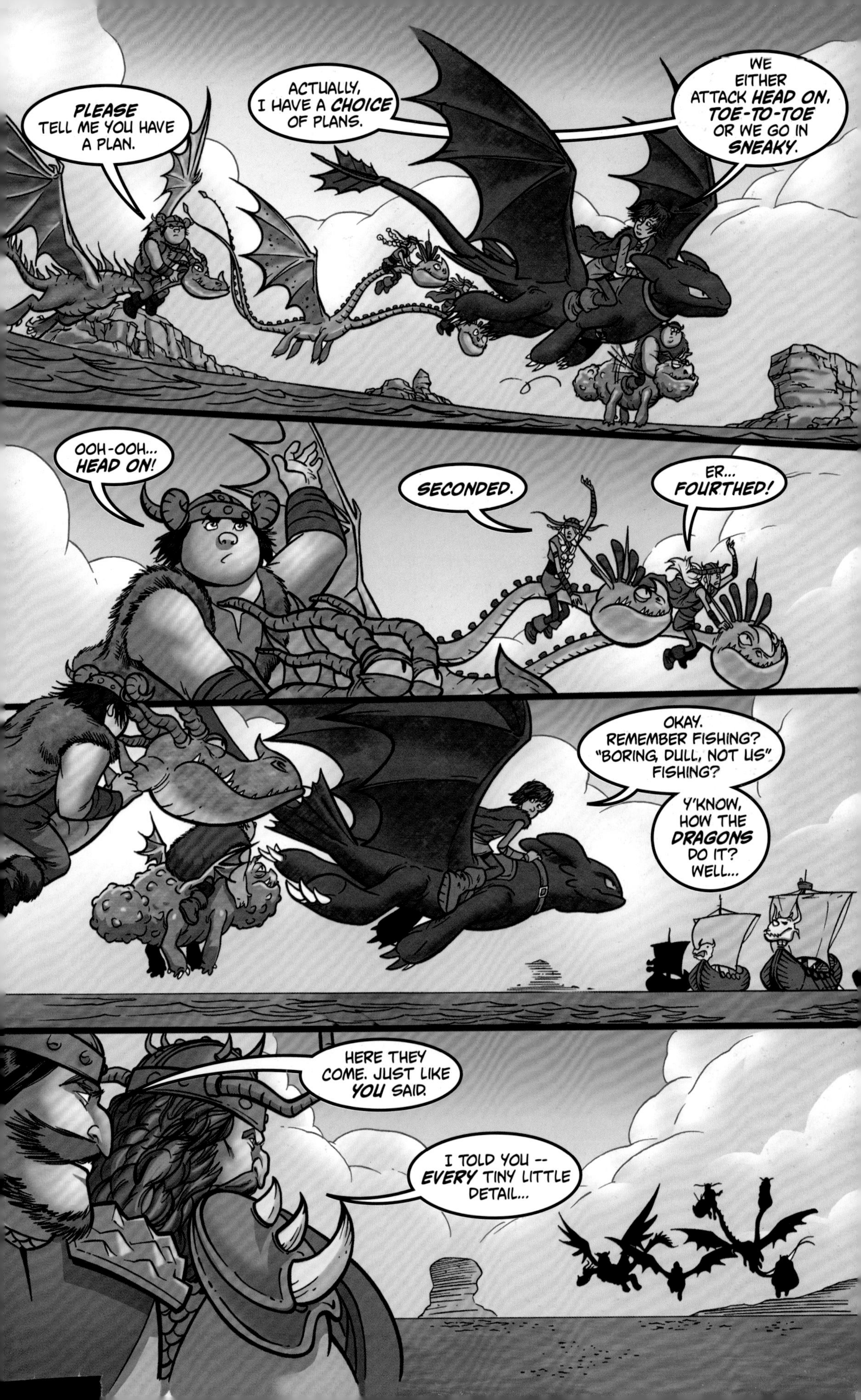
PLEASE TELL ME YOU HAVE A PLAN.
ACTUALLY, I HAVE A CHOICE OF PLANS.
WE EITHER ATTACK HEAD ON, TOE-TO-TOE OR WE GO IN SNEAKY.
OOH-OOH... HEAD ON!
SECONDED.
ER... FOURTHED!
OKAY. REMEMBER FISHING? "BORING, DULL, NOT US" FISHING?
Y'KNOW, HOW THE DRAGONS DO IT? WELL...
HERE THEY COME. JUST LIKE YOU SAID.
I TOLD YOU -- EVERY TINY LITTLE DETAIL...

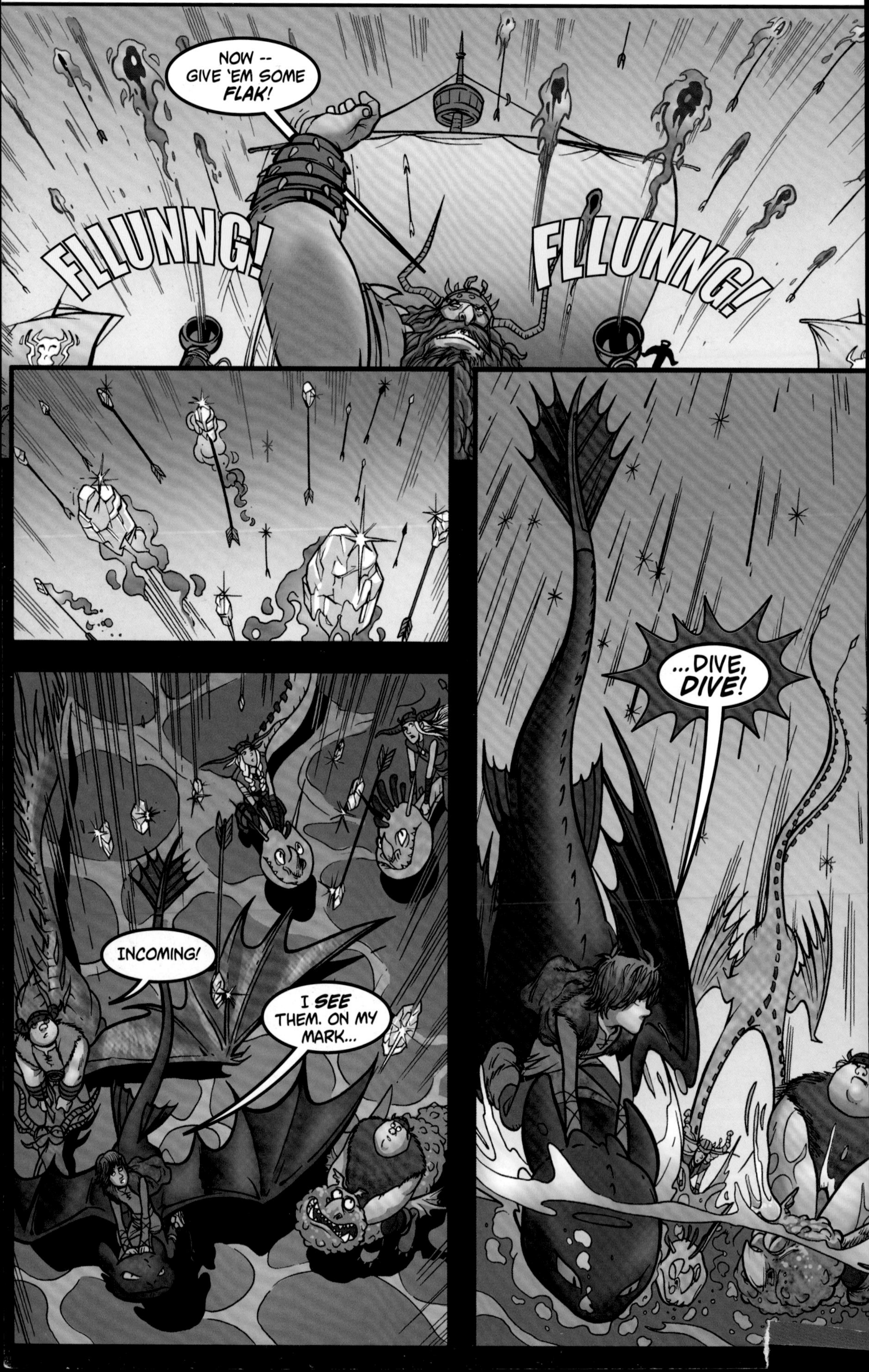
NOW -- GIVE 'EM SOME FLAK!
FLLUNNG!
FLLUNNG!
INCOMING!
I SEE THEM. ON MY MARK...
...DIVE, DIVE!

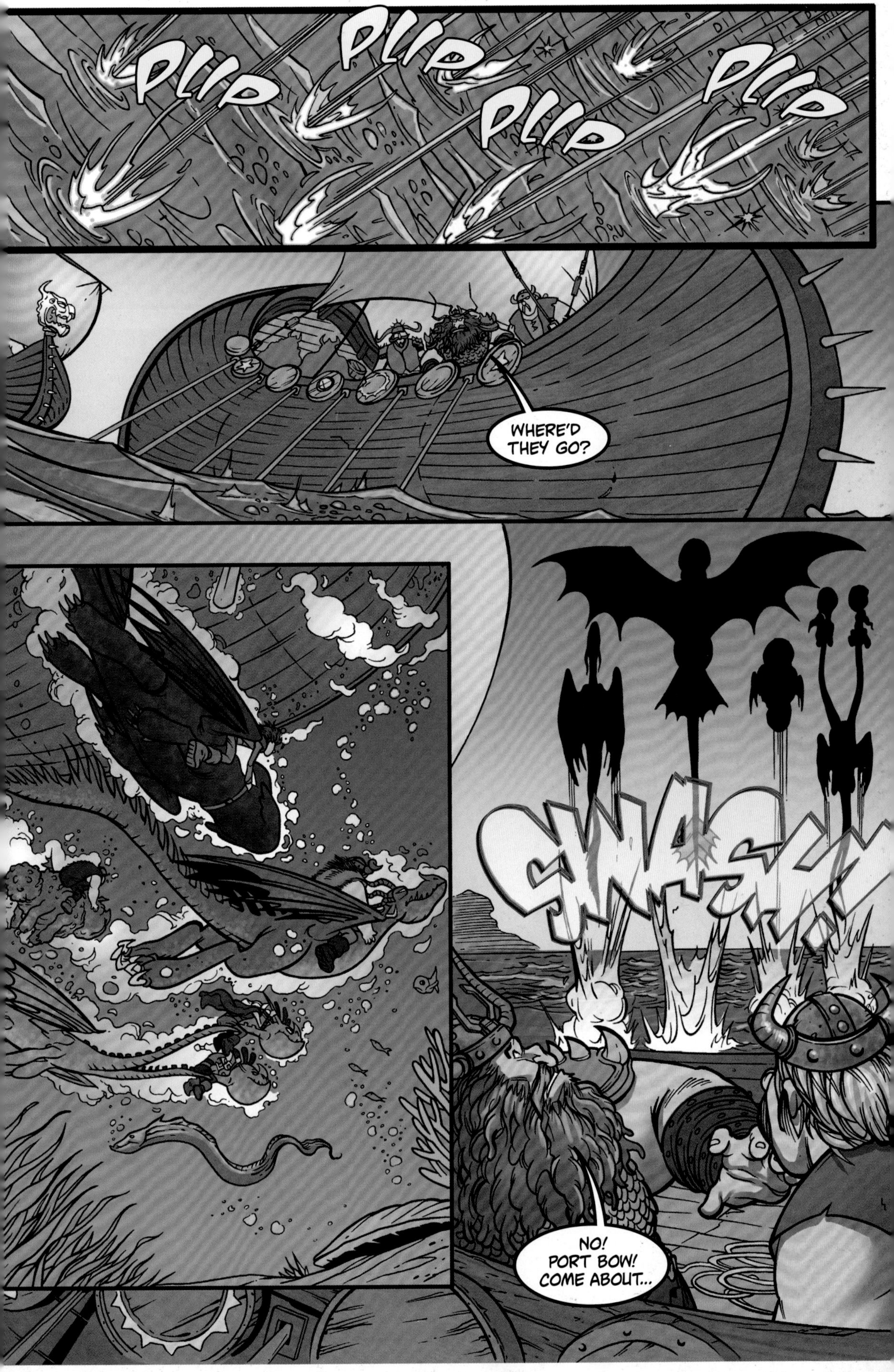
PLIP
PLIP
PLIP
PLIP
PLIP
WHERE'D THEY GO?
NO! PORT BOW! COME ABOUT...

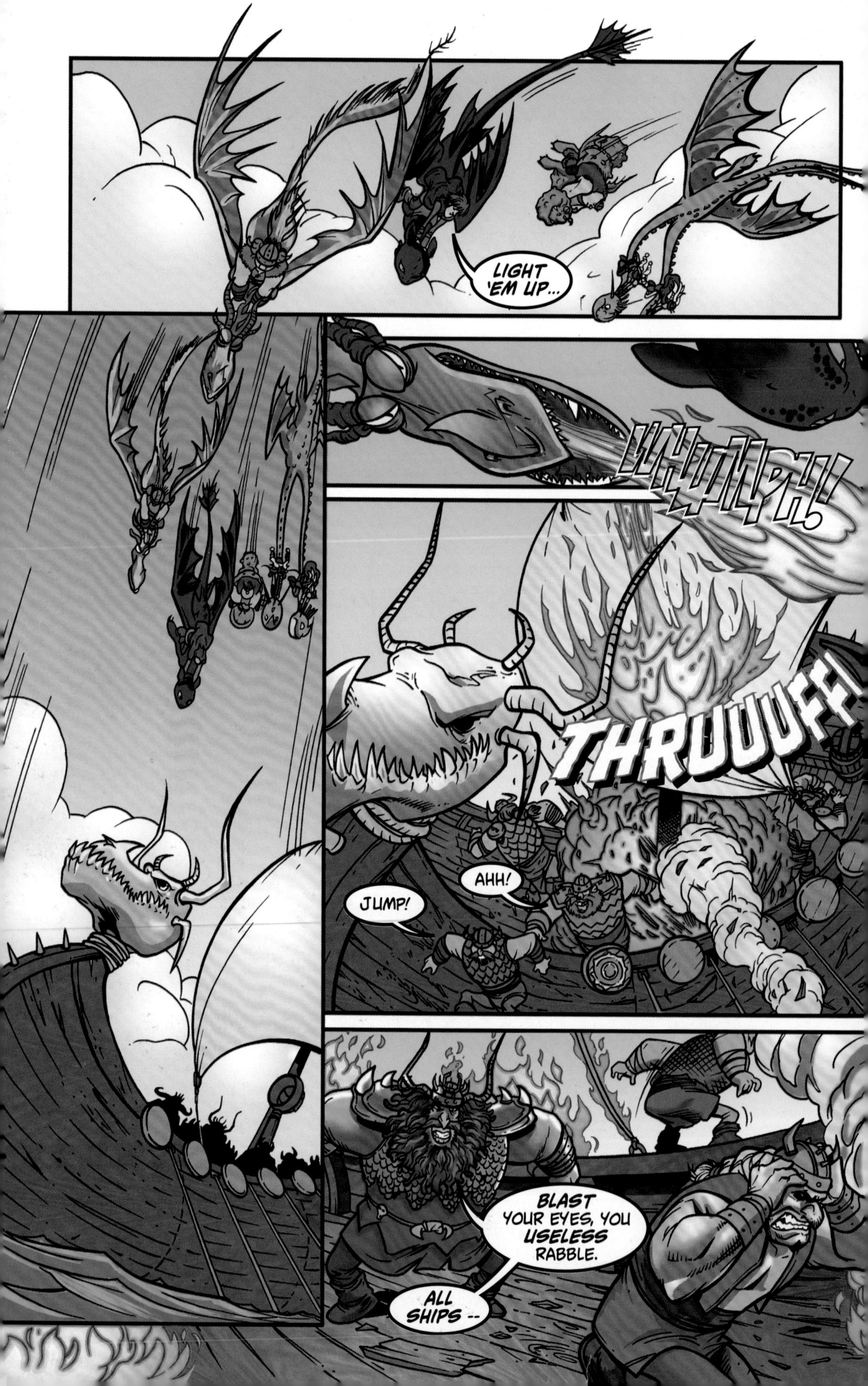
LIGHT 'EM UP...
WHUMPH!
THRUUUFF!
JUMP!
AHH!
BLAST YOUR EYES, YOU USELESS RABBLE.
ALL SHIPS --

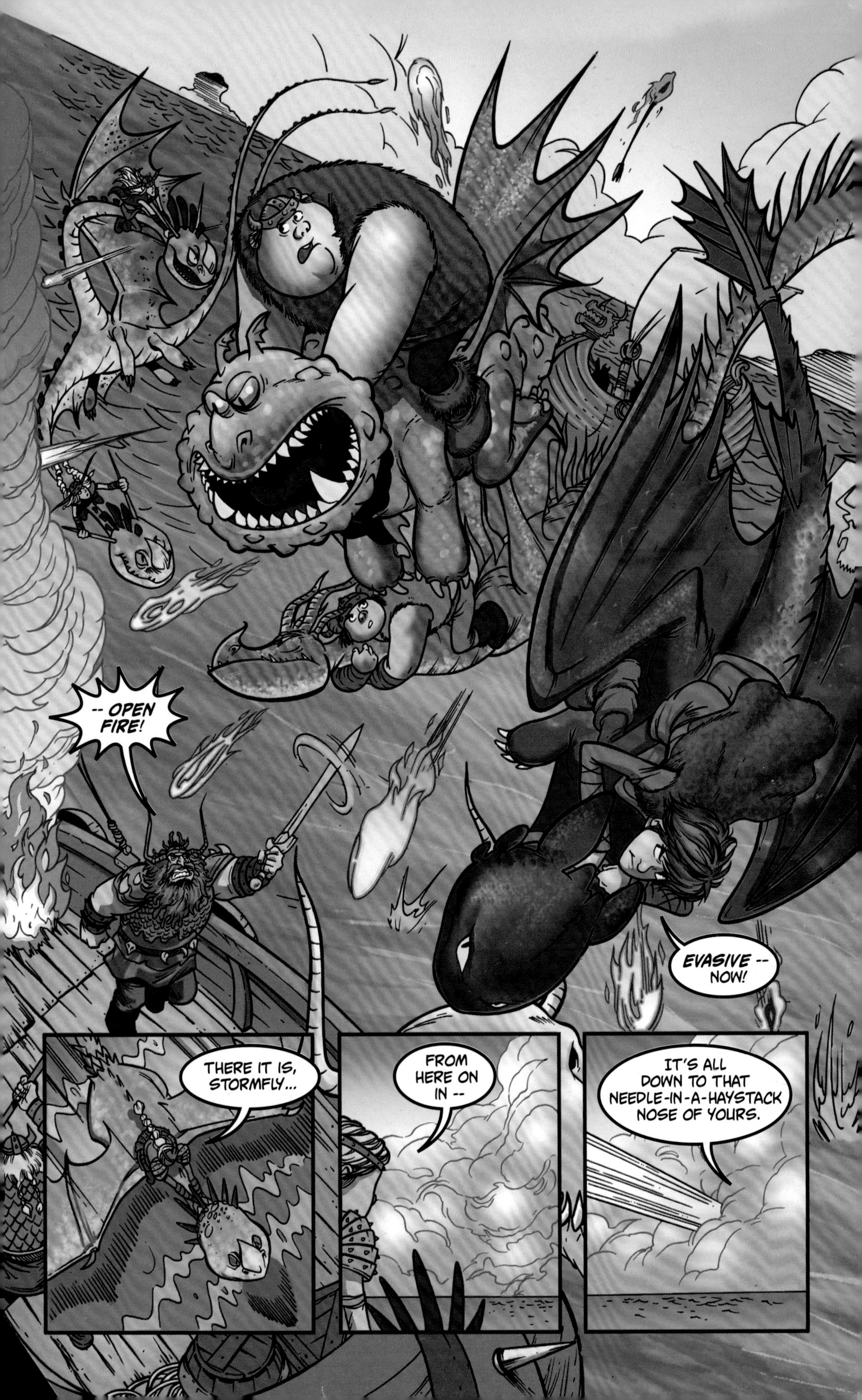
-- OPEN FIRE!
EVASIVE -- NOW!
THERE IT IS, STORMFLY...
FROM HERE ON IN --
IT'S ALL DOWN TO THAT NEEDLE-IN-A-HAYSTACK NOSE OF YOURS.

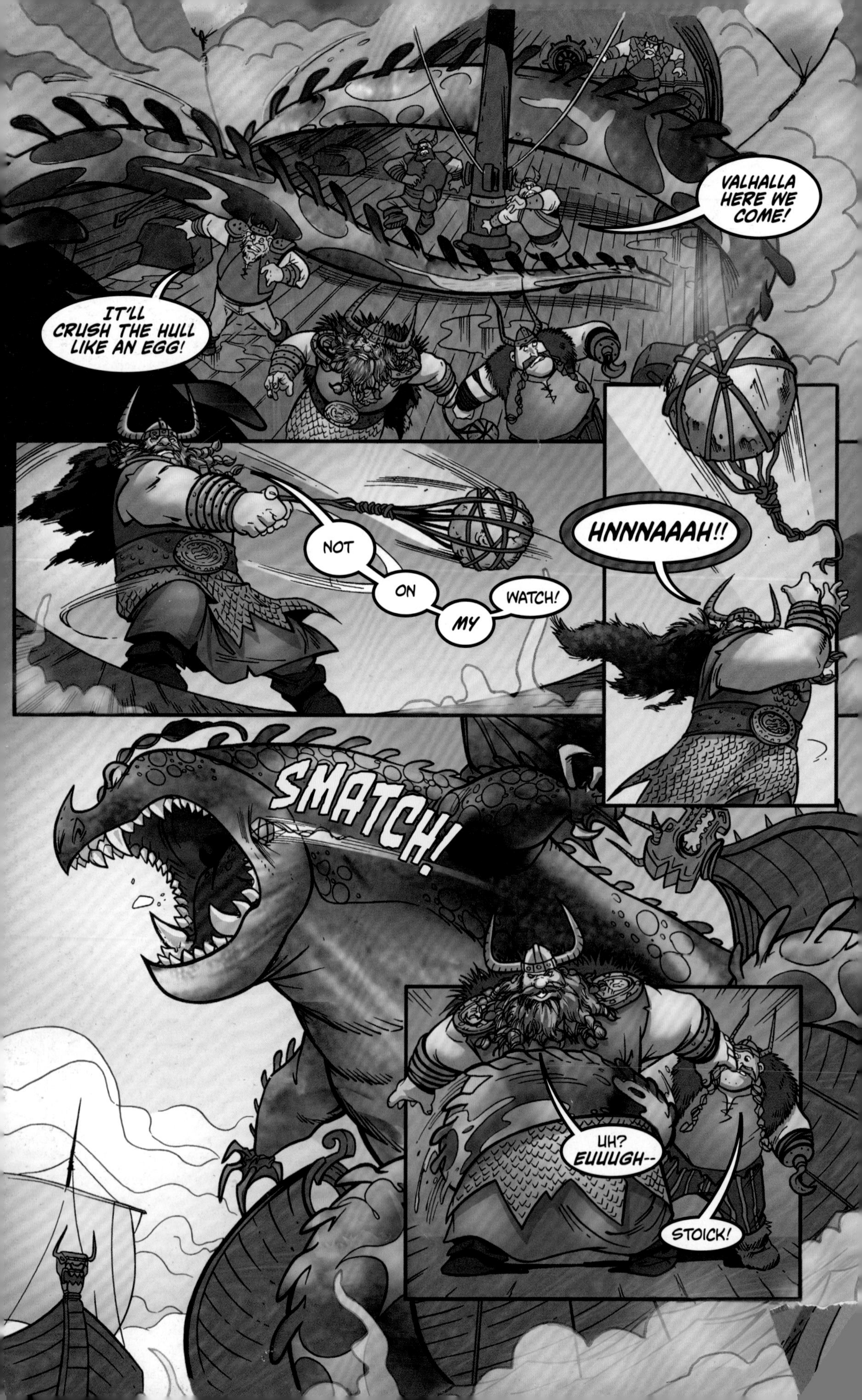
VALHALLA HERE WE COME!
IT'LL CRUSH THE HULL LIKE AN EGG!
NOT
ON
MY
WATCH!
HNNNAAAH!!
SMATCH!
UH? EUUUGH--
STOICK!

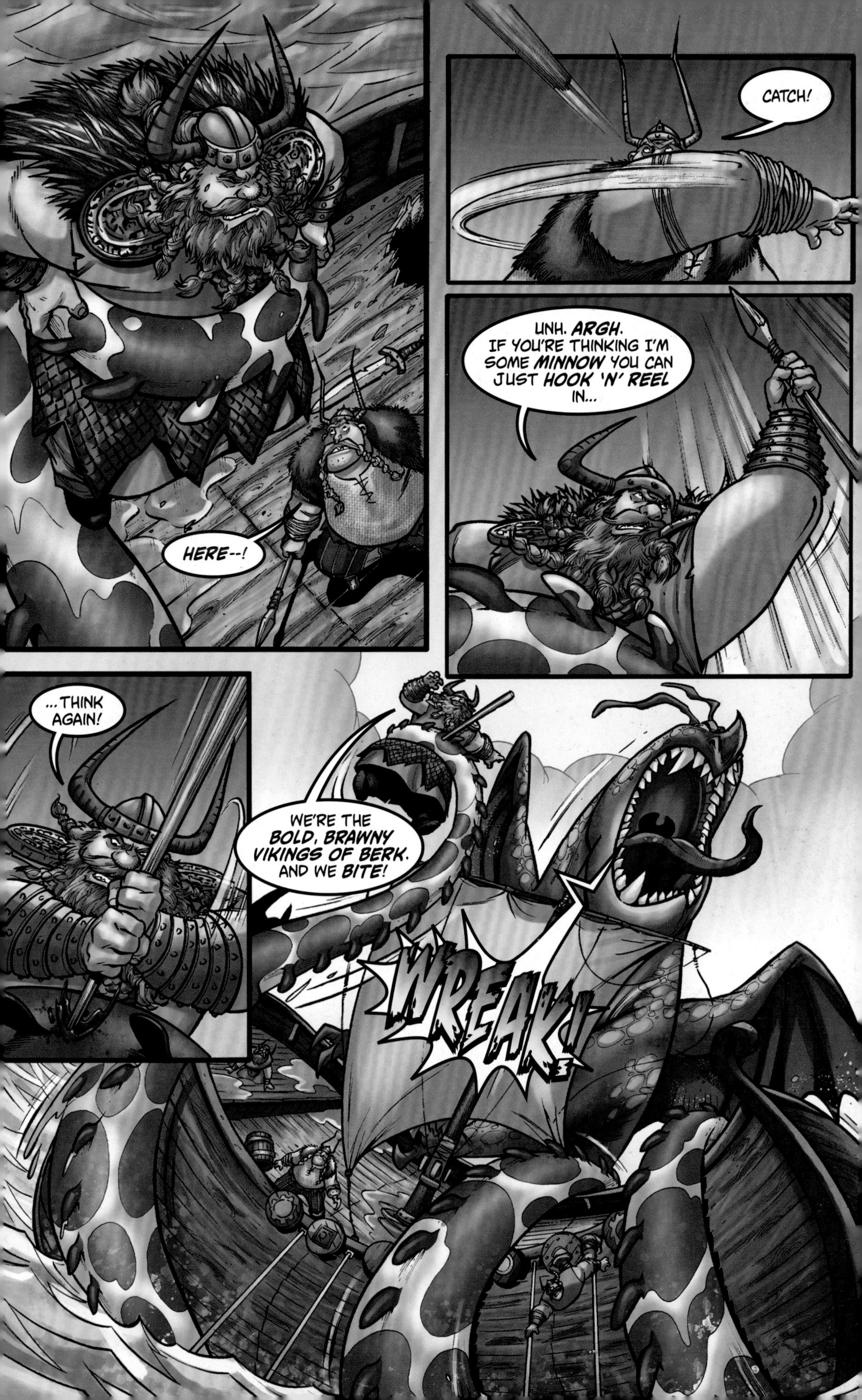
HERE--!
CATCH!
UNH. ARGH. IF YOU'RE THINKING I'M SOME MINNOW YOU CAN JUST HOOK 'N' REEL IN...
...THINK AGAIN!
WE'RE THE BOLD, BRAWNY VIKINGS OF BERK. AND WE BITE!
WREAK!

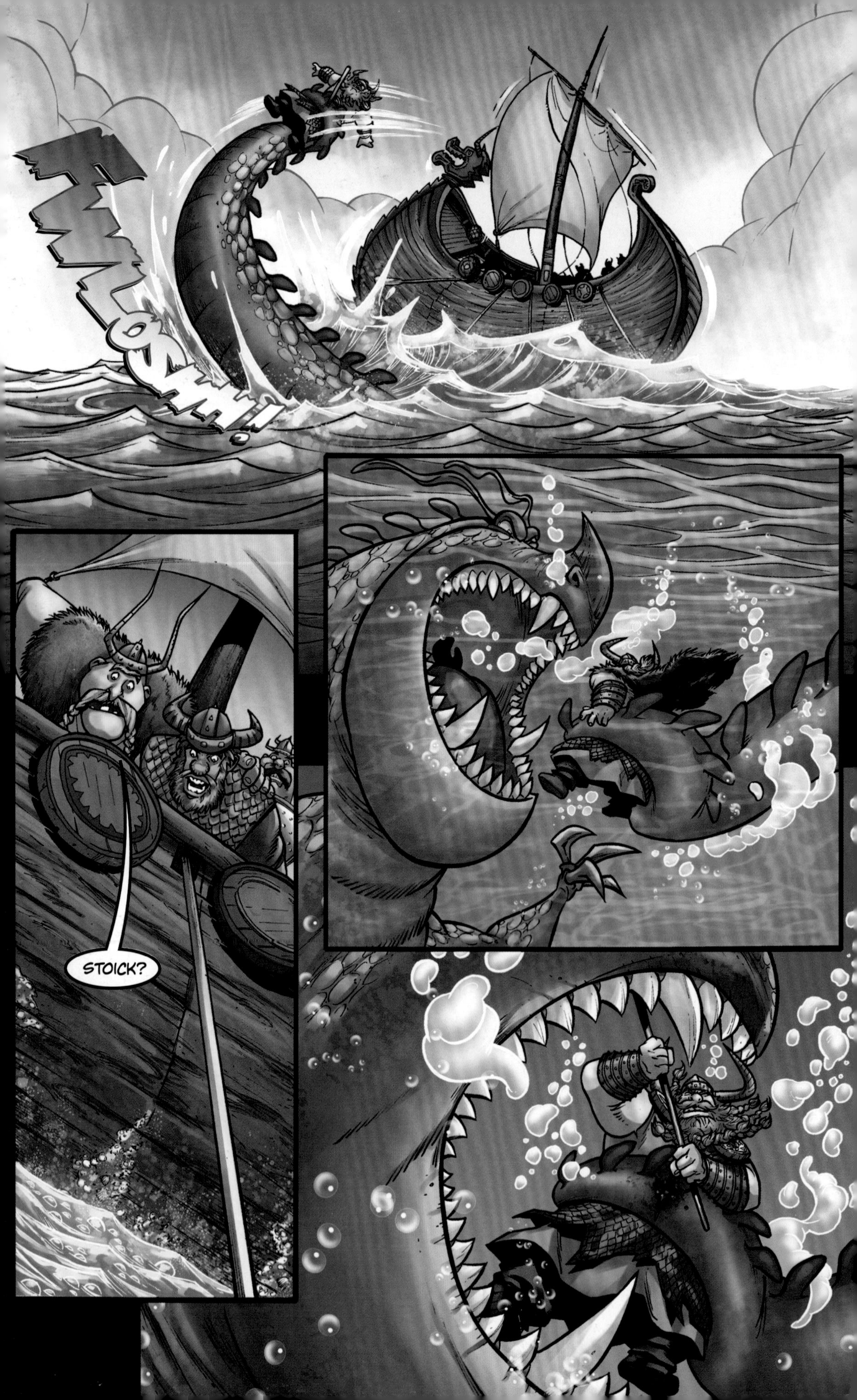
STOICK?

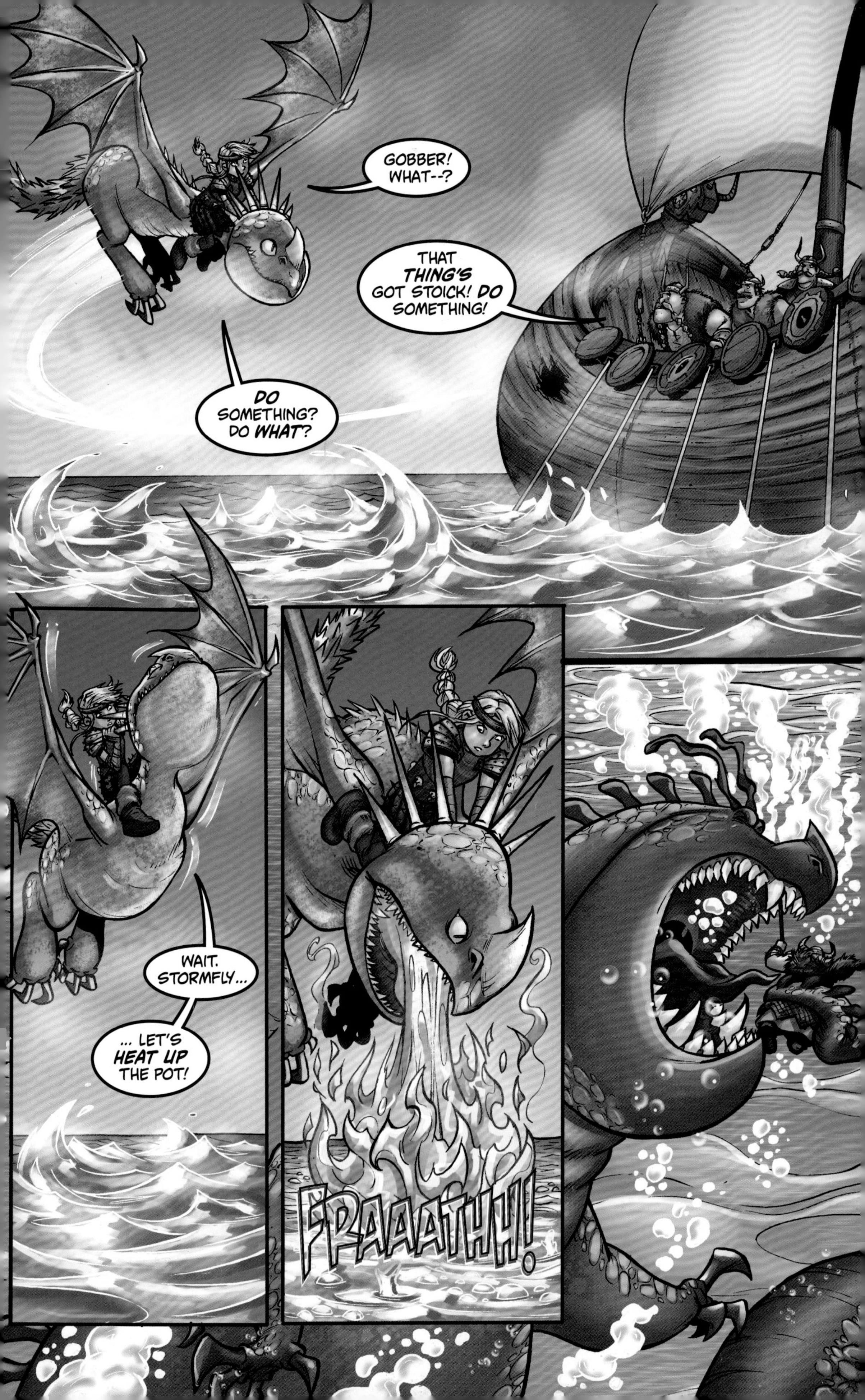
GOBBER! WHAT--?
THAT THING'S GOT STOICK! DO SOMETHING!
DO SOMETHING? DO WHAT?
WAIT. STORMFLY...
... LET'S HEAT UP THE POT!
FRAAATHH!

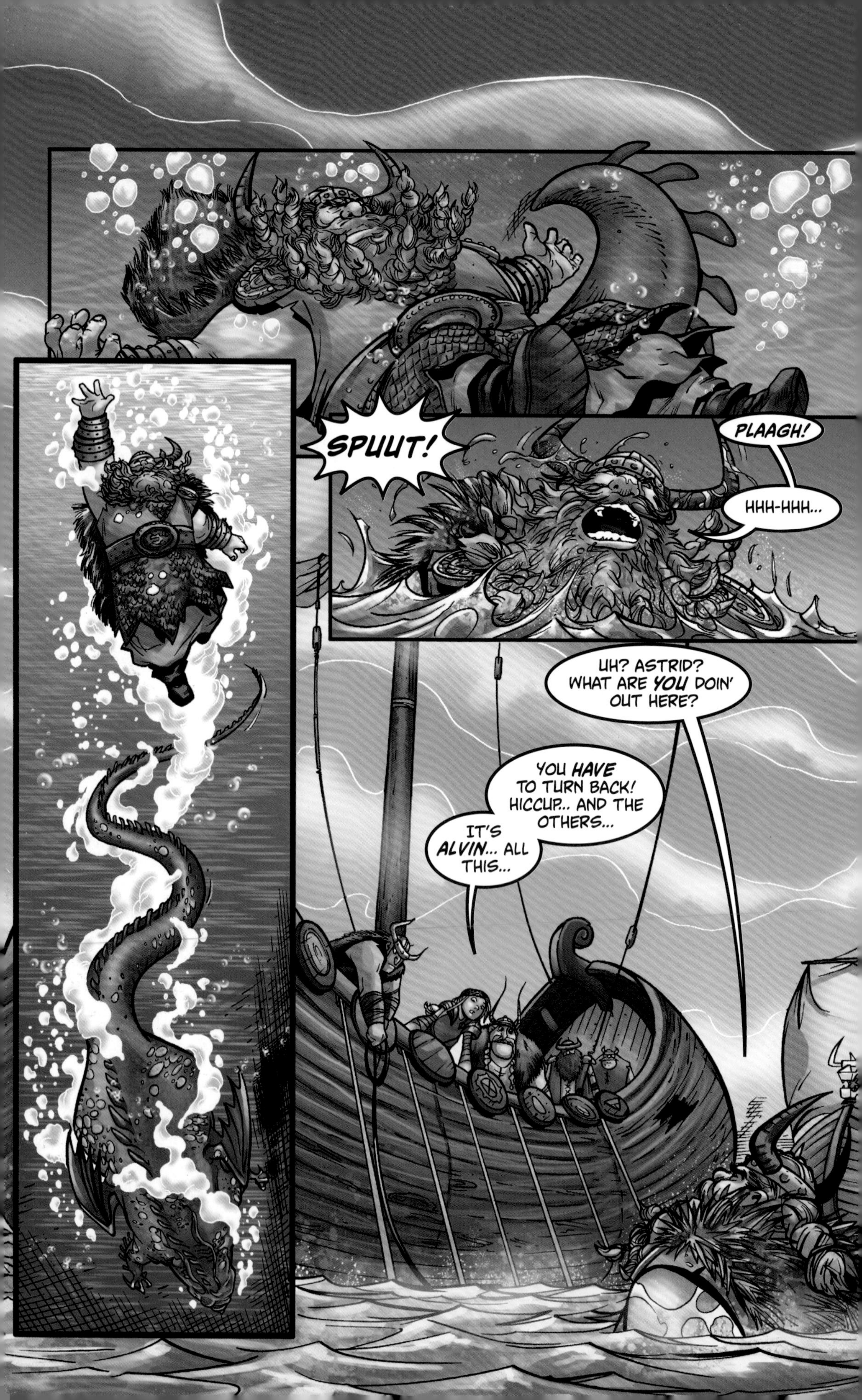
SPUUT!
PLAAGH!
HHH-HHH...
UH? ASTRID? WHAT ARE YOU DOIN' OUT HERE?
YOU HAVE TO TURN BACK! HICCUP... AND THE OTHERS...
IT'S ALVIN... ALL THIS...

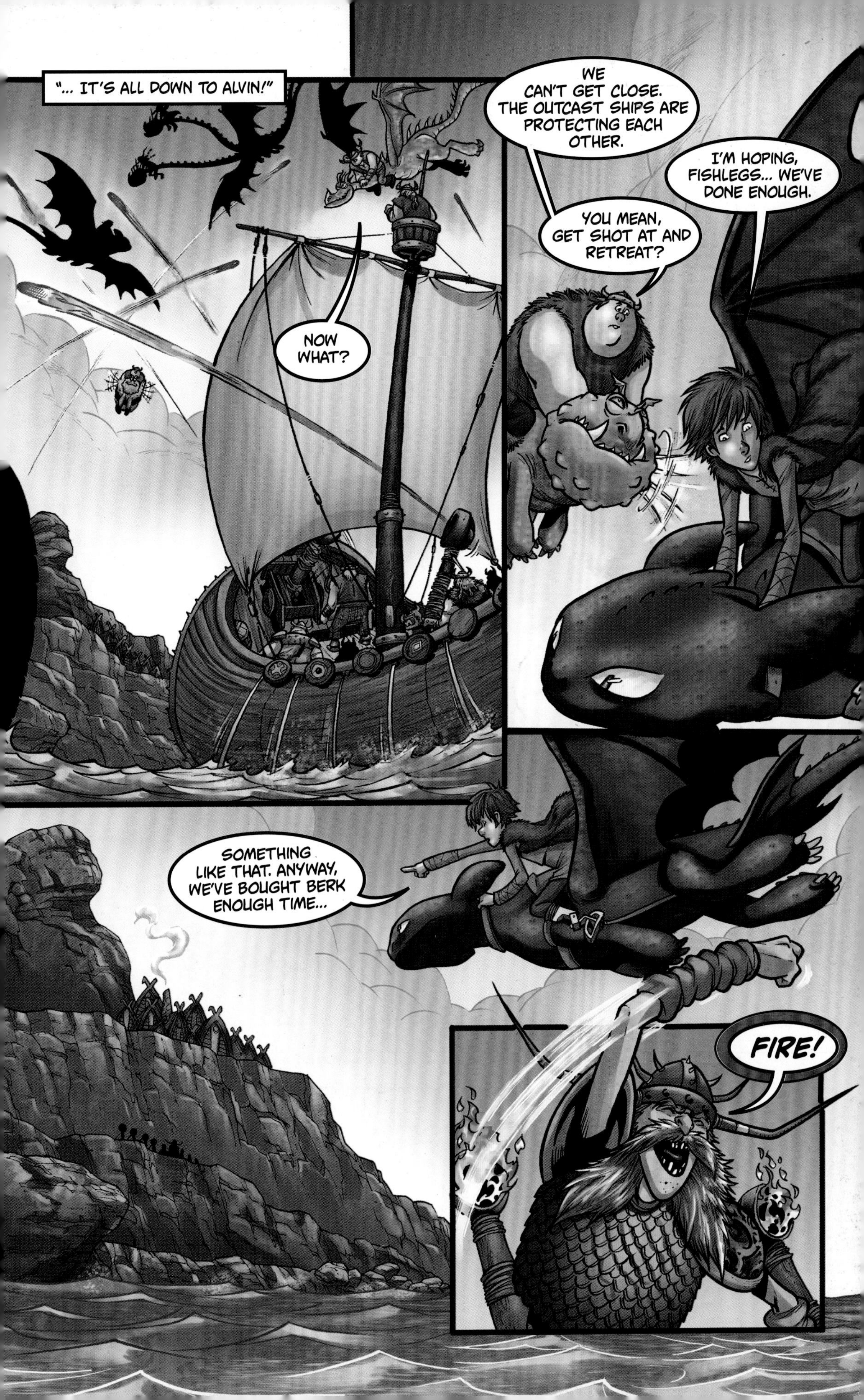
"... IT'S ALL DOWN TO ALVIN!"
NOW WHAT?
WE CAN'T GET CLOSE. THE OUTCAST SHIPS ARE PROTECTING EACH OTHER.
I'M HOPING, FISHLEGS... WE'VE DONE ENOUGH.
YOU MEAN, GET SHOT AT AND RETREAT?
SOMETHING LIKE THAT. ANYWAY, WE'VE BOUGHT BERK ENOUGH TIME...
FIRE!

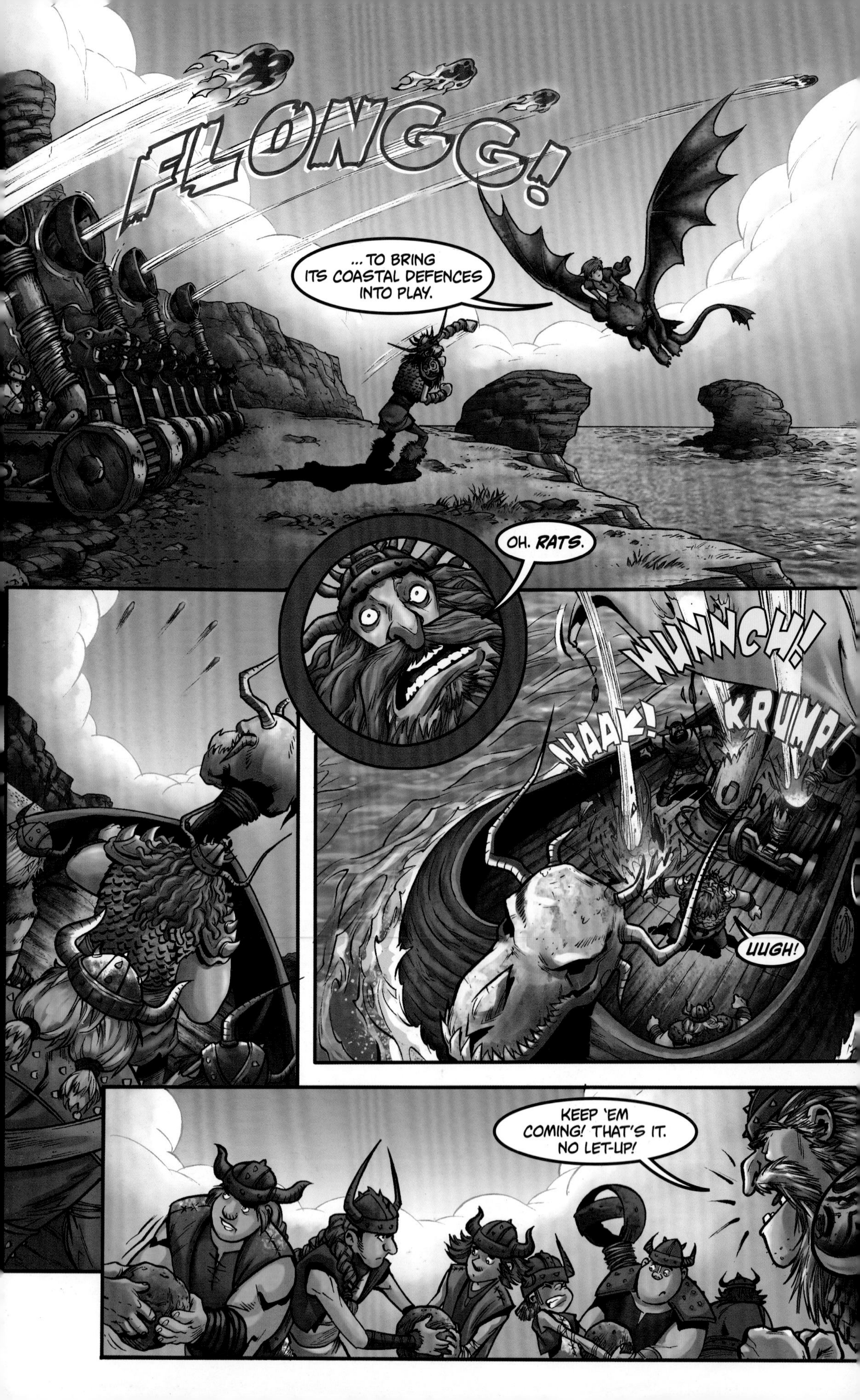
FLONGG!
... TO BRING ITS COASTAL DEFENCES INTO PLAY.
OH. RATS.
WUNNCH!
HAAK!
KRUMP!
UUGH!
KEEP 'EM COMING! THAT'S IT. NO LET-UP!

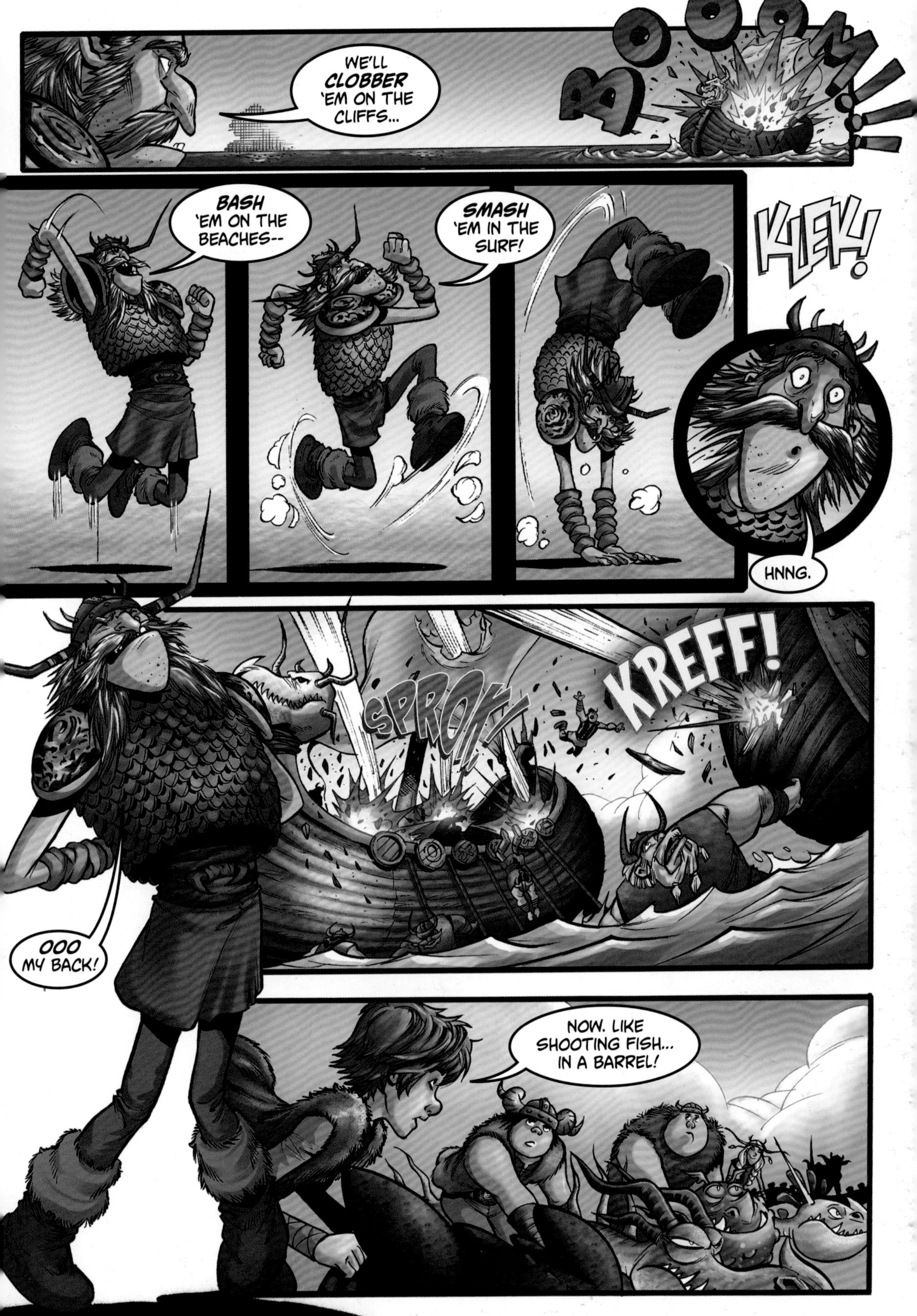
WE'LL CLOBBER 'EM ON THE CLIFFS...
BOOOOM!!!
BASH 'EM ON THE BEACHES--
SMASH 'EM IN THE SURF!
KLEK!
HNNG.
SPROK!
KREFF!
OOO MY BACK!
NOW. LIKE SHOOTING FISH... IN A BARREL!

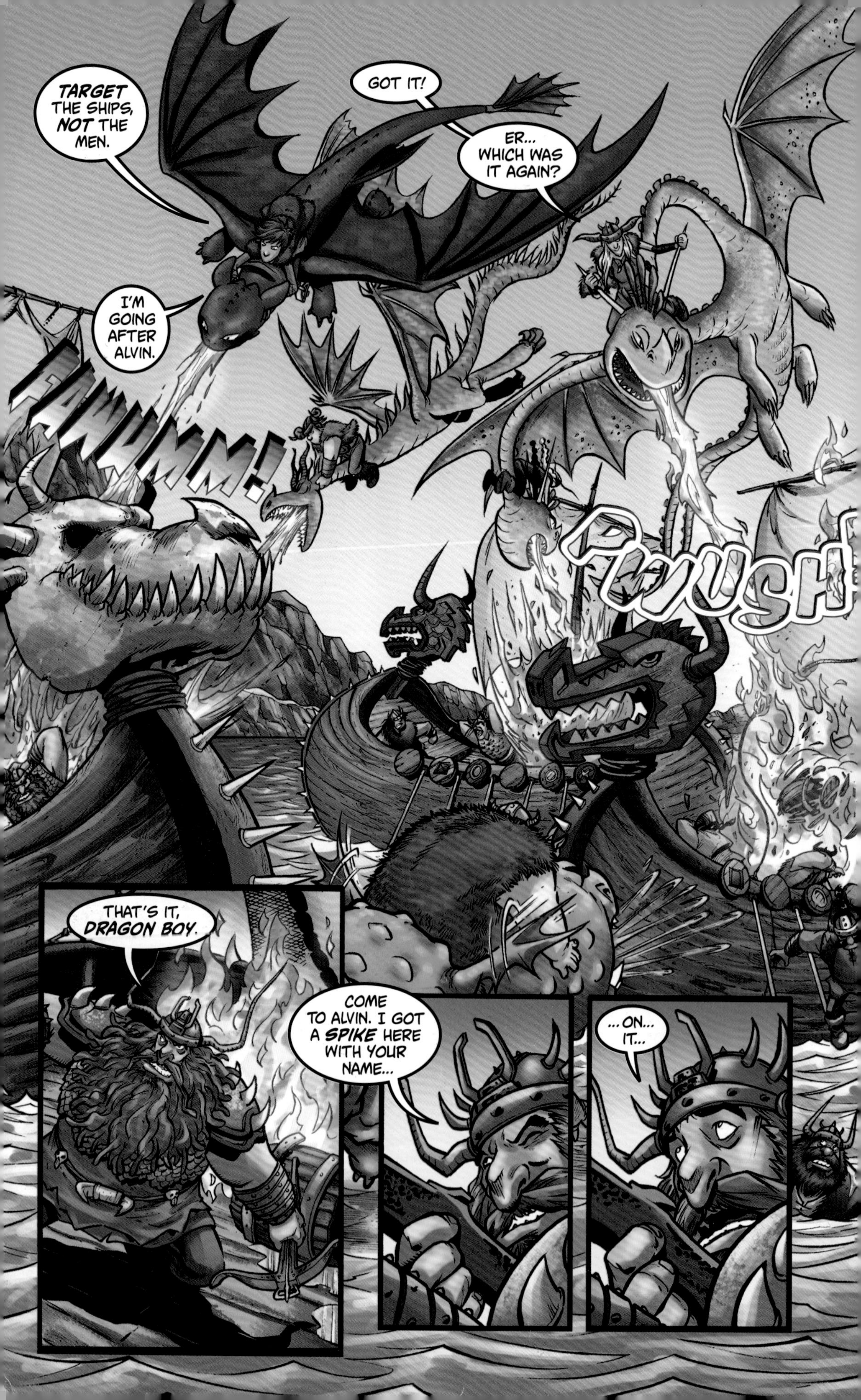
TARGET THE SHIPS, NOT THE MEN.
GOT IT!
ER... WHICH WAS IT AGAIN?
I'M GOING AFTER ALVIN.
FAWUMM!
FWUSH!
THAT'S IT, DRAGON BOY.
COME TO ALVIN. I GOT A SPIKE HERE WITH YOUR NAME...
...ON... IT...

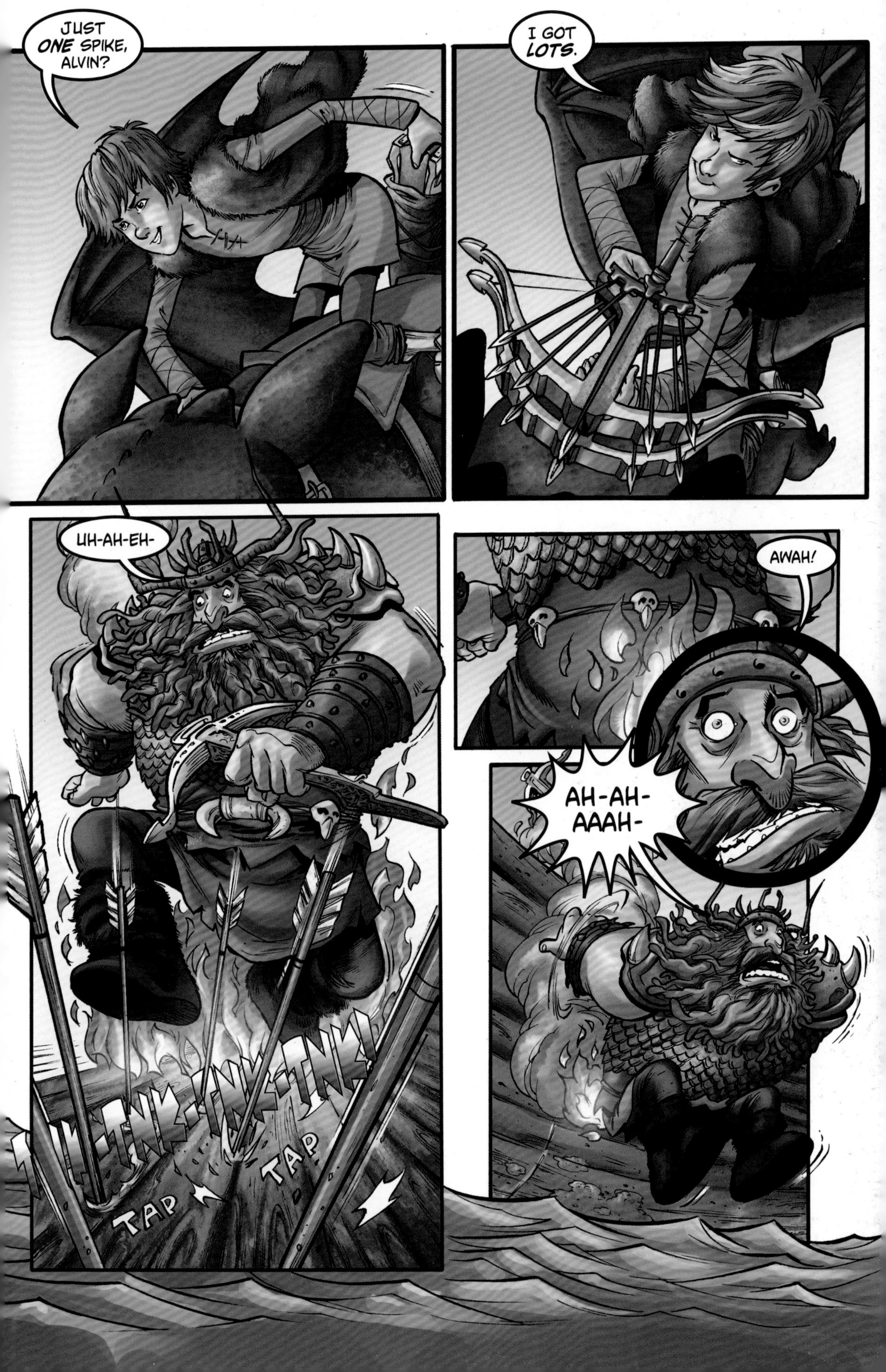
JUST ONE SPIKE, ALVIN?
I GOT LOTS.
UH-AH-EH-
TNK-TNK-TNK-TNK!
TAP
TAP
AWAH!
AH-AH-AAAH-

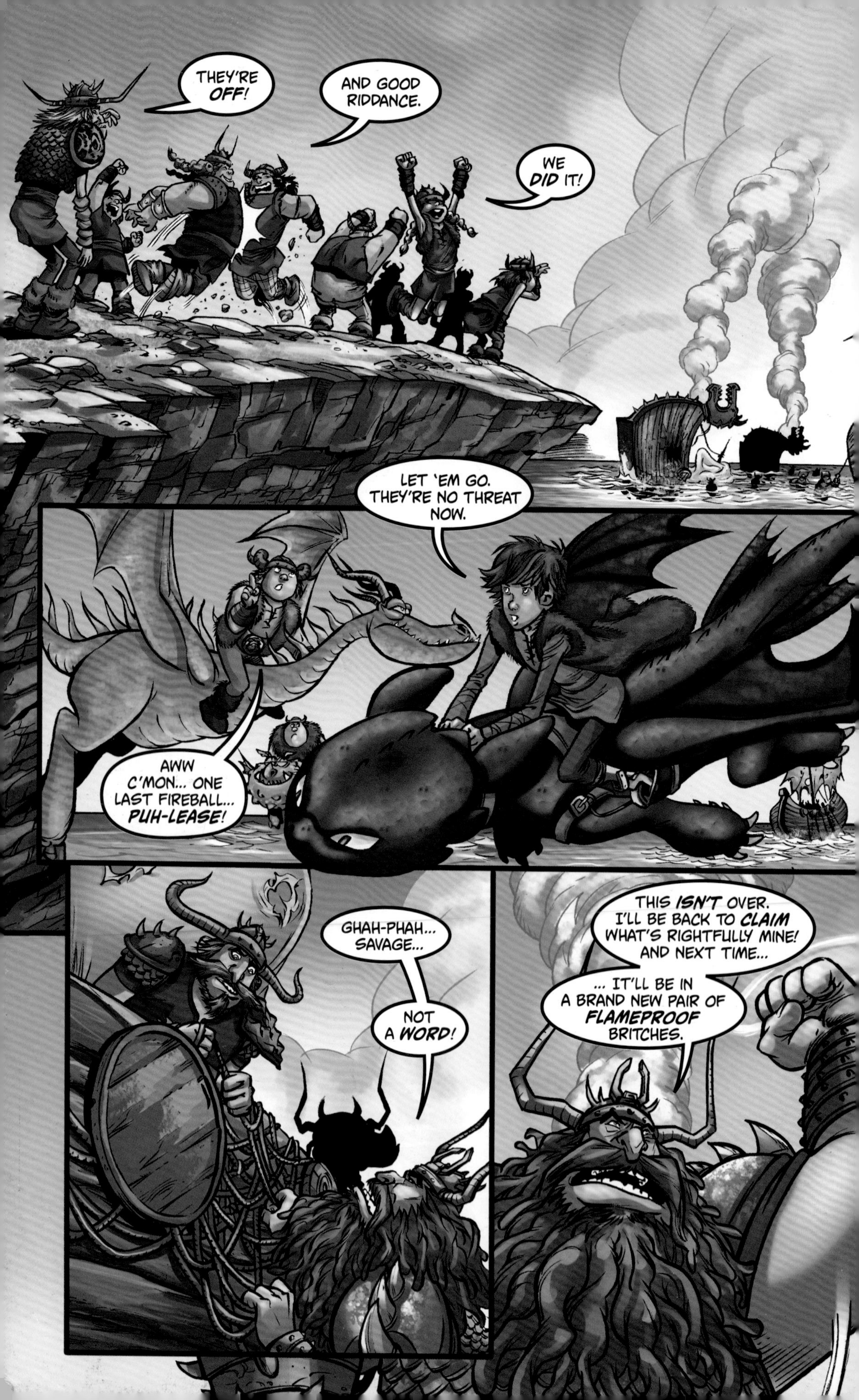
THEY'RE OFF!
AND GOOD RIDDANCE.
WE DID IT!
LET 'EM GO. THEY'RE NO THREAT NOW.
AWW C'MON... ONE LAST FIREBALL... PUH-LEASE!
GHAH-PHAH... SAVAGE...
NOT A WORD!
THIS ISN'T OVER. I'LL BE BACK TO CLAIM WHAT'S RIGHTFULLY MINE! AND NEXT TIME...
... IT'LL BE IN A BRAND NEW PAIR OF FLAMEPROOF BRITCHES.

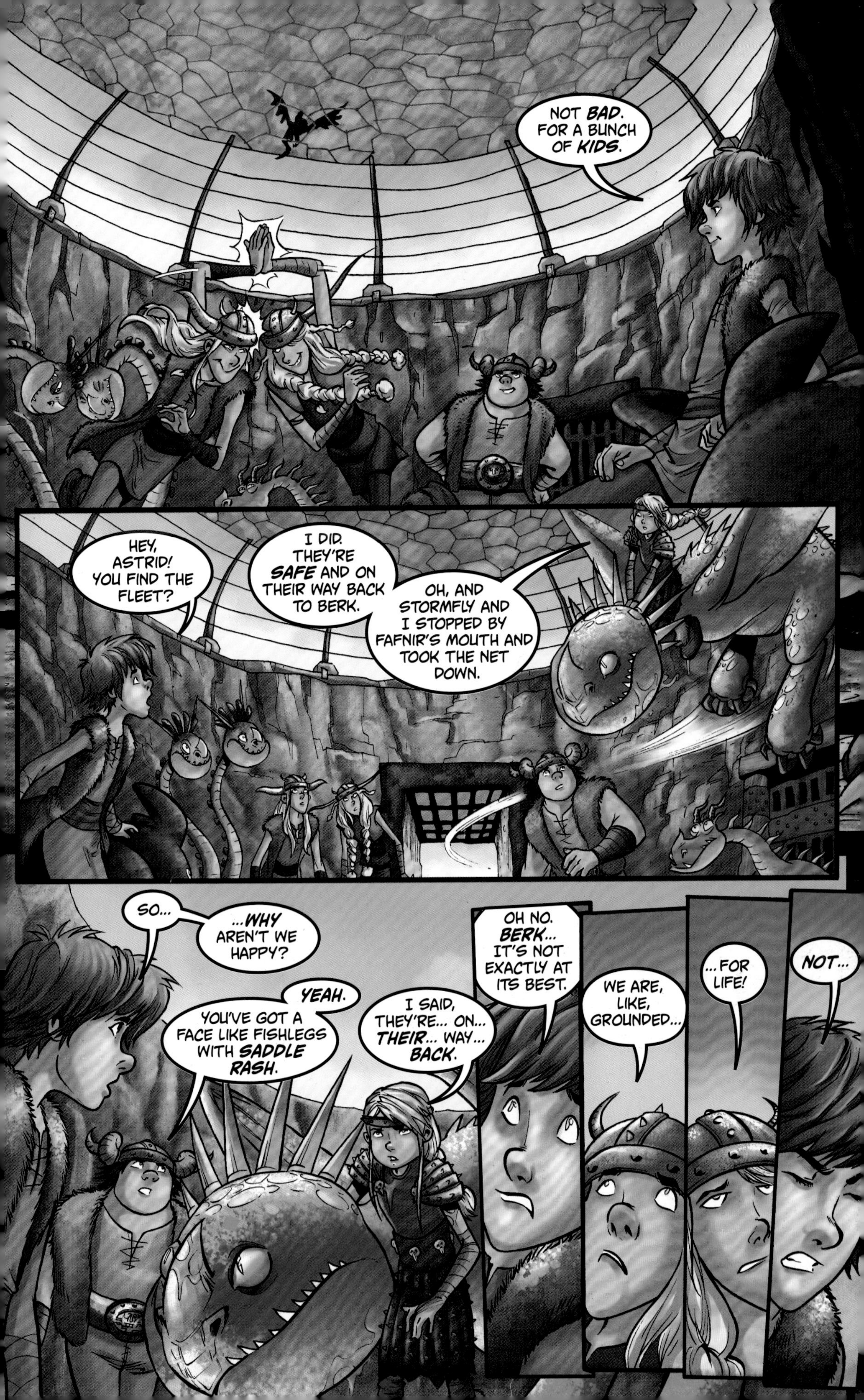
NOT BAD. FOR A BUNCH OF KIDS.
HEY, ASTRID! YOU FIND THE FLEET?
I DID. THEY'RE SAFE AND ON THEIR WAY BACK TO BERK.
OH, AND STORMFLY AND I STOPPED BY FAFNIR'S MOUTH AND TOOK THE NET DOWN.
SO...
...WHY AREN'T WE HAPPY?
YEAH.
YOU'VE GOT A FACE LIKE FISHLEGS WITH SADDLE RASH.
I SAID, THEY'RE... ON... THEIR... WAY... BACK.
OH NO. BERK... IT'S NOT EXACTLY AT ITS BEST.
WE ARE, LIKE, GROUNDED...
...FOR LIFE!
NOT...

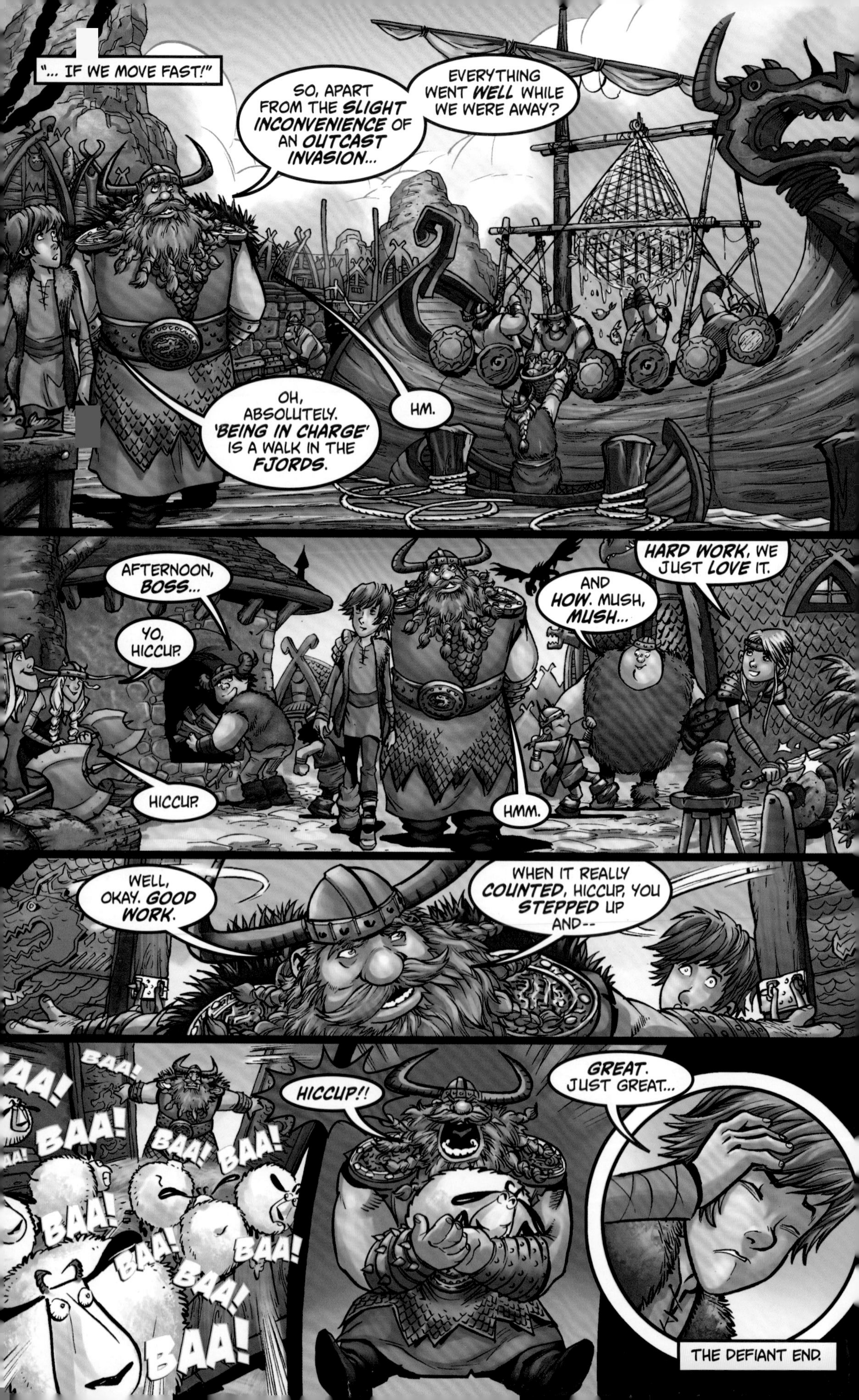
"... IF WE MOVE FAST!"
SO, APART FROM THE SLIGHT INCONVENIENCE OF AN OUTCAST INVASION...
EVERYTHING WENT WELL WHILE WE WERE AWAY?
OH, ABSOLUTELY. 'BEING IN CHARGE' IS A WALK IN THE FJORDS.
HM.
AFTERNOON, BOSS...
YO, HICCUP.
HICCUP.
AND HOW. MUSH, MUSH...
HARD WORK, WE JUST LOVE IT.
HMM.
WELL, OKAY. GOOD WORK.
WHEN IT REALLY COUNTED, HICCUP, YOU STEPPED UP AND--
BAA!
BAA!
BAA!
BAA!
BAA!
BAA!
BAA!
BAA!
BAA!
BAA!
HICCUP!!
GREAT. JUST GREAT...
THE DEFIANT END.

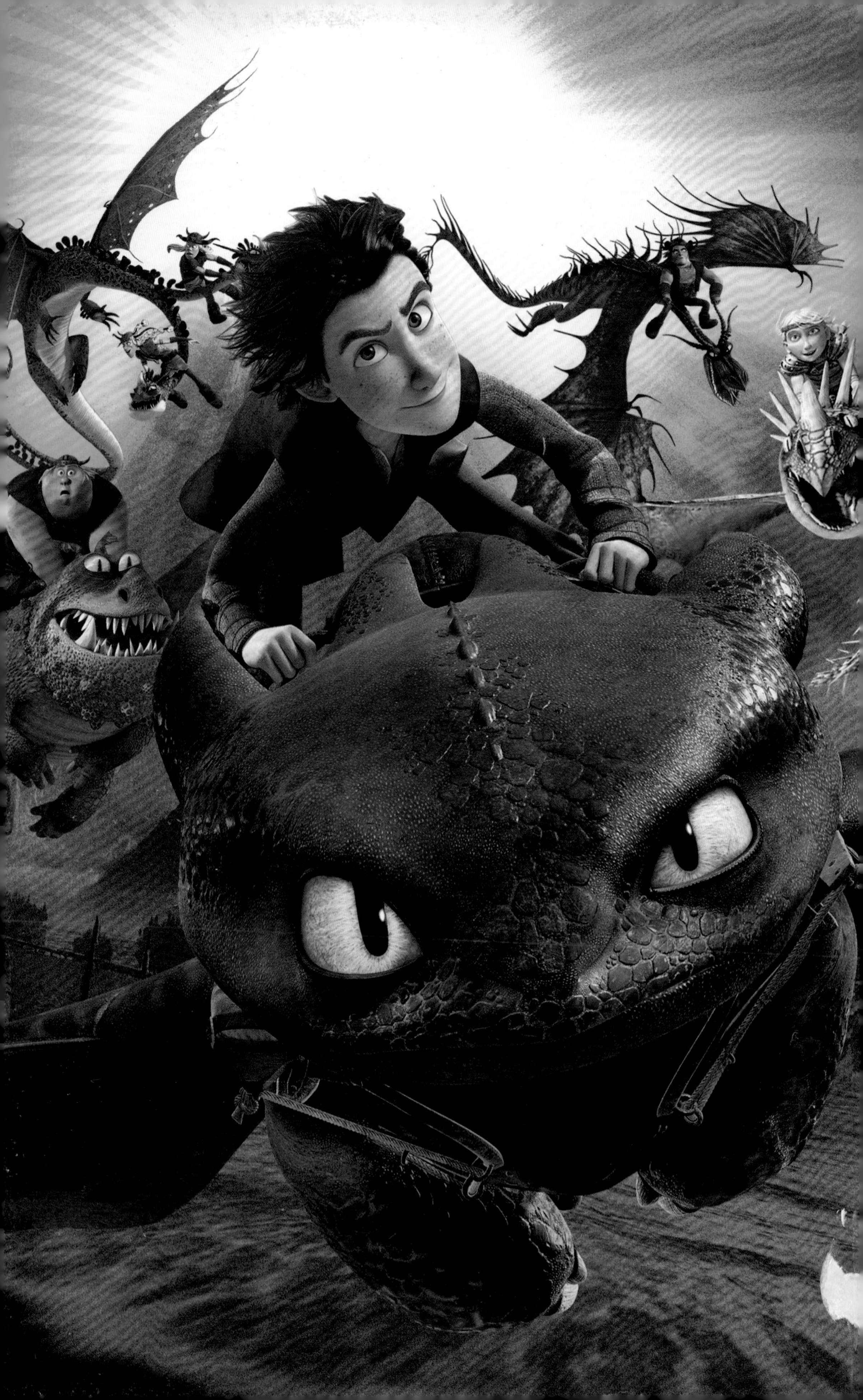

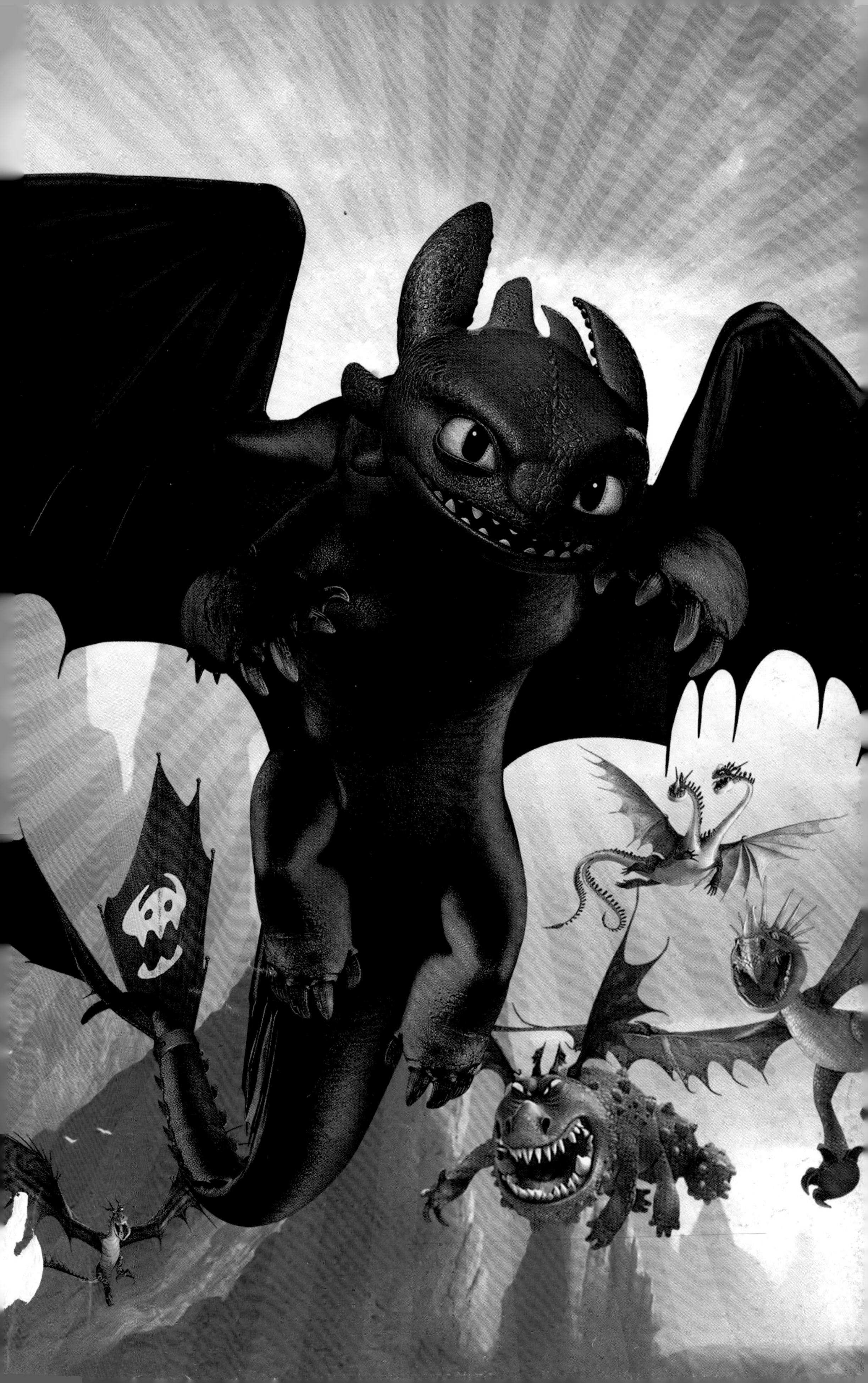

DREAMWORKS

KUNG FU PANDA

BOOKS!

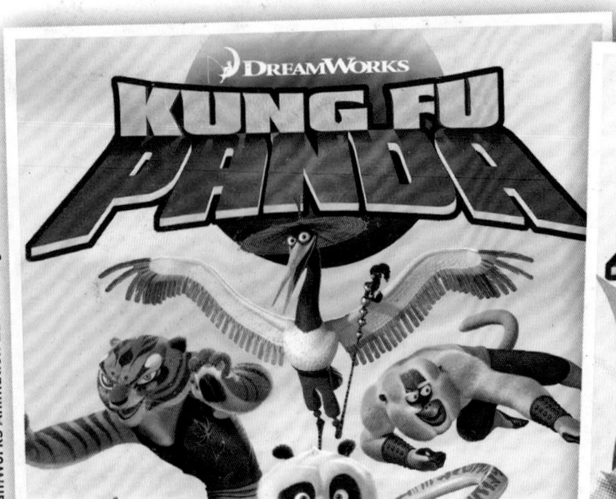
DREAMWORKS
KUNG FU PANDA
DAZE OF THUNDER

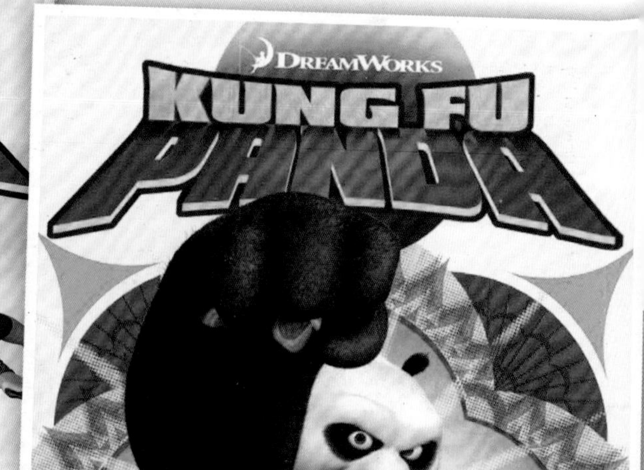
DREAMWORKS
KUNG FU PANDA
SLEEP-FIGHTING

DIGESTS 1 & 2 AVAILABLE NOW!

TITAN COMICS

DREAMWORKS ANIMATION

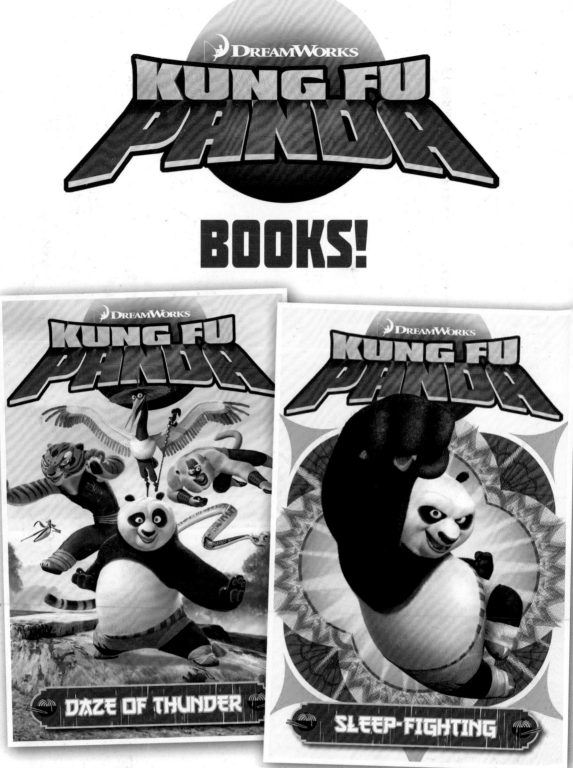

BRAND NEW ADVENTURES!

THE ENDLESS NIGHT

ALL-NEW *DREAMWORKS DRAGONS: DEFENDERS OF BERK* DIGESTS COMING IN FEBRUARY!

DREAMWORKS DIGESTS ALSO AVAILABLE

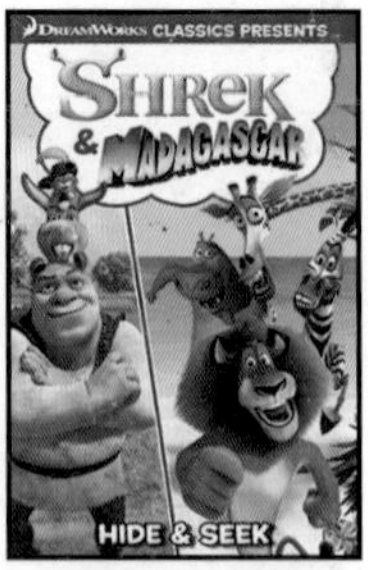
SHREK & MADAGASCAR
HIDE & SEEK
Dreamworks Classics, Volume 1

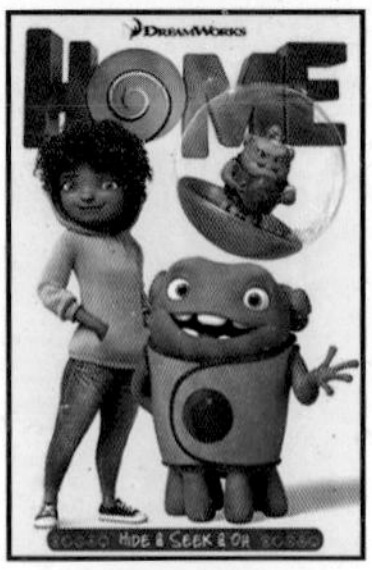
HOME
Home Volume 1

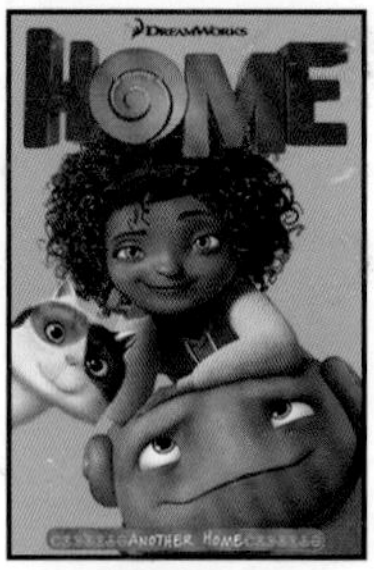
HOME
Home Volume 2

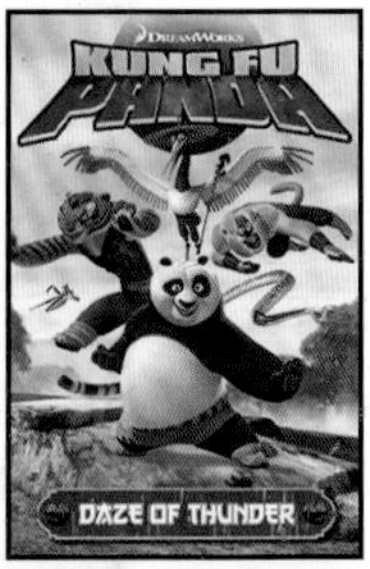
KUNG FU PANDA
DAZE OF THUNDER
Kung Fu Panda, Vol 1 Coming January 2016

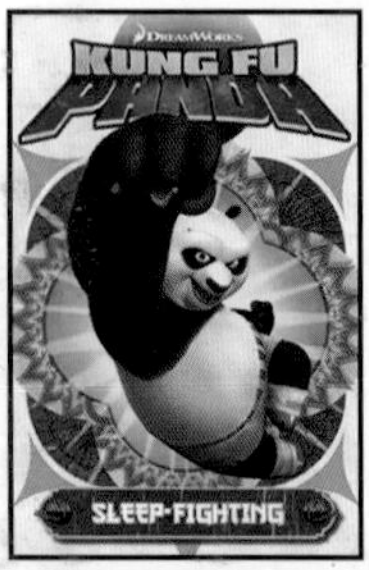
KUNG FU PANDA
SLEEP-FIGHTING
Kung Fu Panda, Vol 2 Coming January 2016

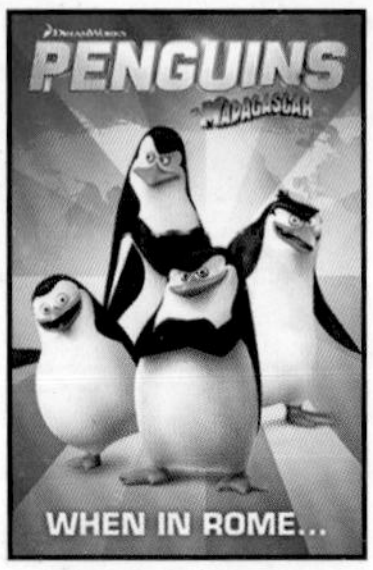
PENGUINS
WHEN IN ROME...
Penguins of Madagascar, Vol 1

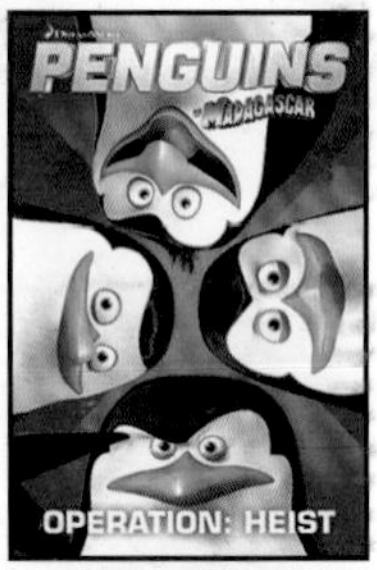
PENGUINS
OPERATION: HEIST
Penguins of Madagascar, Vol 2

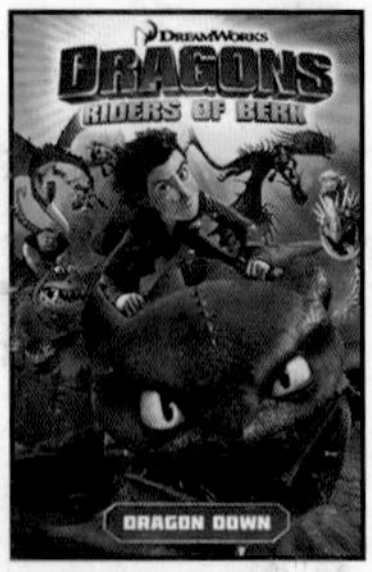
DRAGONS
RIDERS OF BERK
DRAGON DOWN
DreamWorks Dragons: Riders of Berk, Vol 1

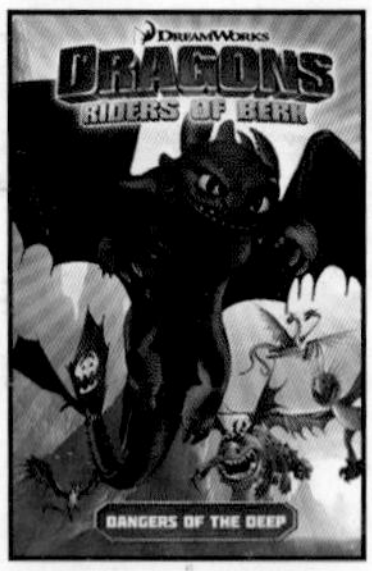
DRAGONS
RIDERS OF BERK
DANGERS OF THE DEEP
DreamWorks Dragons: Riders of Berk, Vol 2

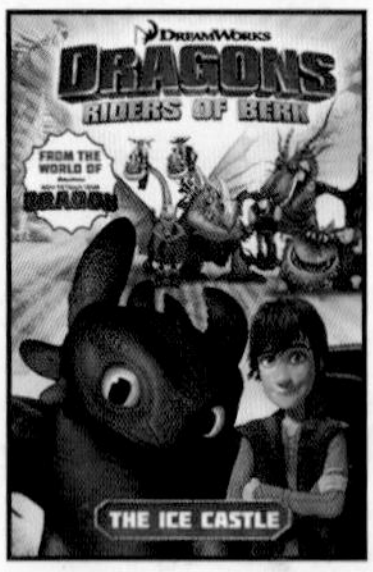
DRAGONS
RIDERS OF BERK
THE ICE CASTLE
DreamWorks Dragons: Riders of Berk, Vol 3

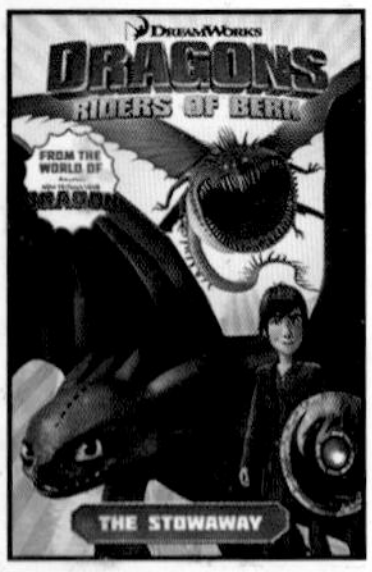
DRAGONS
RIDERS OF BERK
THE STOWAWAY
DreamWorks Dragons: Riders of Berk, Vol 4

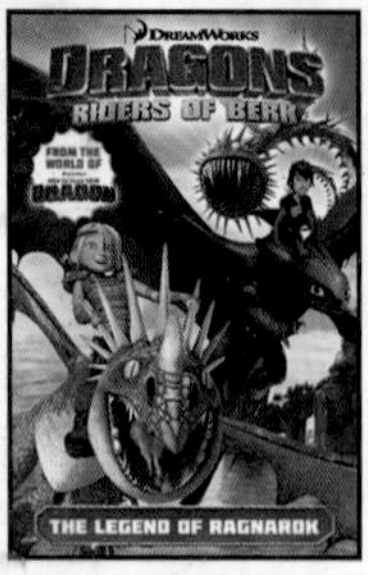
DRAGONS
RIDERS OF BERK
THE LEGEND OF RAGNAROK
DreamWorks Dragons: Riders of Berk, Vol 5

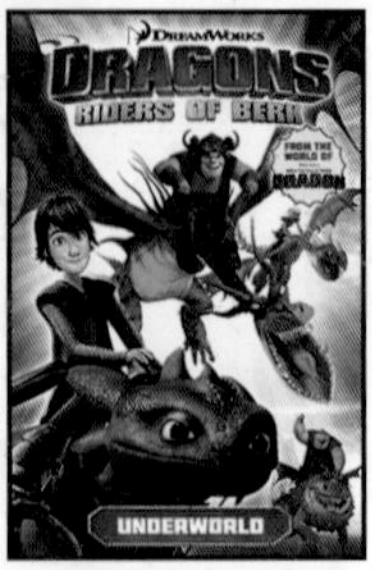
DRAGONS
RIDERS OF BERK
UNDERWORLD
DreamWorks Dragons: Riders of Berk, Vol 6

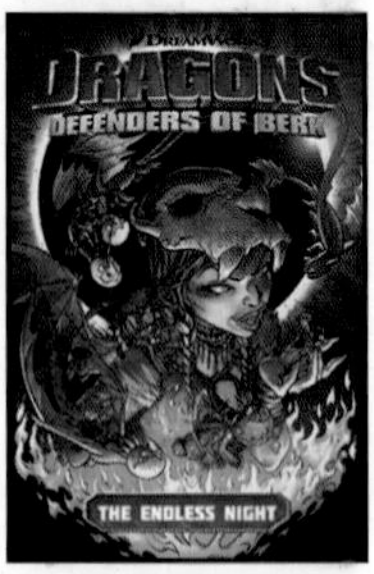
DRAGONS
DEFENDERS OF BERK
THE ENDLESS NIGHT
DreamWorks Dragons: Defenders of Berk Coming March 2016

WWW.TITAN-COMICS.COM

TITAN COMICS

DREAMWORKS ANIMATION SKG